O9-BUD-374

The Haunting of Sunshine Girl

The Haunting of Sunshine Girl

BOOK ONE

PAIGE MCKENZIE

WITH ALYSSA SHEINMEL

Story by Nick Hagen & Alyssa Sheinmel

Based on the web series created by Nick Hagen

WEINSTEIN
BOOKS

For information address Weinstein Books, 250 West 57th Street, 15th Floor, New York, NY 10107.

Printed in the United States of America

Editorial production by *Marra*thon Production Services. www.marrathon.net

Book design by Jane Raese
Set in 11-point Baskerville

Library of Congress Cataloging-in-Publication Data is available for this book.
ISBN 978-1-60286-272-2 (print)
ISBN 978-1-60286-273-9 (e-book)

Published by Weinstein Books
A member of the Perseus Books Group
www.weinsteinbooks.com

FIRST EDITION

4 6 8 10 9 7 5 3

This book is dedicated to Sunshiners everywhere.
Whether you've been there since the beginning
or you're new to the club, this–
and every Sunshine book–
is for you.

Seventeen Candles

She turned sixteen today.

I watched it happen. Katherine, the woman who adopted her, baked her a cake: carrot cake, a burnt sort of orange color with white frosting smothered over the top of it. A girl named Ashley came over to her house with candles, which they lit despite the sweltering Texas heat. Then they sang—Happy Birthday to you, Happy Birthday to you. Our kind don't celebrate birthdays. Except, of course, for when one of us turns sixteen. Just as she did today.

At precisely the time of her birth—7:12 p.m., Central Standard Time, August 14—I sensed the change in the girl named Sunshine. I felt it the instant the spirit touched her. Katherine had just set the cake down on the table in front of her: sixteen—no, seventeen . . . why seventeen?—candles. Sunshine grinned and pursed her lips, preparing to extinguish the flames. But then an instant of hesitation, the smile disappearing from her eyes.

Of course, she hadn't a clue what she was feeling or why she was feeling it. The moment the spirit touched her, her temperature dropped from 98.6 degrees Fahrenheit to 92.3; her heart rate jumped from 80 beats per minute to 110. She pressed her palm to her forehead like a mother checking for a fever. Perhaps she thought she was coming down with something: a cold, the flu—whatever it is that people suffer from. I recognized the culprit immediately: a twenty-nine-year-old male who'd perished in a car accident less than a mile away several weeks earlier, the blood on his wounds still fresh, the glass from the windshield still embedded in his face. Later, I would help him move on myself: his wounds will heal, his skin will be smooth. But for now I keep my focus on Sunshine.

I counted the seconds until her heart rate returned to normal: eleven. Impressive.

She took a deep breath and blew out her candles. Katherine and Ashley applauded. Sunshine stood up from the table and curtsied elaborately, garnering more applause. Her smile was back, planted firmly on her face, her bright green eyes sparkling. Almost as though she never felt anything at all.

My last student's temperature took twenty-four hours to rebound. But Sunshine's was back to normal by the time her mother cut the cake.

Of course, this was just a passing spirit. Soon she'd have to contend with so much more.

CHAPTER ONE

Defending Creepy

"Mom, the house is creepy." We're only halfway up the gravel driveway to our new home, and I can already tell. Even the driveway is creepy: long and narrow, with tall bushes on either side so I can't see our neighbors' front yards.

"I prefer creeptastic," Mom answers with a smile. I don't smile back. "Oh come on," she groans. "I don't even get a sympathy laugh?"

"Not this time," I say, shaking my head.

Mom rented the house off of Craigslist. She didn't have time to be picky, not once she got offered the job as the head nurse of the new neonatal unit at Ridgemont Hospital. She barely had time to ask her only daughter how she felt about being uprooted from the town she'd lived in her whole life to the northwest corner of the country, where it rains more often than not. Of course, I said I'd support her no matter what. It was a great opportunity for her, and I didn't want to be the reason she didn't take it. I'm just not sure that moving from Texas to Washington State is all that great an opportunity for *me.*

Mom parks the car and eyes the house through the windshield. Two stories high, a front porch with an ancient-looking porch swing that looks like it couldn't support a baby's weight. In the pictures online the house looked white, but in real life it's gray, except for the front door, which someone decided to paint bright red. Maybe they thought the contrast would look cheerful or something.

"You can't tell a house is creepy from the outside," Mom adds hopefully.

"Yes, I can."

"How?"

"The same way I can tell that those jeans you bought before we left Austin will end up hanging in my closet instead of yours. I'm very, very intuitive."

Mom laughs. Our little white dog, Oscar, whines from the backseat, begging to be let out so he can explore his new home. As soon as Mom unlatches her seat belt and opens the door, he bounds outside. I stay in the car a second longer, breathing in the wet air blowing in.

It's not just the house. Ever since we crossed the state line the world has been gray, shrouded in fog so thick that Mom had to turn the headlights on even though it was the middle of the day. I didn't picture our new life in Washington as quite so colorless. To be honest, I didn't picture it much at all. Instead, I kind of pretended the move wasn't happening, even as our house back in Austin filled with boxes, even when my best friend, Ashley, came over to help us pack. It wasn't until we were actually on the road that I really *believed* we were moving.

Our new house is on a dead-end street backed up against an enormous, fog-drenched field. Each of the houses we passed before we turned into our driveway was about two sizes too small for the size of its yard; I guess these are the kind of neighbors who want nothing to do with one another. There wasn't a single kid playing in his front yard, not a single dad getting ready to barbeque tonight's dinner, and the street was littered with pine needles from the towering Douglas firs that block out any semblance of daylight. An ugly, rusted, chain-link fence wraps around our new yard.

Judging from the little I've seen so far, I'm pretty sure the whole flippin' town of Ridgemont, Washington, is creepy. I mean, what could be creepier than a place at the foot of a mountain, where the sky is gray even in the dog days of summer? And if it seems like I'm overusing the word creepy, it's not because I don't have access to a thesaurus like everyone else with a smartphone; it's because there is simply no other word that will do.

I shake myself like Oscar does after his bath. It's not like me to be so negative, and I'm determined to snap out of it. I take a deep breath and open the car door. The house is probably adorable on the inside. Mom wouldn't have rented a place that didn't have some redeeming qualities. I reach into the backseat and grab the crate that holds our cat, Lex Luthor. Then I take out my phone and hold it up, taking a picture of me, Lex, and the house in the background, and I text it to Ashley. We promised each other we wouldn't grow apart, even with me living up here in Washington and her back in Texas. I mean, we've been best friends since second grade. If our friendship could survive the middle school cliquey-ness it faced a few years ago, I'm pretty sure it can survive a few thousand miles.

My Chuck Taylors crunch over the gravel driveway as I make my way to the front door. Mom and Oscar are already inside. It might be August, but that doesn't stop Ridgemont from being cold, colder than Austin is at Christmastime, and unfortunately I'm still wearing the ripped-up denim shorts I put on before we left our motel in Boise, Idaho, this morning. The brightly colored mustang on Mom's old high school T-shirt—my favorite shirt these days—looks out of place in the fog, the opposite of camouflage.

I hover in the doorway. "Mom!" I shout. No answer. Just the squeak of the screen door on its hinges while I hold it open, then the whistle of a gust of wind from behind me like it's trying to push me inside.

"Mom!" I repeat. Finally I shout her full name: "Katherine Marie Griffith!" She hates when I call her by her first name, though she claims it has nothing to do with the fact that I'm adopted. We've never made a big deal about it—never had some big talk where my mother, like, revealed the news to me. The truth is, I don't remember a time when I didn't know. There are moments when I wonder who my birth parents are and why they gave me up, but even Mom doesn't know those details. She was a pediatric nurse at the hospital in Austin where I was found—left swaddled in the emergency room: no parents, no paperwork, no nothing—and once she got her hands on me, she says, she knew she was never going to let me go. We were meant for each other, she'd say, simple as that.

Mom and I giggle when strangers comment on how much we look alike, because we don't. We just *act* alike—sometimes too much alike. But unlike me, Mom is a redhead with light skin, almost-gray eyes, pale skin, and freckles. I have long brown hair that's usually trapped somewhere in between wavy and frizzy. And my eyes are green, not gray like Mom's. Ashley says they look like cat's eyes. You know how some people's eyes change color depending on the light or what they're wearing? Not mine. They're always the same milky, light kind of green. And even in the dark my pupils never get big. I've literally never seen anyone with eyes that look like mine. They're so unusual that I'm pretty sure anyone whose eyes matched mine would probably be related to me. Like for real related, by blood.

Anyway, adopted or not, I'm closer to my mom than any other sixteen-year-old I've ever met. Or, at least, I'm pretty sure we're closer than any of the mother-daughter combos I saw walking around the mall in Austin. If they weren't fighting, they were barely talking. Ashley used to pick her phone up and pretend to be deep in conversation every time her mother walked into the room rather than answer when her mom asked about her day. I mean, how many sixteen-year-olds do you know who could spend three days straight locked up in a car with their mother driving across the country? Though I've only been sixteen for a week now.

From somewhere inside the house comes the sound of a toilet flushing. "Where did you think I was, Sunshine?" Mom asks, returning to the front door.

"My name never sounded that ironic in Texas," I mumble, shivering as I step over the threshold. The door slams shut behind me and I jump.

"It's just the wind, sweetie." Mom's got a twinkle in her eye like she's trying not to laugh at me.

"I think it's actually colder inside the house than it is outside." I don't think I've ever felt a cold like this before, not even when

I was nine years old and Mom took me skiing in Colorado, where the temperature was literally below freezing. *This* cold is something else entirely. It's snaking underneath my clothes and covering my skin in goose bumps. It feels kind of like when you have a fever and you're shivering despite the fact that your temperature is rising and you're bundled up under layers of covers in bed. The kind of cold that's damp, as though the whole house needs to be run through the dryer. It's . . . all right, fine, I'll admit it: it's *creepy*. I say it out loud and Mom laughs.

"Is that your new favorite word?" she asks.

"No," I say softly. I can't remember ever having said it much before. But then I never felt like this before.

"No one has lived in the house in months. It's just been empty too long. Once we get all of our stuff in here, it'll feel more homey. It'll be *great*, I promise."

But our stuff—the moving truck full of our furniture and my books and knickknacks and clothes—won't get here until tomorrow. I guess the movers who were driving it from Texas weren't in as much of a hurry to get here as we were. Mom and I ascend the creaky staircase and briefly explore the second floor—two bedrooms and one bathroom with a malfunctioning lock on the door ("I'll ask the landlord to fix it," Mom promises)—but it's hard to imagine how our stuff will look in our rooms when most of our belongings are still a hundred miles away. I go into the room that will be mine and shudder at the bright pink wallpaper and carpet. I am not a pink kind of girl. I decide that I will put my bed in the corner to the right of the door and my desk beside the window across from it. I walk to the narrow window and look out, but the branches of a pine tree in our backyard almost entirely block my view of the street. Even if the sun were shining, I doubt much light would get in. Mom's room faces the front yard, but branches mostly block her windows too.

We blow up our queen-size air mattress on the hardwood floor of the living room and spread blankets over it so the cat doesn't accidentally pop it with his claws when he climbs all over it, which of course he immediately does. We drive into town for pizza, the sound of pine needles hitting our roof in the car chorusing right along with the sound of raindrops. Main Street is mostly empty, nothing like the crowds in downtown Austin.

"It's quaint," Mom says hopefully, pointing out the charming nonchain pharmacy and diner, and I nod, forcing myself to smile. On our way home, the pizza cooling in the backseat, we drive past the hospital, and Mom pulls into the parking lot. She hasn't been here since they flew her in for a job interview a couple of months ago. The hospital is at least half the size of the one where she worked back in Austin. She unclicks her seat belt but doesn't move to get out of the car, so neither do I.

"Guess they don't have as many sick people in Ridgemont as they did back home," I say, gesturing at the nearly empty parking lot.

"It's a small town," Mom shrugs, but she looks wary. She's going to have a lot more responsibility in her new job than she did in Texas, and even though she hasn't said so, I know she's nervous.

"Don't worry. You're going to knock their socks off."

Mom looks at me and smiles. "That's my Sunshine." She reaches across the car to squeeze my shoulder then puts her seat belt back on and restarts the engine. She's turning the car around when the sound of sirens fills the air. An ambulance comes barreling into the parking lot, speeding toward the emergency entrance.

I guess there are sick people in Ridgemont after all.

We eat our pizza in our pajamas, sitting on the air mattress like we're having a slumber party.

"This pizza is better than anything they have in Austin," Mom says as we argue over the last piece.

"Who knew?" I say, ripping the remaining crust from her hands and giggling. "Ridgemont, Washington, pizza capital of the USA."

"See? I knew you'd like it here."

"I like the *pizza*. That's not the same thing as liking the *place*."

"Maybe loving the pizza is just a hop, skip, and jump away from loving the place," Mom counters hopefully. I sigh. The truth is, we've barely been here three hours, and it's really too soon to have an opinion one way or the other.

"Smells funny in here," I say, wrinkling my nose.

"It smells like pizza in here," Mom says, gesturing to the crust-filled box between us.

I shake my head. It smells like something else, a musty, moldy sort of smell, like someone left the air conditioning on too long. Not that you need AC here.

"Anyway, once we have all our stuff moved in, this house is going to smell like us," Mom promises, but I'm not so sure the damp mildew smell will go away so easily.

We read before bed. Mom's tackling the latest thriller to grace the best-seller list—she's a sucker for those kinds of books, even though I make fun of her for it—and I'm reading *Pride and Prejudice* for what has to be the fifteenth time. It's impossible to feel homesick with the familiar weight of the book in my hands. I like all the words no one uses anymore: *flutter* and *perturbation* and *enquiries*. Sometimes I find myself talking like one of the Bennett sisters. Super dorky, I know.

"Do you think maybe I was Jane Austen in a former life?" I ask sleepily when we finally turn off the lights. It must be after midnight. Oscar has weaseled his way in between us on the bed, but I don't mind because even though he takes up half the square footage of the mattress, I'm a lot warmer with him curled up beside me.

"Of course not," Mom says. She doesn't believe in things like past lives. She believes in logic and medicine, things that can be proven with organic chemistry.

"Okay, but I mean if you *did* believe in that kind of thing–"

"Which I don't–"

"Okay, but if you *did*–"

"If I did, *then* would I also believe that you'd been Jane Austen in a former life?"

"Exactly."

"Nope."

"Why not?" I scoff, feigning offense.

I can feel Mom shrug on her side of the bed like the answer is really obvious. "Statistics. Mathematically the chances are infinitesimal."

"You're applying statistics to my hypothetical past life?"

"Numbers don't lie, Sunshine State." Mom calls me that sometimes, even though we've never even been to Florida, the actual Sunshine State. I'm pretty sure Washington is as far as you can get from Florida without actually leaving the contiguous United States. But Mom's always said that as long as she's with me, she's in a state of perpetual sunshine. She says she felt that way from the instant she picked me up when I was a just a newborn baby. That's why she named me Sunshine in the first place.

"Good night, sweetie," she says into the darkness.

"Good night."

The sound wakes me up. I'm not sure what time it is when I hear it. Hear *them.* Footsteps. Coming from the floor above us. I wasn't sleeping all that soundly anyway. Usually when I fall asleep after reading *Pride and Prejudice* I dream about Mr. Darcy, but tonight I was having really weird dreams. I saw a little girl crying in the corner of a bathroom, but no matter what I said or did, her tears kept flowing. I tried to put my arms around her, but she was always out of reach, even when I was right beside her.

"What the freak?" I whisper, rolling over and reaching for Oscar. Dogs' hearing is supposed to be really good, so if he doesn't hear anything, then this is definitely just my imagination, right? But Oscar isn't on the bed anymore, and it's pitch dark in here, so I can't see where he is. He can't be that far away, though, because I can smell the wet-dog-smell of his fur, which hasn't fully dried since we got here. Suddenly the footsteps stop.

"Mom," I whisper, gently shaking her shoulder. "Mom, did you hear that?"

"Hmmm?" she answers, her voice thick with sleep. She was really tired after having driven so far. I should let her sleep. But then the footsteps start again.

Oh gosh, maybe this house doesn't feel creepy because it's been empty for months. Maybe it feels creepy because a crazed murderer has been squatting on the floor above us, waiting for some unsuspecting family to move in so he could strangle them in their sleep. My heart is pounding and I take deep breaths, trying to slow it. But it just gets faster.

The footsteps don't actually sound like a crazed murderer's, though. They sound light, kind of playful–kind of like a child is skipping through the rooms above us.

"Mom," I repeat, more urgently this time. Maybe there really is a kid up there. Maybe he or she got lost or ran away from home.

"What is it?" Mom asks sleepily.

"Do you hear that?" I ask.

"Hear what?"

"Those footsteps."

"All I hear is your voice keeping me awake," she says, but I can tell she's smiling. "It's probably just the cat," she adds, rolling over and putting her arms around me. "Go back to sleep. I promise this place won't seem so creepy in the morning." She emphasizes the word *creepy* like it's some kind of joke.

"It's not funny," I protest, but Mom's breathing has resumed its steady rhythm–she's already fallen back to sleep. "It's not funny," I repeat, whispering the words into the darkness.

The last thing I expect is an answer, but almost immediately after I speak, I hear it, clearly and softly as though someone is whispering in my ear. Not footsteps this time but a child's laugh: a giggle, light and clear as crystal, traveling through the darkness.

I squeeze my eyes shut, willing myself to think about anything else: Elizabeth Bennett and Fitzwilliam Darcy, Jane and Mr. Bingley, even Lydia and Mr. Wickham. I try to picture them dancing at the Netherfield ball (even though I know Mr.

Wickham wasn't actually there that night), but instead, all I can see is the little girl from my dream, her dark dress tattered with age, playing hopscotch on the floor above me. And again I hear laughter. A child's laugh has never sounded quite so scary.

Before I know what I'm doing, I crawl out of bed and head for the stairs. If there's a little girl up there, she's probably just as frightened as I am, right? Though she didn't sound frightened. I mean, she was laughing.

I place my foot on the bottom step and look up. There's nothing but darkness above me. Oscar appears at my side, leaning his warm body against my leg. "Good boy." My voice comes out breathless, as though I've been running.

I put my foot on the second step and it creaks. Then there's nothing but quiet—no laughter, no footsteps, no skipping. My heart is pounding, but I take a deep breath and it slows to a steady beat.

"Maybe it's over," I say. Oscar pants in agreement. Other than our breathing, the house is silent. "Let's go back to bed," I sigh finally, turning around.

Oscar curls up beside me on the air mattress, and I run my fingers up and down his warm fur. I expect to lie awake, staring at the ceiling, for hours. Instead, my eyelids grow heavy, my breathing slows until it keeps time with Mom's.

But I swear, just as I'm drifting out of consciousness, in that place where you're more asleep than awake anymore, I hear something else. A phrase uttered in a child's voice, no more than a whisper:

Night-night.

CHAPTER TWO
Pink Irony

"How pink can it possibly be?" Ashley sounds almost as skeptical about the color of my new room as my mother did about the possibility that this house might be haunted.

Even though she can't see me through the phone, I shake my head. The movers left an hour ago, and Mom and I have been unpacking ever since. My new room is a crooked sort of rectangle. I thought I'd be able to see how our life would fit into these rooms once our belongings were here with us—how my life would fit into my new bedroom. But I'm not sure I will ever fit into a room that looks like *this.*

"I swear, Ashley." I keep my phone on speaker as I sift through all the items I packed so carefully just a few days ago in Austin: my antique typewriter, which now sits on my desk beside my laptop, my taxidermied owl—Dr. Hoo—currently perched on a shelf above my desk like he's about to swoop down and lift up my collection of glass figurines. "You've never seen a room this pink. You've never seen a *pink* this pink." Ashley laughs, but I'm being totally serious. The pink in my new room is everywhere: in the roses on the wallpaper, the shaggy carpet on the floor. Even the light switch is painted pink.

When I woke up this morning I immediately raced up the stairs to search for any trace of a child hiding up here. But there was nothing. No footprints, no dirt tracked over the carpets, no sticky fingerprints on the windows, and certainly no little girl hiding in the closets or the bathroom. Mom said that whatever I thought I heard last night was probably just a bad dream, but I shook my head. I know what I heard. Plus, it's even colder on the second floor of this house than the first floor. Maybe the air is too damp to move here; the mildewy smell is even stronger on the second floor, the carpet almost damp, as though it flooded a few months ago and never had a chance to air out.

"My room used to be pink," Ashley offers. Clearly she still doesn't grasp the gravity of the situation.

"Yeah, until you turned thirteen and outgrew it."

"Didn't you see pictures of the house online before you moved?"

"Obviously they neglected to include pictures of *this* room."

"So move into another room."

"There isn't any other room. There's my mom's bedroom and there's this bedroom and a bathroom in between."

"What about a guest room for when your best friend comes to visit?"

I laugh. "Nope. You'll join me inside this giant Pepto-Bismol bottle."

I pick up what might be my most prized possession, removing it from a cocoon of Bubble Wrap: the Nikon F5 camera my mother bought me for my sweet sixteen. I place it gingerly on the bed. Ashley thought I should have asked for a car. *Every teenager in America asks for a car when they turn sixteen*, she'd said. She got one, a bright blue, shiny, four-door hybrid that she proudly drove around town with the windows down and the music loud. But what I really wanted was an old-fashioned camera to shoot with real film. And boy, did Mom deliver.

My high school in Austin offered photography classes, and I signed up the first day of my freshman year, borrowing a camera from the photography teacher, Mrs. Soderberg. She patiently taught me how to develop film in the school's basement darkroom. Most everyone else used digital cameras, but those pictures never looked as true to me as the ones taken with film.

Ashley has always teased me because I'd rather spend hours in the darkroom with a teacher instead of staring at a screen looking at the status updates of people I see at school all day anyway. She said that was the reason I didn't have more friends. And she said my collection of stuffed birds didn't help either. *Normal girls are grossed out by dead animals.*

It's only one stuffed bird, I'd insisted. Mom and I found Dr. Hoo at an antique store just outside of Austin. I can't explain it, but the instant I saw him I knew I just had to have him. He was snowy white with black speckles on his soft head and wings, and even though he'd clearly been dead for a long time, he just *felt* so alive to me.

It's not like I needed more friends. Ashley and I were different, but we'd bonded in second grade over a shared love of colorful construction paper and glitter-glue, and we've been close ever since. Besides, she and my mom had always felt like enough in the friends department. Mom always said I was all she needed, and truth be told, between me and her work, it never seemed like she had time for much else. Anyway, why would I want friends I had to act fake in front of? I don't want to pretend to be scared of dead things and to prefer digital to film. I don't mind that I'm old-fashioned.

"Just promise me you're not going to be as antisocial in Ridgemont as you were in Austin."

"I've lived in Ridgemont for less than twenty-four hours. I haven't had time to be antisocial."

"Will you at least promise to wear something *normal* on the first day of school?"

I fold my arms across my chest. "Define normal."

"It is not normal for a sixteen-year-old to have pajamas with feet."

"That was one sleepover, and we were in the eighth grade!"

"Do you still have them?" Ashley asks, knowing the answer.

I laugh and close my eyes. I can picture Ashley now, her pretty blue eyes sparkling, her blond hair blown dry straight and smooth down her back. She's probably planted next to the air conditioning vent in her (normal-colored) room, wearing normal denim shorts and a normal T-shirt. She always refused to come with me whenever I went to Goodwill in search of vintage blouses and boots and bags. I don't dress like a crazy person or anything like that; I just don't dress like most of the other kids I know either. I like crocheted hats and scarves, T-shirts with funny little icons on them, and long sleeves that hang past my wrists.

"Maybe the kids at Ridgemont High will dress the way I do."

"Maybe," Ashley agrees, though I can tell she doesn't really think so. "Or maybe they'll think your style is some really cool import from out of town. You could pretend to be from New York. Or London!"

"Who would believe I'm from London?"

"You could do a British accent. Boys love British accents."

I shake my head. "If I'm going British, I'm doing it for British things like afternoon tea and carriage rides across the castle lawn."

"So you won't just be British, you'll be royalty too?"

"As long as I'm inventing a new reality, I may as well make it count."

"You'll be the most popular girl at school in no time."

I nod in agreement. "The boys will be falling all over me the second I say my first *Right-o, jolly good!*"

Ashley giggles. "Now what's so funny?" I ask.

"Nothing," she says, but her giggles just get louder. I bet her cheeks have turned nearly as pink as my carpet. When she speaks she can barely get the words out. "I'm just trying to imagine you sneaking a boy up to your room. What would be more mortifying—the dead bird or the pink walls?"

"He'd run away as fast as his legs could carry him," I agree, and I'm laughing too. The mere idea of a boy in my room is absurd all on its own. Ashley knows full well that I've never so much as kissed a guy.

From downstairs my mother's voice is calling my name. "Ash, I gotta go," I say. "Mom needs me."

"Tell Kat I say *Hi*."

"I will," I promise. "Miss you."

"You too," Ashley says before hanging up.

I step into the hall. The carpet out here is a nice neutral color: tan. Nothing like the pink monstrosity going on in my room.

Wait. *The hallway is carpeted.* So is Mom's room. So is mine. I pace back and forth, then skip a little, trying to imitate the sounds I heard last night.

"Hey Mom, do you hear that?" I shout.

"Hear what?"

I skip more, into my own room, into Mom's, and then back to the hallway. The carpet is so thick that I can feel its plushness even with shoes on. "Hear that!"

"I hear your voice, yelling at me!" she calls back, an echo of what she said when I woke her in the middle of the night. Now I race down the stairs, two at a time. My mother is in the kitchen, leaning on the enormous counter in the center of the room, surrounded by half-unpacked boxes of pots and pans and Tupperware. The cat mews at her feet, wondering which box his food is in. The counter was probably white once, but it's taken on a gray tinge, just like the outside of the house. Mom's turned all the lights on, but it still seems dark in here. Rain beats against the window above the sink. Thunder rumbles in the distance.

"I'm making a grocery list," Mom says. "What do you need?"

"The floor is carpeted," I answer.

"What?"

"Upstairs. It's hardwood down here, but the entire second floor is covered in carpet." Lex mews insistently, rubbing up against my legs. I bend down to pet him. He's got a patch of white fur on his chest and face, but otherwise he's all black. Having a black cat never seemed like bad luck before.

"I know," Mom shrugs. "It said so on Craigslist."

"Did it say on Craigslist that the color pink almost certainly originated in the second bedroom?"

Mom wrinkles her nose. She hates pink as much as I do. "I'm going to ask the landlord if we can paint over that wallpaper."

"Why would anyone want to paint over pink roses the size of my head?" I joke.

"Just be glad they're not the size of your head plus your hair."

"Now you're just being mean." Mom knows I'm jealous of her hair, which is always perfectly straight—unlike mine, which bursts into a ball of frizz the instant even a milliliter of moisture has the nerve to enter the atmosphere. "This climate is not doing my hair any favors."

"Sweetie, you're going to have to pick one thing to complain about at a time. I can't keep track of it all."

"I'm not complaining," I say, but I stick my lower lip out into a babyish pout so that Mom laughs. I am complaining and I know it. The weather, the noises, the creepiness. The pink.

"Wait." I interrupt my own train of thought. "I wanted to tell you about the carpet."

"What about the carpet?"

"It's carpeted upstairs. You didn't hear me skipping around, did you?"

"No."

"So then how did I hear those footsteps last night?"

Mom smiles, walking across the room to put her arm around my shoulders. "Sunshine, I know you think you heard something last night—"

"I *did* hear something."

"Okay," she concedes. "You did hear something. But don't you think it's more likely that it was just a branch hitting an upstairs window, or the wind blowing through the trees, or—"

"I know the difference between branches and footsteps. Between the wind and an actual voice."

"Okay," Mom says patiently. "But like you said, it'd be almost impossible to hear footsteps coming from the second floor."

"Exactly," I nod, snapping my fingers and spinning around in a not-particularly-graceful attempt at a victory dance.

"Exactly what?"

I stop spinning. "I've been saying it since we got here. This house is just plain strange."

"I know this is a tough transition for you." Mom reaches out to rub my back up and down. "Last night was your first night living anywhere but our house in Austin. It's going to take a while to adjust."

I shake my head. It's not as though I've never slept anywhere but our old house. I've slept at Ashley's more times than I can count. Mom and I have gone on vacations and shared hotel rooms. What I felt last night was not just homesickness. Homesickness makes you *sad*, not *scared.*

"I *did* hear something. And not just footsteps. I told you—I heard laughter too. There was a little girl upstairs. I know it."

"A little girl?"

"Well, maybe the ghost of a little girl."

Mom shakes her head. She doesn't believe in ghosts. I wasn't so sure I believed in them either. Until now.

"I'm going to prove it to you," I promise.

"How?"

I have no idea how to prove a house is haunted, so I wrinkle my nose just like she did a few minutes before.

Finally Mom sighs and says, "Do you want to come with me to the grocery store?"

"I've still got a lot of unpacking to do." My desire to get everything in its proper place trumps my fear. Plus, how will I prove to her that something fishy is going on here if I'm not in the house to experience it?

"You sure you feel safe being left all alone in a haunted house?" Mom asks as she reaches for her car keys. "Mwa, ha ha," she adds in a silly deep voice like the Count's from *Sesame Street*, waving her fingers in front of her.

"I'm not alone," I say, trying to ignore the fact that my voice is shaking. "I've got Oscar and Lex to protect me."

Mom kisses the top of my head before she heads out the door. Oscar and I climb the stairs and go into my room, where I close the door behind us. You'd think all this pink would make the room feel less creepy, but if anything, it has the opposite effect. Thunder rumbles again, closer this time. I turn to my desk, my back to the window. In Austin I kept my glass unicorns lined up in size order, tallest on the left, shortest on the right. Here I decide to arrange them by color. I've been collecting unicorns since I was five years old and my kindergarten teacher read our class a book called *The Last Unicorn*. Mom gets me a new figurine every Christmas. I have eleven total, and that's not counting the ones that broke over the years. They're made of glass, and they're all in different colors, from purple to green to blue to clear and, yes, even a pink one. I place that one front and center.

Suddenly I feel a chill down my spine, as though a breeze is coming in through the window behind my desk. But the window is closed. Not just closed—locked. I press my hands against the glass: it's icy cold, but no breeze is coming through. I guess with a climate like Ridgemont's, a house would need to be well insulated.

"What do you think, Oscar?" I say, talking to our dog like he can understand me. And like he's not color-blind. I go back to concentrating on the shelf above my desk. "Do you think the purple should go next to the pink or the red one? The pink? Okay, if you say so."

Again, a chill. This time the breeze is so strong that it softly blows my hair back from my face.

"Where do you think that's coming from, Oscar?" I'm trying to sound as cheerful as I did about my unicorns. I don't want poor Oscar to get scared. "It's an old house, right? Maybe there's a draft or something. You've heard about drafty old houses." *Drafty old houses* sounds like something Jane Austen might have said. That's not so bad. I imagine that Oscar is nodding with agreement.

I adjust the pink unicorn, trying to ignore the fact that my hands are shaking. The breeze comes again, stronger this time, lifting my hair off my shoulders. I back away from my desk, dropping the unicorn. Its horn snaps right off with a sad little *ding* sound. "Oh, no," I moan. He made it all the way from Austin in one piece, and I had to go and drop him. Suddenly Oscar dives under my bed.

"You feel it too, don't you, boy?" I ask, but Oscar just whimpers. I pull my sleeves down over my wrists, covering up the goose bumps dotting the skin on my arms.

Bang. I spin around. My door has flown open; that *bang* was the wood hitting the wall behind it.

"Good golly!" I shout, folding my arms across my chest and balling my hands into fists. My heart is racing. Another chill runs down my spine, and then another, and another, until it feels like I'll never be warm again. I sit on my bed and shiver, my heart pounding.

Mrs. Soderberg used to say that you could capture things on film that were impossible to detect with the naked eye. Slowly, so that I won't scare away whatever might be in this room with me—I can't catch it on film if I frighten it away—I reach for my camera. I filled it with black-and-white film before we left Austin, excited about having a new place to photograph. Now I press my eye into the viewfinder and adjust the lens for optimal focus. I take the pictures methodically, adjusting the shutter speed for a lengthy exposure, careful to hold my hands steady.

Click, click, click. The sounds the camera makes are somehow comforting. Even Oscar sticks his head out from under the bed.

Mom was just teasing when she asked whether I felt safe being left alone in a haunted house. But now I know: once you move into one, you're never really alone again.

CHAPTER THREE
School Daze

By the time school starts I'm totally exhausted. I haven't slept through the night once since we moved here a week ago. And we've had literally one sunny day! I'm thinking of asking Mom to get me one of those UV lights that are supposed to simulate the sun for Christmas, though that seems a million years away. Don't get me started on what all this fog is doing to my curls either. I've never understood girls who complain about having straight hair. Try living with frizz for one day, and you'll change your tune. Between the rat's nest on my head and the bags under my eyes, I'm not exactly looking hot these days.

Every night I get into bed hoping for the best. Maybe tonight will be the night I don't hear footsteps or laughter or a tiny little voice wishing me good night. Maybe tonight will be the night I don't feel a phantom breeze wafting across my room, lowering the temperature so that I'm cold no matter how many blankets I pile on the bed.

So far, no such luck.

I never minded being home alone when we lived in Austin, but since we moved to Ridgemont I get nervous every time Mom leaves the house, like I'm a little kid who still needs a babysitter. Two days ago she had to work an overnight shift. I lay in her bed with the door closed so that Oscar and Lex had to stay in the room with me. I called her at, like, three in the morning to report the latest, but I couldn't get her on the phone because she was with a patient. When she finally called me back she seemed more exasperated than concerned. She said that the sound of a door creaking open was "just the old house settling on its foundation," that footsteps were "probably branches hitting the windows," that laughter was "just the wind howling through the trees."

There's no such thing as ghosts, Sunshine is quickly becoming her mantra. She must have said it a dozen times in the last week alone. I mean, I know she's a skeptic, but it's not like her to just dismiss me like that. When I was little she stayed up with me after every bad dream I ever had, rocking me back to sleep when I was convinced there were monsters under my bed and letting me sleep in her room when I was too scared to be alone in my own.

Now she explains away every sound, every breeze, every drop in temperature. I'm starting to worry that it's only a matter of time before she decides I'm going nuts and sends me to sit on some psychiatrist's couch. Even Ashley thinks I'm losing my mind; at first she laughed every time I mentioned our haunted house, but last night she said I sounded nuttier than a fruitcake.

But I don't think I'm crazy, and I'm determined to prove it.

I've been putting my camera to good use, taking pictures of the breeze blowing back the curtains in my room when the window is closed. A few days ago I caught a shot of the door swinging open. Two nights ago I slept with my camera in my bed so that when I heard the laughter I could take a picture of my room; the flash was superbright, and I had the shutter speed on the slowest setting possible, hoping that a long-exposure photograph might be able to pick up something I couldn't see with my eyes alone.

I'm walking to school this morning with two rolls of film in my bag. All I need is a darkroom, and maybe I'll finally have some proof to show my mother. My backpack feels like it weighs a million pounds.

The fog is so thick that from our driveway, about halfway down the street on either end, I can't see the dead end to my right or the next street over on my left. The streetlights on our block are spread out even more than the houses, and what with the near-constant rain and the shadows from the randomly placed Douglas firs everywhere, it's always dark here. None of the other houses on our street look quite as creepy as ours, not even the two vacant ones across the way. We live near the hospital, and I'm pretty sure I'm the only person under thirty living on our block. There are no tricycles on the front lawns, no swing sets. Just the pine needles covering every surface and the occasional sound of sirens from the ambulances going to and from the hospital where my mother spends most of her days (and nights). A siren wails now, so loud that I literally jump.

"Doesn't exactly make for the coziest neighborhood in America," I say out loud, kicking the ground with my sneakers.

At least some of the houses are painted pretty colors: peach and yellow and even pale blue or, even better, plain wood or brick. The other homes are ringed, like ours, by ancient-looking trees, as though a long time ago they carved this street out of a pine forest. Mom thinks that most of the sounds I'm hearing are probably low-hanging branches batting against the roof when the wind blows. Walking down our street, I can actually see why she'd think that. But I know the difference between a branch and footsteps, and I certainly know the difference between the wind and laughter.

To be honest, I'm sort of upset that my mother isn't taking this more seriously. I have literally never lied to her. I know, that's superlame for a teenager to say, but it's the truth. (See? I never lie!)

As I get closer to Ridgemont High, more cars appear on the street. A few kids on bikes whiz past me. Everyone looks so excited for the first day of school, hugging each other hello and wearing bright, shiny new outfits that practically glow in fog. It may be the first day of school, but I'm clearly the only new kid. Everyone else seems to know each other, and no one seems as bothered by the cold as I am. They're all wearing T-shirts and jeans, nothing like me in my long skirt and sweater, but it's not like anyone dressed like me at my old school either. I tighten my blue owl-print scarf around my neck and pull my sleeves over my wrists, patting my hair into something that looks less like a frizz helmet. Ashley would tell me I should smile, so I plaster a grin onto my face.

In homeroom the teacher makes me stand at the front of the room and introduce myself. I probably blush as pink as my bedroom carpet. Most of the kids in the classroom don't even look up from their cell phones when I say my name. It's junior year—looks like everyone has had the same group of friends for a while now, and no one is looking to befriend the new girl. People aren't mean or anything. I mean, a group of cheerleader-type girls don't even acknowledge me, but a few of the girls smile and wave before looking away, and at least two boys wink at me. Ashley would say that I should wink back, but just the thought makes me want to hide behind my hair.

First period is algebra—not exactly my favorite subject—but I'm relieved to discover that the teacher is covering equations my old school introduced last year, so I allow myself to zone out a little bit and count the minutes until third period, the only class I really care about: visual arts.

Finally I walk into a room that looks more like a camp arts-and-crafts tent than a high school classroom. Three long wooden tables crisscross the center of the room; splotches of paint dot the linoleum floor. Various student projects hang on the walls—everything from collages to charcoal sketches to an enormous quilt. But no photographs.

I scan the room anxiously, looking for the black door that indicates a darkroom is on the other side, the telltale red light that photographers mount outside to let visitors know whether the room is in use.

But the only doors inside this room are wide open—one that leads to a supply closet and the other that leads to what must be the art teacher's office, a cramped little alcove with a messy desk inside.

"Darnit!" I say out loud.

"What was that, dear?" a woman's voice rings out behind me, clear as a bell. I adjust my scarf.

I turn around and face a strikingly pale woman with long hair that's so dark it's almost black. If it weren't for the purple circles beneath her eyes, she'd actually be quite beautiful.

But instead she just looks like she doesn't get much sleep. Her clothes are as dark as her hair, a long, black sort of caftan over a long black skirt. If she were a student and not a teacher, she'd fit right in with the Goth kids.

"I'm Sunshine Griffith. I'm new here. I was just looking for the darkroom . . ." My voice lifts hopefully at the end of the sentence.

The woman eyes me carefully. I tell myself there's nothing creepy about that. Usually art teachers are artists themselves, so maybe this is just how she looks at people. In case she might want to draw them one day or something. "I'm sorry, dear, we don't have a darkroom here."

Here. In *this* room. "Is there a darkroom someplace else in the school?" I ask, playing with my backpack's straps, knowing the film is in the front pocket, waiting to be developed. Surely the school has a darkroom *somewhere*, right?

"I'm sorry, dear," she says again, shaking her head. She really does look sorry. "Ridgemont High doesn't have a darkroom."

For a second I remain frozen in place. How am I going to develop my film? Was all that time I spent taking pictures just a waste? I ball my hands into fists and tuck them into my sleeves. It's almost as cold in here as it is at home.

Other students walk past me, and I realize I'm standing in the middle of the room. I force my feet to walk me toward the long table near the center of the room and sink onto one of the stools. There are kids scattered on the stools throughout the classroom; they're all chattering happily, catching up after a summer spent apart or just gossiping about which teacher they got for Algebra II and which jock got the best car for his birthday. Clearly none of them cares about the fact that their school doesn't offer a photography class, and none of them have a clue that I'm sitting here feeling devastated about it. There's plenty of room at the table, so no one sits on either side of me. Finally the bell rings, signaling that third period has officially begun, and the woman with the sad eyes walks to the front of the classroom and announces, "I am your visual arts teacher, Victoria Wilde. Let's make some art, shall we?"

Everyone makes a run for the supply closet. Wait, that's it? *Let's make some art, shall we?* No further direction, no actual *assignment?* Just go to the supply closet, grab your medium of choice, and get started?

Ms. Wilde glances at me. She seems to be waiting to see what I'm going to do before she disappears back into the alcove where her desk sits. Her dark eyes have a sort of laser focus that makes me feel her gaze like actual fingerprints on my skin. I bet she's the kind of person who can see out the back of her head too.

I look around. At my old school visual arts was kind of serious business. I mean, we weren't, like budding Picassos and Ansel Adamses, but at least we took our work seriously. But the drawings on these walls are little more than rough sketches; the collages appear to have no rhyme or reason. The lights in the classroom are dim, not nearly bright enough to allow students to really focus on their paintings and sketches. At Ridgemont High visual arts is, apparently, a total blow-off class.

"Everything okay?" a deep voice asks. I spin around on my stool and discover a tall, slim boy standing over me.

"Am I in your way?" I ask, scooting my stool farther under the table and managing to bang my knee against the table in the process. "Ow!"

"You okay?"

"Just klutzy," I nod, rubbing my knee. Later I'll discover a big purple bruise blossoming beneath my clothes. "I could trip over my own two feet," I add. The boy cocks his head to the side almost exactly the same way Oscar does when he's trying to understand the gibberish that comes out of my mouth. "It's something my mom says."

The boy smiles, then makes his way around the table and plops down on the stool across from mine. He adjusts his brown leather jacket. It doesn't really fit him, and it looks old, the leather cracked and faded, just the kind of thing I always hoped I'd come across at Goodwill back in Austin. But no one would ever give anything that nice away. He lays the supplies he's taken from the closet out in front of him: a glue stick, pipe cleaners, construction paper. Like this is a kindergarten class. I narrow my eyes to squint at the door to the supply closet, wishing it would morph into a darkroom.

"I know, right?" the boy acknowledges my look. "I could be in AP English right now, but my mom insisted I take this class. She thinks I need to 'broaden my horizons,' you know?" He has straight dirty-blond hair parted in the middle, and I notice that his eyes are an amber sort of brown. He's cute in a nerdy way, like he popped out of an eighties movie or something. If Ashley were here, she'd be kicking me under the table, trying to get me to flirt with him. But flirting has never come as easily to me as it does to her.

"My old school had photography class," I say, reaching into my backpack and bringing out the two rolls of film. What did I think would happen anyway? That I'd develop this film and see something that I wasn't able to see in real life? That I'd run home and hold the photos up for my mother to see and then she'd turn from a cynic into a true believer? I wrap my hands around the film canisters and shiver. They're cold—like blocks of ice, not plain old pieces of plastic.

I pull my camera from my bag. I'd been planning on showing it to my new photography teacher so she'd know just how serious I was.

"Wow," the boy says. "Is that a Nikon F5?"

I realize that I feel strangely, wonderfully warm. I look around: if I'm warm, then everyone else in this room must be sweltering. But my new classmates look completely normal: none of the boys are wiping sweat from their brows; none of the girls are pulling their hair back into ponytails. Whatever this is, no one else is feeling it. It's my own private heat wave. For the first time in two weeks I can literally feel the color rising to my cheeks. But I don't feel hot—I just feel *comfortable.*

"Yeah," I answer, smiling. "It was my birthday present."

"Awesome." He grins, revealing teeth that are just slightly crooked. He pulls a pair of round, wire-rimmed glasses from his pocket and puts them on, though they quickly slide down his nose so it looks like he's wearing bifocals. "I'm Nolan, by the way," he adds as he bends over his construction paper, running his glue stick up and down the length of the pipe cleaners, bending them into strange, squiggly shapes until it looks kind of like they're laughing. "Nolan Foster."

Feeling ever warmer, I lift my hair off my shoulders and coil it into a messy knot. "I'm Sunshine."

I unwrap my blue scarf and head for the supply closet, trying to ignore the way Ms. Wilde stares at me when I come back with an armful of pipe cleaners.

CHAPTER FOUR
Playtime

"Is he cute?"

I can hear Ashley's smile through the phone. I roll my eyes. "Whether or not he's cute isn't the point."

Ashley sighs. "I know, I know. The point is that being near him made you warm, just like being in that creepy house makes you cold, blah blah blah." Ashley sounds even more tired of hearing me talk about creepiness than Mom does. I imagine her twirling her blond hair dismissively. I had sent her four text messages before she wrote back today. And she didn't call me until it was nearly midnight in Austin. While we're on the phone I change into my pajamas—puppy-printed, but no feet—and climb into bed. "Does it at least smell any better?" she asks.

I wrinkle my nose. "Nope. Still reeks of mildew."

"Gross."

"I know."

"You'd think it would smell like you and Kat by now."

"You'd think," I agree.

"But back to the boy. Maybe you were warm being near him because he was, you know, *hot*."

"What?"

"There's a reason they call it hot, Sunshine! Wait till I tell you how hot I felt sitting next to Cory Cooper in his car yesterday."

Cory Cooper is the boy Ashley spent most of sophomore year crushing on, and I know she's waiting for me to squeal with delight—*Cory Cooper took you for a ride in his car yesterday?!* But I can't squeal because I just noticed that Dr. Hoo isn't on the shelf he was on when I left for school this morning. Instead, he's on the window sill, his face turned outward, as though he's surveying the yard below.

"Ashley . . ." I say softly, whispering as though I'm worried that whatever it was that moved Dr. Hoo might hear me.

"Sunshine . . ." she replies, trying to whisper back, but giggling instead.

I want to giggle with her. Really, I do. But I can't stop staring at my stuffed owl.

No one has been home today. Mom left for work before I left for school, and she hasn't come home yet. She texted me about an hour ago to tell me not to wait up.

Mom loves her new job. And anyway, these long hours are temporary. Just until she gets things up and running, just until her bosses see how valuable and amazing she is.

"Seriously," Ashley says now, "Sunshine, what's going on?"

"I'm not sure," I say, getting out of bed. I reach for Dr. Hoo and put him back on his shelf, and that's when I notice that beneath him, my unicorns have been moved; someone didn't like the way I arranged them by color and instead rearranged them by size, the way they used to be in Austin.

I pull my hand away as though I've touched something hot.

Okay: worst-case scenario, a ghost snuck into my room and moved my stuff around when I was at school. Best-case scenario . . . a robber came into the house, didn't steal anything, but just moved stuff around? Or the dog developed opposable thumbs and stood on his hind legs to move things around? Or I moved Dr. Hoo and the unicorns myself and don't remember doing it because I'm losing my mind?

Wait, which is the best-case scenario here?

I reach into my backpack and remove the two film canisters, place them side by side on my desk. "Hey Ash," I say hopefully, "if I send you some film, can you take it to Max's to get developed?"

Max's is a camera store in downtown Austin. In the summertime, when I couldn't access the school's darkroom, the employees there let me use theirs.

"Why? There must be a studio in Ridgemont you can use."

I shake my head. "No," I say firmly, "it has to be Max's." They're the only people I'd trust to develop the film. "It's important."

"Why, are there ghosts on the film?"

When I don't answer, Ashley bursts out laughing. "Wait a minute, Sunshine. Do you actually think you have photographic evidence of the paranormal? Dude, we'll sell it to the highest bidder. We'll make a fortune!"

"This isn't a joke, Ashley," I say.

"Listen, I know you must be homesick–"

"What?" I ask, spinning around defensively like maybe I think Ashley is behind me and I need to face her head on. Of course, because it's me and I'm a klutz, I lose my balance in the process, but I manage to stay more or less upright. "Why do you think that?"

"Oh, I don't know, maybe because you're convinced your house is haunted and you can't even be bothered to notice whether the boy sitting next to you in art class is *cute*? If you're trying to convince Kat to move back to Austin, you'll probably have better luck with something a little more practical." Ashley knows as well as I do that my mom prefers science to fairy tales.

"I'm not trying to get Mom to move back to Austin," I say.

"Then what exactly are you trying to do, Sunshine?" Ashley has never sounded so impatient with me, not even when she tried to get me to buy a normal white T-shirt at the Gap and I bought a vintage blouse from a thrift shop instead, not when I dragged her to an antique store in search of a first edition of *Pride and Prejudice*, not even when I tricked her into coming with me to a screening of *Roman Holiday* by telling her I actually wanted to see the latest new release at the theater.

The temperature in my pink room drops about twenty degrees. I'm literally shivering, and when I exhale, I can see my breath. I turn around to face my desk again; the film canisters I'd set side by side are now stacked one on top of the other. My heart starts pounding so hard I can hear its beat in my ears.

Okay, that definitely isn't a robber, and it's not the pets, and I guess technically it could be me losing my mind, but I really, really, *really* don't think so.

"Just promise me you'll bring the film to Max's," I beg Ashley finally.

"Fine," she says, but I can tell she's pouting.

"And tell me all about Cory Cooper," I say, exhaling. Living in Creep Central is no excuse to be a bad friend. Though maybe it is an excuse to at least get out of this room. I hop down the stairs and greet Oscar and Lex in the kitchen, get some ice cream out of the freezer, set it on the kitchen counter, and concentrate on the sound of Ashley's voice telling me that Cory put his hand on her thigh when he drove her home from school today.

"He hasn't kissed me yet," Ashley says. "But I know it's coming. You know how you can just tell sometimes?"

I lick ice cream off my spoon like a little kid with a lollipop. "No," I say, sighing dramatically, "I really don't."

"Aw, poor Sunshine," Ashley giggles. "Wait, what are you eating?"

"Ice cream."

"What flavor?"

"Vanilla."

"Boring."

"Classic," I counter, grinning.

"Did you at least dress it up with some syrup and whipped cream?"

I shake my head, smiling. Ashley knows the answer will be no, but she likes teasing me almost as much as Mom does. "Why mess with perfection?" I say, and Ashley laughs. I hear the sound of Mom's key in the lock. "I gotta go, Ash. Keep me posted about Cory and the Kiss with a capital K."

"I will."

"And you'll bring the film to Max's for me?"

Ashley groans. "Jeez, yes, I said I would."

"Good night," I say, "and thanks."

"Night," Ashley replies, "say *Hi* to the ghost for me."

I'm putting the ice cream away when Mom wanders into the kitchen. She looks surprised to see me here. "Sunshine, what are you doing up?"

"Ashley and I were just catching up. First day of school, that kind of thing."

I wait for her to ask me how school was, to ask me for minute details about the kids at Ridgemont High—what do they wear, who did I sit with at lunch, how were my classes, that kind of thing she used to ask me. Back in Austin she asked how even the most uneventful of days were.

But instead, she pulls a sheaf of papers from her bag and says, "You really shouldn't be up so late on a school night."

"You're up late, and you have to get up earlier in the morning than I do," I say. I pause, sure that she's going to tease me in response, make a smarmy remark about how I'm still a growing child, not a grown-up like her. But instead she sits at the kitchen counter and stares at her papers.

"Mom?" I prompt.

"Hmm?" she says, looking up at me like she'd already forgotten I was here in the room with her. She hasn't even said hello to Oscar and Lex, who are circling her stool anxiously. "It's late. You really should go to bed."

I don't say it out loud because I would sound like a whiny little kid, but I don't want to go to bed. I want to stay down here and tell her about Dr. Hoo and the unicorns. I don't want to go back into the room with them.

"New patient?" I ask, gesturing to the papers that Mom's studying.

Mom shakes her head. "Budgets," she says dismissively, like I couldn't possibly understand. I think about her face our first night here in Ridgemont, how nervous she looked when we sat in the hospital parking lot.

"Okay, then," I say, turning on my heel. "Good night."

Mom looks up, just for a second, and smiles. "I'm sorry, sweetie. Believe me, I'd much rather be hanging out with you than working on budgets."

"Don't worry about it."

"I'll come home earlier tomorrow. I want to hear all about how you wowed them at your new school."

"Not so much wowed them as bumped into every table and corner, resulting in some fabulous new bruises."

"I'm sure you'll accessorize the heck out of them," Mom says, then drops her gaze back to the papers spread out in front of her. I'm pretty sure she's not actually going to come home early tomorrow.

Things will be better once she's had time to settle in to her new job. And, they'll be better once I get the film developed and can show her that something creepy is happening in this house. I'll take some more pictures tonight before I send the film to Ashley; I'll photograph the unicorns and Dr. Hoo and the canisters on my desk. Something will show up, something that can't be seen by the naked eye. Mom will apologize for dismissing me, but I won't be mad. After all, I can't blame her for not believing in ghosts. Most people don't.

By the time I open the door to my room I feel much better. Excited even. Maybe Ashley's right—maybe we'll sell these photos to the highest bidder and I'll become famous: *The Girl Who Discovered Ghosts.* My face will be plastered on the cover of magazines. Kids will start dressing like me; vintage shops will be sold out of flowing blouses and printed scarves.

But on the other side of the door my room is a mess. The stuffed animals who'd been neatly lined up on a shelf above my bed, my teddy bears and my favorite stuffed dog, are now lying across my bed; the stuffed giraffe that Mom got me for my sixth birthday is perched on top of my pillows. The board games I'd left in a box in my closet, Connect Four and Jenga, checkers and Monopoly—hadn't gotten around to unpacking them yet—are scattered on the floor.

I open my mouth to scream for Mom. She can't explain this away with branches on the windows or the sounds a house makes when it settles. But then I close my mouth before any sound escapes. She won't need to explain it away. She just won't believe me.

I step inside my room, the pink carpet plush but cool beneath my feet. What does all this mean? I reach for my camera and take pictures. Looking at the world through the viewfinder is usually comforting, but tonight I can't make heads or tails of what I'm seeing.

Slowly I begin putting all the toys away, first the board games and then the stuffed animals. I brush my teeth and pile extra covers on my bed to keep out the cold. Just as I'm about to turn off the light I notice that Dr. Hoo is back on the windowsill, looking outside again. I throw off the covers and march across the room to turn him back around; I like the idea of his plastic eyes focused on me while I sleep, like he's standing guard or something.

I reach for him, my fingers itching to touch his soft feathers. And that's when I feel it. He's *wet.* Not completely, not all over, but there are a few stripes of moisture down his front, as though someone reached out with wet fingers to pet the soft tuft of his feathers.

I leave my owl by the window. Evidently someone wants him that way.

CHAPTER FIVE
Leather Jackets

Despite the lack of photography, visual arts class is quickly becoming my favorite part about life at Ridgemont High. Not because of my increasingly silly collage—I'm adding a layer of glitter and confetti to the left of the pipe cleaners—and certainly not because of Ms. Wilde's tutelage. She might just be the oddest duck in the pond that is my new school.

No, I like visual arts class because Nolan Foster always sits directly across from me. And for whatever reason—whether it's because he's hot like Ashley says or because of something else entirely—I continue to feel warm when I'm near him. Or at the very least, not freezing.

Actually I'm pretty sure Ashley wouldn't think Nolan is hot. He's nothing like Cory Cooper, who has a bright red car and a letterman's jacket. Every day Nolan wears the same leather jacket that he wore on the first day of school. Maybe if I were his girlfriend, he'd let me borrow it. Just the thought makes me roll my eyes at myself. You're not supposed to want to date a boy just for jacket access. Not that the jacket is the only reason I might want to date Nolan. Not that I want to date Nolan. I mean, I don't *not* want to date him . . . oh my goodness, Sunshine, get a grip.

Nolan has stuck with pipe cleaners for his collage, raiding the supply closet for all the black, white, gray, and cream-colored ones. They're twisted into a million different shapes on the table in front of him. When Ms. Wilde leans over me to study Nolan's creation across the desk, the fringe from her lacy black shawl falls into my eyes.

I know I'm in no position to judge—it's not like anyone else in town dresses the way I do—but seriously, I'm pretty sure our art teacher is the only person in Ridgemont who outfits herself like a witch in mourning.

I brush the fringe from my eyes as Ms. Wilde says, "Such *intense* work, Nolan. Where do you get your inspiration?" Without waiting for an answer, she keeps talking. "It's so clear what you're communicating about our mortality—all that black, all that death, but the dusting of white pieces in between—symbolizing hope, I assume?"

Nolan nods. "Of course," he says, his voice low and serious. "What could be more hopeful than white pipe cleaners?" Ms. Wilde keeps her eyes on his collage, so Nolan can wink at me without her seeing.

"All that death," she repeats softly, spinning Nolan's collage in circles on the table. "Have you always found yourself drawn to death?"

"What?" Nolan sputters, caught off guard by such an odd inquiry. Man, this teacher is weird. I'm pretty sure you're not supposed to ask your sixteen-year-old student a question like that.

"I mean, do you find yourself drawn to relics from an earlier time? Tools that were used by extinct peoples, technology from past decades, clothes that were worn by people now dead?"

Nolan doesn't answer her. Instead, he turns pale. I eye his obviously vintage leather jacket. As soon as Ms. Wilde walks away I'm going to tell him that I like vintage clothes too.

But Ms. Wilde doesn't walk away. Instead, she hovers at our table, waiting for an answer.

From across the room a student shouts, "Ms. Wilde, are we out of charcoal?" But our teacher doesn't even look away from Nolan's collage. "Ms. Wilde?" our classmate repeats, louder this time. Instead of answering, she leans closer to Nolan's collage.

"Ms. Wilde?" I prompt. She turns sharply from Nolan's collage to me, as though noticing my presence here for the first time. "I think, ummm—" I don't know the name of the student across the room. "I think she needs you over there."

"Tabitha Chin," Nolan supplies. "Tabitha was asking for more charcoal."

Ms. Wilde shakes her head. I get the idea that she's not particularly interested in what her students are asking for. But Tabitha stands up and walks over to our table. She taps Ms. Wilde on the shoulder, finally forcing her to take her eyes off of me.

"I'm sorry to interrupt, but I really wanted to finish this sketch before next period. I couldn't find any fresh charcoal in the supply closet." Tabitha pushes a few strands of her dark hair behind her ear.

Across the room the other students at her table giggle. I may not have spoken to anyone in this class besides Nolan, but I'm pretty sure we all agree on one thing: Ms. Wilde is the weirdest teacher we've ever had. She might be the weirdest teacher anyone's ever had. She lets out a sigh as she walks across the room with Tabitha, off in search of sketching charcoal.

"Lucky," Nolan mutters once she's out of earshot.

"Me?"

"Yes, you."

"Why's that?"

"Tabitha distracted her before Ms. Wilde could comment on your project."

"She probably wouldn't have liked it anyway. All this glitter and confetti aren't nearly deathly enough for her taste."

Nolan nods. Now Ms. Wilde is holding up Tabitha's sketch—a vase—asking whether it's meant to be a metaphor for the containers in which we live, how fleeting our bodies are, fragile as glass.

"No," Tabitha shakes her head, "I just thought it was a pretty vase."

Looking disappointed, Ms. Wilde drops the sketch back onto the table and moves on.

"Guess she's not interested in pretty things," I say. Some of the blue glitter from my collage must have stuck to her shawl as she leaned over me; she practically sparkles under the fluorescent lights as she moves from student to student.

"That woman looks for death in everything," Nolan shrugs. "Give her time. She'll find a way to argue that your glitter is a symbol of something maudlin." He points to the left side of my collage and puts on a high-pitched voice. "We start out young and sparkly, but the passage of time ravages us, until we fade away." He points to the other—so far, glitter-free—side of my project.

"Well, I can't have that," I say jokingly, upending a jar of glitter all over the other side of the collage. I lean down to blow away the excess.

And promptly unleash a storm of glitter all over Nolan.

"Ohmygosh, ohmygosh," I stammer, standing up. "I'm such an idiot. I didn't put glue down before I sprinkled the glitter."

"Don't worry about it," Nolan says, standing up to brush the glitter from his jacket.

I run to the back of the classroom and grab a stack of paper towels. "I'm so so so so so sorry. *Sunshine strikes again*," I moan, rushing to his side. The rest of the class seems utterly oblivious to the emergency going on down at our end of the table.

"Really, Sunshine, it's okay. Believe me, this jacket has been through worse than a glitter bomb."

"But it's literally the nicest jacket in the entire world and I had to go and–"

"Really?" Nolan grins. "You like it?"

"Are you kidding?" I ask, reaching out to brush some of the glitter away. The leather is warm under my fingers, wrinkled and ridged from what looks like decades of use. I bet it has that amazing old smell, the kind you can usually only find along the spines of ancient books or inside antique furniture. I lean a bit closer, just to get a whiff, even though it must make me seem like the weirdest girl in the entire world, even stranger than Ms. Wilde.

But before I can inhale I draw back. I step away from him and head back to my side of the table. "Here," I say, holding out the paper towels, far enough away from him that I have to straighten my arm for him to reach them.

Okay, seriously, what the heck just happened? One second I was the weirdest girl in the world because I wanted to smell an old jacket, and *now* I'm the weirdest girl in the world because as soon as I got close enough to sniff said jacket, I felt the irresistible urge to pull away.

Something is seriously wrong with me.

I've never been boy-crazy like Ashley. I've never even been boy-mildly-insane. Back in Austin, a few days after my birthday, Ashley dragged me to one last sweaty Texas party. She said I had to get my first kiss while I was still on southern soil. I ended up dancing with Evan Richards, a boy I kind of knew from history class. He was perfectly nice and cute and willing, and by the end of the evening his hands were on my hips and butterflies were in my stomach as his face drew close to mine. And I was ready. I mean, at the very least I thought I should get my first kiss over with already like Ashley suggested. But at the last second I pulled away. It didn't feel right.

Ashley said later that my expectations were too high; she thinks I want to be swept off my feet like a Jane Austen heroine. "It's just a kiss, Sunshine," she'd moaned. "You're probably the last sixteen-year-old in America with virgin lips."

Maybe she was right. Maybe I expect too much. *Don't be ridiculous*, Ashley would say if she were here. *Stop wasting your time on ghosts and ghouls and wacky feelings, Sunshine,* she'd add, *concentrate on that boy instead.*

Which is why I will never tell Ashley that being close to Nolan feels like I'm a magnet pressing up against the wrong side of another magnet.

"Sunshine? Earth to Sunshine?"

I look up. Nolan has taken all the paper towels from my outstretched arm. I drop my hand, folding my arms across myself.

"Sorry," I say quickly. "Just spaced out there for a second."

"No worries," Nolan shrugs. "And seriously, don't worry about the jacket. Like I've said, it's been through a lot worse, believe me. You don't get to be this old without a few bumps and bruises." He slides the jacket off and holds it up, twisting the arms so I can see the dark brown spot on the left side. "See that? That's a patch from when my grandfather literally burned off the left elbow by leaving this thing too close to a campfire." He swings the jacket onto the table, splayed open so I can see the silky brown lining inside. "And see that?" he says, pointing to a seam along the collar, "That's where my grandmother had to sew in a whole new lining when my grandfather's dog chewed out the old one."

"It belonged to your grandfather?" I say, reaching out to trace the lining with my finger. His grandmother's stitches are perfect–tight and precise.

Nolan nods, his voice dropping so Ms. Wilde won't hear. "It freaked me out when she asked about dead people's clothes. Like maybe she's a mind reader or something."

"Don't let Ms. Wilde freak you out," I say. "She's just our kooky art teacher, not a psychic."

Nolan nods, but he looks unconvinced.

"Plenty of people wear used clothes," I add quickly, unwrapping my scarf from my neck. "I got this at a vintage shop back in Austin." I hold it out. "Who knows what happened to the person who owned it before I did, right?"

Nolan nods, pulling his jacket off the table and sliding back into it. He sits back on his stool, so I sit on mine too. "Actually, after my grandfather passed away, my grandmother sent half his clothes to a vintage store."

"What happened to the other half?"

Nolan grins. "Somehow or another it all ended up in my closet. Though I never wear anything but the jacket."

"Why not?"

"I'm not sure. Guess nothing else ever fit this well."

I smile. "Then why keep it all?"

Nolan smiles. "My grandfather was my favorite person. I was pretty wrecked when he passed away. Guess I was just trying to hold on to him, you know?"

I nod, but the truth is, I don't know. My mom's parents were gone long before I came along, and I've literally never known anyone who has died, certainly not well enough to miss them. I never really gave much thought to what happens after we die. Well, not until we moved to Ridgemont and I started sharing a room with a ghostly presence who I'm pretty sure likes to play with my toys.

"What was he like?" I ask.

"He was kind of a weird old guy, but I loved him," Nolan smiles a sad sort of smile, then shrugs. "I don't know. He was just my grandfather. He'd lived in Washington State his whole life and could trace our family back for a half-dozen generations. His own great-grandfather had crossed the country on the Oregon Trail."

"Wow."

"I know. There's actually a street named after him in Portland. My grandfather kept a framed photo of the street sign on his desk." He pauses. "I haven't really ever talked about this with anyone. He only passed away six months ago."

"I'm so sorry," I say softly.

"I asked my grandmother if I could have the photo, but she said no. In fact, pretty much the only thing she was willing to part with was his clothes."

"So you took whatever part of him you could."

Nolan shrugs. "I guess. I don't know. Maybe. Or maybe . . . I know, it sounds insane, but maybe part of me thought he might show up one day, looking for his stuff."

I nod, smiling. Right now it doesn't sound so insane to me.

CHAPTER SIX

Night Terrors

It's already dark when I walk home from school (not that it was ever all that light to begin with), and the houses closest to school glow and twinkle beneath a layer of Halloween decorations. But the closer I get to our house, the fewer the decorations. I guess there's no need for inflatable ghosts and iridescent skeletons when it's already so creepy here.

Anyway, I don't think there are any kids around to trick-or-treat. I considered hanging a black cat on our front door, but it seemed kind of pointless. Our driveway is so long and surrounded by hedges that no one but Mom and me would even see it, and I don't exactly need a reminder that Halloween is less than a week away. Besides, Mom is so busy that she probably wouldn't even notice it.

Lex and Oscar greet me when I open the door. I make sure there's water in their bowls and tell them it's nearly suppertime before trudging up the stairs to my room. I brace myself before opening the door, wondering what kind of disaster awaits me on the other side, but today, at least, my room is in the same condition it was in when I left it this morning.

Well, almost the same condition. As I step inside and slip off my backpack, I see that someone retrieved my checkerboard from the closet and set it up in the center of the bed, black checkers arranged neatly on one side, red on the other.

For some reason seeing just the one game set up neatly on the bed is even creepier than when I opened the door to find every single toy I owned strewn across the room. This is so much more *specific.* I take a deep breath, the cold air chilling my lungs.

This is someone asking me to play with her.

I've decided the ghost must be a ten-year-old girl. I mean, not in real years. For all I know, it's been a hundred years since she died, so maybe technically she's 110 years old. But I think she must have been around ten when she died. She seems to want to play board games most of all—they're on top of the piles of scattered toys in my room—and I feel like that's the kind of thing you get into around fifth grade, right?

All I have to do is take a few steps across the room, reach out my arm, and move a single checker, and the game will begin, right? But then what? Would an invisible hand move a piece on the other side?

Before I can do anything I hear the sound of the front door opening and closing, of Oscar barking with excitement. I turn and run from my room, the checkerboard almost forgotten on the bed. Because, honestly, Mom coming home at a reasonable hour might actually be even more miraculous than a ghost trying to play with me.

"Will wonders never cease!" I shout, running into the kitchen and throwing my arms around her.

"I'm taking the night off," Mom says, grinning. "It's been too long since we've had a proper girls' night." She heaves a bag of groceries onto the kitchen counter.

"Are you *cooking?*" Since we moved to Ridgemont, it's been a lot of take-out and microwave dinners.

"Roast chicken," she says with a smile.

"Ladies and gentleman, meet Katherine Griffith!" I shout in a game show host kind of voice. "She's a mother, she's a nurse, she's a . . . five-star chef!"

Mom curtsies. "I'm a woman of many talents, Sunshine. What can I say?"

I rush through my homework, feeling grateful that the Ridgemont school system is about six months behind the Austin school system so I can breeze through at least half of my assignments and be done in time to set the table and mash the potatoes. After dinner we pile the dishes in the sink—"Let's clean up in the morning," Mom says—and curl up together on the couch, arguing over which of us is hogging the blanket.

We're watching *The Tonight Show* when it happens. At first it doesn't seem like much: the lights flicker, the TV turns off and on.

"That was weird," Mom says, and I shrug, trying to ignore the fact that I'm suddenly freezing, despite the fact that I won our earlier blanket battle. I slide across the couch and rest my head against her chest like I'm ten years old myself and silently beg my little friend not to play any of her games tonight.

Please, I plead. *Please just let me have this one nice night with Mom.*

But then the lights flicker again, and this time they don't turn back on.

Please, I plead again. *I promise to play checkers or Monopoly or Go Fish or whatever you want with you tomorrow.*

"A storm must have taken down the power lines," Mom says, sitting up.

"What storm?" I say. It's raining, but there's no thunder or lightning. "There's not even any wind tonight."

"Not again, Sunshine!" she groans, the littlest bit of a smile playing at the edges of her lips.

I fold my arms across my chest with a huff. "Not again what?"

"I know you're just dying to blame this on your ghosts. But you know as well as I do that blackouts happen all the time."

"Not ghosts," I mumble into the darkness. "Ghost. One ghost. I told you. I think it's a little girl."

"I know. A laughing little girl about ten years old."

"It's not just laughing, Mom, I swear. She wants to play with me."

"Sweetie, I know you're lonely. But believe me, you're going to make friends at your new school soon, and the idea of this ghostly playmate will disappear."

I look at her seriously. "She's a ghost, not my imaginary friend."

"I don't want to argue with you, sweetheart. Let's find some candles."

Mom reaches for my hand in the dark, and together we walk toward the kitchen. The blanket slides to the floor, and I shiver.

"Ow!" I shout suddenly as I bang my shin.

"You okay?"

"Coffee table."

"You sure it wasn't your ghost?"

"Very funny."

We take another step. Moonlight streams in through the kitchen windows so that the countertops and floor seem to glow. Oscar and Lex are curled up on the floor, fast asleep. "At least the blackout isn't bothering them," Mom says.

She pulls candles and a book of matches from the junk drawer in the kitchen and sets about lighting them. But no matter how many times she tries, the matches won't light.

"What the heck?"

"Let me try," I offer, reaching for the matches, but once they're in my hands, I know it's hopeless. Because they're wet.

"Must be a leak or something," Mom says, shrugging. She takes the matches from my hands and goes back to her futile attempts to light them. As if on cue, a drop of water splashes onto my nose.

"Where did that come from?" I ask, looking up. We're on the first floor. Even if the roof is leaking, we shouldn't be able to feel it down here. I pull my phone from my pocket and shine its flashlight on the ceiling.

"Mom?" I ask. "Did you leave the water on upstairs or something?"

Mom looks up and gasps. The ceiling above us is soaking wet, drops of water beading across the cream-colored paint and falling to the floor. "Did you take a shower when you got home from school?" We're directly below the bathroom. "Maybe you left the water running."

I shake my head. I haven't even been on the second floor since she got home—didn't want to see the checkerboard waiting for me.

Then I hear it, a sound coming from above.

"Mom," I whisper urgently, but she's frozen in place. "Mom," I repeat, but she shakes her head, her hair brushing my face as her head moves back and forth.

"Do you hear that?" she whispers, and I nod.

It's the most terrible sound I've ever heard. Not laughter. Not *Night-night.* Not the sound of my things being arranged in the room above us. Not even the sound of water running. Instead, it's the sound of crying. But it's like no crying I've ever heard before.

She's not crying, I realize with a start. She's *begging.* And suddenly, she screams.

Mom turns from the kitchen and makes a dash for the stairs.

"There's a little girl up there!" she shouts, and I follow. "We have to help her!"

Mom opens the door to my room first. Because of the tree blocking my window, only the smallest sliver of light streams in from the moon outside. Actually, wait, not the moon. I walk to the window and peer out through the branches: our neighbors' lights are on.

"Mom," I say softly, "I don't think it's a blackout—"

But she just turns around and runs into her own room.

"Where is she?" Mom shouts desperately. "She's not in either of our rooms."

The crying is louder, and louder still. *Please. Please. Please!*

As the cries get louder, it becomes clear: the sounds are coming from the bathroom.

Mom and I crouch down onto the floor and crawl to the bathroom door. Mom reaches for the knob and starts to turn it. I brace myself for what we're going to see on the other side.

Maybe it won't be that bad. Maybe it will be like *Alice in Wonderland.* Maybe the ghost is crying so hard that she's drowning in her own tears, flooding the floor beneath her.

Can ghosts even cry?

"It's locked." Mom drops her hand.

"What?" I reach up and try the knob for myself. The metal is cold and slick with condensation. "How can it be locked?"

"Whoever's inside must have locked it," Mom says, pulling

herself up to stand. She presses her body against the door like she thinks she can knock it down.

I shake my head. "That lock is broken, remember? You were going to call the landlord and ask him to fix it?"

I shine the light from my phone on her face. Her skin is about three shades paler than usual, practically blue.

A sound makes me drop the phone, plunging us into darkness.

Splashing. But not the sound of a little kid splashing around in the bathtub having fun.

On the other side of the bathroom door someone is trying to keep her head above water. Trying and failing.

Splash. Splash. Splash.

Mom tries the doorknob again, pressing her weight against the door.

"Help me, Sunshine!" she shouts, so I grab my phone, get up, and stand beside her, pressing against the door with all my strength.

Something presses back and we both jump away.

Splash. Splash. Splash. And in between the sound of someone coughing, sputtering, gasping for air. A child's voice saying *Please!*

I close my eyes. I don't want to imagine what's happening on the other side of that door, to the little girl who just wanted to play. Maybe if I'd just played with her . . .

I jump when something cold touches my socked feet; I shine my phone's flashlight on the carpet. Something is seeping out from under the bathroom door. I crouch down to look more closely. I don't think it's just water.

Whatever it is, it's a reddish sort of brown, darker than the tan of the carpet. I take a deep breath. I hope it's not blood. I'm not so good with blood.

"Mom?" I say as I back away from the door. "What is that?"

Mom doesn't answer. Instead, she pounds her fists against the door, making me jump all over again.

"Whoever you are, don't you dare hurt that little girl!" she shouts.

"You said there was no little girl."

Mom ignores me. "Don't hurt her!" she shouts again, louder this time. "Do *not* hurt her!"

Splash. Splash. Splash. Please!

I start shouting too. "Don't hurt her!" I echo. "Don't hurt that little girl!" I put up my fists and pound against the door with all my might. And in between the pounding of our fists I listen for the sound of splashes. As long as she's splashing, she hasn't lost. As long as she's splashing, she still has enough life in her to put up a fight.

Please don't do this again, I hear her beg, her voice thick with effort.

Again? What does she mean, *again?* How many times has this happened before?

Splash. Splash. Splash. More brown water rushes out from under the bathroom door, soaking the carpet, drenching the bottom of my jeans.

I pound even harder, and Mom does too. Between the two of us we'll knock the door down before we give up.

All at once the sound of splashing stops. The bathroom is suddenly horribly silent. Mom and I look at each other in the darkness.

Just as suddenly the lights come back on. The door swings open. I was in midpunch, so I fall face first into the bathroom, knocking my nose against the tile, face down in a puddle of murky water.

I start shaking uncontrollably.

"It's just rust, Sunshine," Mom explains breathlessly. She knows I'm kind of phobic about blood.

"Rust?" I echo.

"From the pipes," she says, gesturing to the tub. I nod, struggling to get my bearings and looking up at the room around me. It doesn't make sense: the water from these pipes has never been rusty before. Maybe this water is different. Older. Rotten. I inhale—the smell of mildew is so strong I can taste it.

The bathroom is a disaster area. Though the faucet isn't running, the tub is overflowing with water, like it's being filled from below. The tiles around the tub are all scratched up, as though someone was gripping both sides, hanging on for dear life.

I pull myself up to stand. It's so cold in here that I'm surprised there's any water at all; you'd think it would be frozen solid.

My heart is pounding so fast, and I can barely breathe. No one else is in here. It's just Mom and me—no little girl, no evil man standing over her, forcing her to beg for her life.

But why would a ghost have to beg for her life anyway?

Mom reaches into the tub and releases the stopper; water begins to disappear down the drain. The mirror above the sink is broken, cracked right down the center, and it's all fogged up so that it takes me a second to see my own reflection.

I'm soaked and shivering. My white T-shirt is stained brown with rust.

"Mom?" I say, turning around to face her. She just shakes her head. Unlike me, she's covered in sweat, hot from the effort of pounding on the door.

"Mom?" I say again, but she still doesn't answer. Instead, she backs into the hallway, her soaked shoes leaving footprints on the carpet.

"What the heck happened in there?" she asks finally. She looks at me like she thinks I have an answer, like maybe all my obsessing over ghosts for the past few weeks has given me some insight, some knowledge into what's going on in this house.

I can't believe I ever complained over a few gusts of wind and a messy floor. What was all of that? Just a warm-up for what happened tonight, the grand finale?

"Sunshine?" Mom prompts. "Was that your ghost?"

I Am Watching

Sunshine has no idea that I am watching. This is a first for me—normally I observe spirits, and spirits always sense when they are being watched. In fact, it's nearly impossible to hide from a spirit, though the ability would come in handy from time to time.

But it is easy to hide from a girl, even a girl like her. To her I am just another car in the school parking lot; perhaps my windows are tinted a bit more than her classmates', but not enough to draw attention. I am a stranger in the aisle of the supermarket, searching for the ripest avocado. And right now I am the man taking an early morning walk in her neighborhood, enjoying a brief respite from the rain.

I perceived the creature's arrival last night, even from across town. It was even more powerful now than it had been before, stealing strength from the rain and the damp, a long wet trail of misery in its wake. I left my motel and drove to the house, parked right outside. I wasn't worried that Sunshine or Katherine would see me. They were too troubled by what was going on inside to notice the stranger in the black car staring at their front door, straining to hear the sounds of their screams.

It tried to touch Sunshine first. I wonder if she even noticed, preoccupied as she was with the suffering of the little girl on the other side of the door.

She hasn't honed her skills yet, doesn't know how to perceive a demon's touch. The creature pulled away as though Sunshine's flesh burned it.

It latched on to Katherine easily, wrapping itself around her, soaking into her skin. Did she notice the layer of moisture that sprang up on her flesh? Probably not. Most don't. Like her adopted daughter, she reserved her focus for the cries on the other side of the door. It will take hours for the shift to occur in her body and mind, days for her eyes to dim almost imperceptibly, weeks for her hair to lose its luster and her skin to grow pale. The creature isn't in a rush. It knows exactly how much time it has.

I drove away not long after midnight, but now, just a few hours later, I am back. There is other work I could be attending to, but I tell myself that none of my work is more important than this. Than her.

And so I am watching.

CHAPTER SEVEN

The Morning After

Mom and I sleep in the living room. Well, *sleep* might not be the right word for what we do. First, I scrub my face and hands clean, using the kitchen sink because I can't stand being in that bathroom a second longer, wondering what kind of monster could hold a little girl under water even as she struggled so hard that there are scratch marks in the tile. We debate over whether to call the police. "And report what?" I ask. "A flooded bathroom with a malfunctioning lock?" Then we collapse onto the couch in the living room. We don't turn off the lights; I don't particularly feel like being plunged into darkness again anyway. We just sit there, holding hands, staring at the wall across from us. At some point I guess I must have fallen asleep because the next thing I know, it's morning, and the scent of Mom's coffee is wafting in from the kitchen, and I'm stretching my arms above my head, blissful in that brief moment between being asleep and being fully awake when I don't yet remember that the scariest thing that ever happened to anyone happened to us last night.

Okay, maybe not the scariest thing that ever happened to anyone. But it's gotta be up there on that list somewhere. It's certainly the scariest thing that ever happened to *me.*

"Mom?" I say, padding into the kitchen.

"Morning, sweetie," Mom says as she pours herself coffee. "My goodness, what a night."

"Understatement of the year."

"My neck is killing me," she says, tilting her head back and forth. "Maybe after work tonight you can rub it for me?"

I shrug.

"That's the last time I sleep on the couch," Mom says with a sigh.

I shake my head. "I'm not heading up those stairs anytime soon."

"Planning on going to school in the clothes you slept in? Very glamorous."

"I don't care." Who cares what I go to school wearing? I notice that she's fully dressed, her hair drying down her back. "Did you take a *shower*?" I shudder, trying not to imagine her having to step over a puddle of dirty water in order to get to the tub.

"Of course I showered," she replies. "I shower every day. And you should really get a move on if you're planning on taking a shower before school. I can give you a ride today if you hurry."

I shake my head and reach for a mug and pour in some coffee. I add a ton of sugar—I don't exactly feel like filling my mouth with bitterness this morning; I can still taste some of last night's mildew—and make my way toward the stairs. I close my eyes, and a flash of what happened last night fills my imagination. I shake my head. Mom's right. I can't wear these clothes to school today. I look down and see that my shirt is filthy: stained brown with the rusty water.

I remember the fear I felt when I fell into it, terrified that it might be blood. I've never been good with blood. When I was six and lost my first tooth while biting into an apple, my mouth filled with blood and I actually fainted. Mom loves telling people that story. *A nurse's daughter, scared of the sight of a little blood*, she'd laugh.

Apparently I'm not so good with rust either. Did I really sleep like this?

Slowly, clutching my coffee mug to keep warm, I walk up the stairs, concentrating on putting one foot in front of the other. I have to walk past the bathroom to get to my room, and Mom has left the door open, the lights on. I want to walk right past it without looking in, but I can't help myself; before I know what I'm doing I've turned my head and looked inside. I brace myself for rusty brown stains on the floor, the broken mirror, the scratches on the tile.

But what I see is even scarier. "Mom!" I shout, my voice is so loud that it startles me.

"What?" she shouts back, running up the stairs. "Are you okay?"

I shake my head. "Of course I'm not okay," I answer. My hands are shaking so hard that coffee is splattering out the sides of my cup. She takes it from me, then looks me over like she's trying to find a cut or a broken bone, trying to figure out what could have made me shout for her the way I did.

"You're spilling this everywhere."

"Did you . . . did you clean it all up?" I ask, but then I shake my head. She could have wiped up the water, but you can't scrub away scratch marks. You can't replace a broken mirror at seven in the morning. Beneath my feet the carpet that was damp just a few hours ago is dry. The scent of mildew hangs in the air, but then again, this house always smells damp.

"I'm going to try to, but seriously, Sunshine, coffee leaves a stain. It's a good thing this carpet is tan . . ."

"What are you talking about?"

"You splashed coffee all over the carpet," Mom says, pointing to the floor just outside the bathroom door. I haven't actually stepped inside yet.

I shake my head. "No, I mean . . . how did the bathroom get like this?"

She sighs. "Get like what? Listen, honey, I know I said I could give you a ride to school, but you really have to get going or else I'll be late. The way you shouted–my gosh, I thought you must have been dying or something. Don't scare me like that."

"No," I say slowly. "I'm not the one who was dying."

"What are you talking about? Is the dog hurt?"

My skin prickles, making me want to scratch myself. "What are *you* talking about?" Mom doesn't answer. Instead, she crouches down and starts blotting the fresh stains on the carpet with a paper towel. A cold chill makes goose bumps blossom on my arms and legs. "What do you remember about last night?"

Without looking up at me, she answers, "We had roast chicken and mashed potatoes with too many lumps in them. We made ice cream sundaes, and you spilled chocolate syrup on your shirt, and we fell asleep on the couch watching *The Tonight Show*, and now I've woken up with a crick in my neck so bad that I think I might have to find a chiropractor."

I take a step backward, away from the bathroom, away from her.

"That's all you remember?" I ask, my voice shaking. "Nothing else? Nothing at all?"

"Is there something you think I'm forgetting?"

Yes.

A scream so bloodcurdling I can still hear it echoing in my ears.

A little girl's voice begging for mercy.

A darkness so black, it felt like I'd never see the sun again.

Mom stops blotting, sits on her heels, and looks up at me. "Did you have another bad dream or something?"

Did I have a bad dream? No. It was real. I have the ruined shirt to prove it. But she says the stain on my shirt is chocolate syrup. One of us is going crazy. One of our minds has invented memories of what happened last night.

I close my eyes, willing myself to keep calm. *Take a deep breath, Sunshine. The answer is right in front of you.*

Or on you, I think, looking down at my shirt. I *hate* chocolate syrup. I never, ever, ever put it on my ice cream. I like plain vanilla. Boring, just like Ashley says. Mom knows that. So there's no way the stain on my shirt is syrup. It doesn't even look like syrup; it looks like exactly what it is: a dried-out patch of rusty water.

She's the one with the made-up memories, not me.

But now what? I can't make her believe me. All my proof is gone: the scratches on the floor, the shards of glass in the sink from the mirror above. I should have gotten my camera last night, should have taken pictures. In my terror I guess it never occurred to me that I might need more evidence. I thought she finally believed me; that was the one part of the night that wasn't scary. I actually felt better, even with everything going on, knowing she was finally on my side.

I need some time to think. To figure this out. Alone.

So I say, "You're right. I'm just moving too slowly this morning. You should get going without me. I can walk to school."

"You're sure?"

I nod.

"All right," she says, pressing her hands against her thighs, pushing herself up to stand. She leans over and kisses the top of my head. "I know you're having a tough time adjusting, Sunshine. Maybe . . . I don't know. Maybe if things aren't better for you in a few months, we should consider moving back to Austin."

Her voice sounds so sad when she says it that I shake my head. "I'll be all right," I say, and I don't watch her walk down the stairs. Instead, I turn around and head for my room, closing the door shut behind me before I collapse onto the floor in a little ball, hugging my knees to the chest.

That's the first time I've ever lied to my mother.

CHAPTER EIGHT

A Good Old-Fashioned Haunting

I take my time getting dressed, even though it means I'm missing first period, the first time I've ever cut a class. It's turning into a day full of firsts. Ashley would be so proud of me, doing normal teenage things like lying to my mom and ditching. That is, she would be proud of me *if* she knew, but she doesn't know because she hasn't answered any of my texts. I didn't go so far as to say it was an emergency, because then she might have called my mom, and that wouldn't do me any good. So I just said I really, really, really, really needed to talk. I was kind of hoping she'd think it was about *that hot guy* (how she refers to Nolan) and call back right away, but so far, no such luck.

Before I walk out the door I check my phone to find out the outside temperature: it's in the fifties, supposedly going up to the sixties. There's a chance of rain this afternoon, but what else is new? "I'm going to need a scarf," I say out loud, wondering who is left in this house to hear me. Is the little girl gone? She couldn't have been killed last night, not if she was already dead, but maybe she was . . . I don't know, *destroyed* or something? Just the thought makes me shudder.

I run up the stairs and into my room, searching for my favorite blue-owl scarf. That's when I notice the checkerboard, right where it was when I got home from school yesterday, on the bed I didn't sleep in last night.

"I guess there's one way to figure out if you're still here," I say sadly. I lean down over the board and slide one of the black checkers forward. I should be hoping that when I get back home later the checkers won't have moved. If they're just as I left them, then maybe ghost girl is gone. But part of me hopes I'll come home to a countermove instead.

"Freak," I mutter to myself as I close my bedroom door behind me.

I walk to school slowly, going over the events of the past twenty-four hours in my head.

Splash, splash.

When we were nine Ashley's mom took us to the pool at the local rec center. There was a nasty kid there, a bully, and Ashley and I knew enough to stay out of his way. But some little kid accidentally cut him in line for the bathroom, and the bully was so angry that he picked the kid up and tossed him into the deep end of the pool before anyone could move quickly enough to stop him. The lifeguard dove in and saved him, but before she could get to him, the little boy splashed around desperately, trying to keep his head above water, gasping for air. I never forgot the sound of it. I hoped I would never hear it again. And I never did.

Until last night.

Splash, splash.

I get to school just in time for visual arts, second period on Fridays. I sit down across from Nolan, particularly grateful when the warmth of being near him washes over me.

"You okay?" he says, looking up from his collage. "You don't look so good."

I must blush crimson. I mean, okay, I know I don't look good—I barely slept last night, and after my mom left, I was still avoiding the bathroom. I brushed my teeth in the kitchen sink and skipped a shower altogether, then ran to school through a fog of spitting, drizzling rain. My hair is probably sticking out like a cartoon of someone getting electrocuted.

Well, I guess that's appropriate. I mean, I've certainly had a shock.

Still, I hate for Nolan to see me like this. I mean, I know I have much, much, much more important things to worry about, but he's a boy and I'm a girl, and . . .

"Sunshine?" he prompts. "You okay?"

"Sorry," I say, nodding frantically. "Yeah. Of course. Yeah. Just. I didn't sleep much last night. It happens, right? Blah!" I giggle nervously. Why do I feel the need to ramble on when Nolan just asked a simple question? I did that the day we met, when he asked whether I was okay after I bumped into the table.

"Blah?" Nolan echoes.

"Yeah, I just say that sometimes. When I can't think of something else to say."

I expect Nolan to laugh at me, but instead he says, "Supercalifragilisticexpialidocious."

"I'm sorry?"

"You know, from *Mary Poppins.* A word to say when you can't think of anything else to say?"

"Exactly!" I grin. I spent most of preschool carrying a *Mary Poppins* DVD like I thought it was a clutch bag. "Wow, I can't believe I didn't think to say that instead of *blah*!"

"Blame it on the bad night's sleep," Nolan offers.

"Good idea."

A voice behind me says, "Oh, I couldn't sleep either. I just had the worst nightmares." I jump and turn around. Ms. Wilde is standing over me. Her skirt is so long that it looks almost like she's floating. The dark circles under her eyes are even more pronounced than usual, her skin a shade paler, as blue as my mom's looked last night. And her eyes are bloodshot, as though she's been crying. Actually, as though she's still crying, just a little bit.

Wow, I can hardly believe it, but I think Ms. Wilde is in even worse shape than I am.

"What is it that kept you awake, Sunshine?" she asks.

"Bad dreams?" Nolan tries, but I shake my head. I'm not about to tell them what really happened, but I'm not going to lie either. I've done that enough for one day.

"It's . . . complicated," I reply. Ms. Wilde leans down over me so I have to crane my neck to look up at her face. She squints.

"You have very . . . unusual eyes."

"I know," I say, dropping my gaze.

"I don't know how I didn't notice that before." Her usually melodic voice is an octave lower than usual, like maybe she's getting over a cold.

I turn around on my stool, pretending to be concentrating on my collage, but the truth is, I just want Ms. Wilde to leave me alone. I'm too tired to make small talk about my weirdo eyes. After what seems like forever, I hear the swish of her skirt as she walks away.

"She is the weirdest teacher ever," Nolan whispers, and I nod in agreement.

During lunch, instead of eating, I sprint to the library. Maybe I can find something—online, in a book, somewhere—to help me explain all of this to my mother, to help me convince her. I sit in front of a computer and Google haunted houses and demonic possession and poltergeists and ghouls, but 90 percent of the results are ads and reviews of horror flicks. I plant my elbows on the table and rest my head in my hands, closing my tired eyes. This is getting me nowhere.

"Got a thing for ghosts?"

For the second time today a voice from behind me makes me jump. Well, I'm sorry to be such a spaz. If people knew what was happening to me, they'd hardly blame me for it.

This time, when I turn around, it's not a teacher standing over me but Nolan, his lips curled into a grin as though he's just heard the funniest joke in the history of funny jokes.

Great. Someone else who thinks ghosts are every bit as absurd as Mom and Ashley do.

I shake my head. "Not exactly. I mean, I never used to. I mean . . ." I trail off. "It's complicated," I sigh.

"Of course it's complicated." Nolan pulls out a chair to sit beside me. I feel just a tiny bit warmer with him near, and I resist the urge to lean into him, like I'm in an old cabin and he's the fireplace.

"Of course it is?"

He grins. "Sure. Only a fool would expect the paranormal world to be simple."

I can't tell if he's making fun of me or not, so I keep my mouth shut.

"I mean, my grandfather–"

Oh my gosh. What an idiot. Me, I mean, not him. Here I am, talking about ghosts to someone whose beloved grandfather passed away a few months ago. He must hate me. "Nolan, I'm sorry, I didn't mean–"

"Didn't mean what?"

"To, I don't know. Make light of . . . I don't know. You know. Death." Butterflies flutter in my stomach when I say the word *death.* I must have said that word a thousand times before: you know, *Jeez, Mom, you scared me to death* (when she snuck up on me from behind back home in Austin), *Golly, Ashley, I'm bored to death* (every time she made me go to the mall with her). I don't think I ever fully appreciated what the word meant before. Now, it seems to me that it's the kind of word that *should* give you a jolt of adrenaline when you say it out loud.

"What?" Nolan asks, narrowing his eyes in confusion. I don't answer, just shake my head, and somehow Nolan seems to understand. "Oh, I didn't mean anything like that," he adds quickly. "I meant that my grandfather used to tell me these amazing ghost stories. Tales that he'd been told by his father, who'd been told them by his father, and so on as far back as he knew. Stories of spirits and ghouls passed down from generation to generation, from one side of the country to the next." He smiles wistfully, and suddenly I can picture him as a little kid, that same sort of wide-eyed wonder on his face, sitting in front of an old stone hearth in his grandfather's house, listening to story after story.

I wonder what Mom's parents were like. Maybe I'd have been close with them. Maybe I'd have complained about being forced to visit them every summer like Ashley did about her grandparents. Either way, it's only now, here with Nolan, that I understand that I missed out on something big, not having had grandparents.

"Sounds nice," I say to Nolan.

"Nice?" he echoes, and bursts out laughing. "Are you kidding? It was terrifying!" Soon I'm laughing too, so loud that the librarian comes over to shush us. Quietly Nolan continues. "Most kids are raised on fairy tales, but not me. My bedtime stories had more blood and guts and gore than they did fair maidens and gallant princes."

"Guess you had your share of nightmares."

He shrugs. "Not really. I mean, like I said, I was raised on those stories. I know it sounds strange, but I always found them kind of comforting."

"Plus you knew they weren't real," I add. Just like I knew the fairy tales my mom told me weren't real.

"No way." Nolan shakes his head. "I believed every one of them. My grandfather believed them too, no matter how much the rest of the family made fun of him. He'd been a believer his whole life. My mom used to refer to him as 'that crazy old man.'" He sets his mouth in a straight line as he recalls his mother's words, like even now, months after his grandfather's passing, he can't stand knowing that people talked about him that way. It's clear that Nolan never thought his grandfather was anything but perfectly sane.

Wait a minute . . . does this mean Nolan believes in ghosts? What would he say if I told him what's going on in my house, the stories that do nothing but bore Ashley and irritate my mother?

"I'm actually writing an extra-credit report for my history class about ghosts of the Northwest. Thought if I could back up some of his stories, get an A out of it, it might . . . I don't know—"

"Keep your mom from calling him crazy?"

Nolan nods. "Pretty much. I was going to check out some of the places where my grandfather swore he saw specters this weekend. You interested?"

I sit up a little straighter. *Am I interested?* He means do I want to come with him, right? If Ashley were here, I'd have to step on her foot to keep her from squealing. She'd say that a ghost hunt—though, in her opinion, totally fake—could be the perfect first date. So many opportunities to grab a boy's hand—*Oh, no, did you hear that too?*—and warm embraces—*I'm so scared that I'm shivering.*

"Earth to Sunshine, Earth to Sunshine," Nolan singsongs. I blink and look up at him. "Searching for sketchy old haunted houses not exactly your cup of tea?"

"If only you knew," I mutter.

"If only I knew what?" Nolan says, his eyes widening just a little.

I hesitate. Should I really tell this boy about what's going on? I mean, it's great that he believes in ghosts and everything, but that doesn't mean he'll believe *me.* Maybe, like Mom, he'll take one look at our house and say that the sounds I'm hearing are probably just branches hitting the windows, pine needles falling on the roof. Maybe he'll think I'm just crazy, and then he'll tell everyone at school that I'm crazy, and he won't even sit next to me in visual arts anymore and I'll have to go back to being freezing absolutely everywhere.

But . . . what if he *does* believe me? What if he doesn't explain away the sounds and smells and actually remembers what happened the morning after the scariest night of my life? Then I would have an ally. Someone to talk to about how terrifying all of this is. And maybe someone to help me figure out how to prove it.

So, slowly, I tell Nolan about our house. I tell him about the creepiness that's settled over everything since we moved in, about the laughter and the toys, about the film I sent off to Austin to be developed, about the chill in the air (I leave out the fact that the chill diminishes when he's close). Finally I tell him about what happened last night and the even scarier thing that happened this morning, when my mother woke up oblivious once more.

"Wow," Nolan whistles. "Sounds like you've got a good old-fashioned haunting on your hands."

"I don't know what I have on my hands."

The bell rings, signaling that lunch period is over and it's time to go to class. I turn and close the window on the computer. All my ghost Googling disappears. I pick up my bag from the floor and start to walk to class, but Nolan doesn't budge.

"What are you doing?" I ask him.

"Waiting," he answers.

"Waiting for what?"

"Waiting for you to invite me over after school today so I can help you try to figure out what's going on in your house. I'd invite myself, but I don't want to be rude."

I grin. In my entire life I've never been so relieved to issue an invitation (and yes, I know, *issue an invitation* is total Jane Austen–speak).

When Ashley finally texts me back—*everything okay?*—I write back: *Sorry. False alarm.* There's no point in telling her what happened last night, not when she won't believe me. Not when there's someone so much closer to home who actually does believe me.

Although I am tempted to ask for her advice about having a boy over for the very first time.

CHAPTER NINE

Photography

At home later I hesitate before opening the door to my room. Nolan isn't coming over until five o'clock, and I'm tempted to wait till he gets here before checking on the state of my checkerboard. But I force myself to turn the knob and step inside.

The checkers are exactly where they were when I left this morning. Maybe I invited Nolan over for nothing after all. I drop my backpack in the center of the room with a sigh and spin around on my heel, closing the door behind me.

Nolan knocks on our front door at precisely five o'clock. I'd suggested we walk home from school together, but he said he had some work he wanted to get done first. Turns out, the work was research. About our house. He walks into the door shaking his head.

"I couldn't find anything unusual about this house or your neighborhood. No reported hauntings, no mysterious disappearances, and no little girls murdered in the bathroom."

I shudder at the mere mention of a little girl murdered in the bathroom as I lead him into the kitchen. He's barely stepped foot inside the house, and he's already as skeptical as Mom and Ashley.

Great.

"I thought all the scary stuff happened upstairs?" he asks, though he takes a seat at the kitchen table.

Flustered, I nod. I mean, it's not like my mother ever handed me a list of rules about being alone with a boy in the house or whether he's allowed in my room. Still, I can't help thinking about what Ashley said a couple of months ago: *What would be more mortifying: the dead bird or the pink walls?*

It doesn't matter. Or anyway, it *shouldn't* matter. Nolan isn't here for *me*. He's here for the ghost—and of course, now that I finally have another believer in the house, I'm not even sure she's still here. There's no laughter, no creaking footsteps, no tears.

I shudder. Did the ghost actually drown last night? I mean, I know ghosts are already dead, but maybe they can . . . I don't know, die a second death. A *horrible* death, I think, remembering the sounds of her struggle.

I swallow a sigh. Maybe I should just admit I'm going crazy, like Ashley would say. Maybe I should let Mom send me to a shrink in her hospital every day after school. At least then I'd have a chance of seeing her before dark.

"Ummm," I say finally, leaning against the island counter in the center of the kitchen. "Do you want something to drink or something? I could make coffee."

"No thanks," Nolan says, standing up.

Great, he's going to leave. He's been here for less than five minutes. But instead, he leans against the counter across from me and smiles.

"Don't worry, Sunshine. Just because I came up empty-handed doesn't mean I don't believe you."

Now I do sigh—a sigh of relief, feeling that familiar Nolan-centric warmth wash over me. "I'm sorry I don't have anything to show you. The ghost isn't exactly at my beck and call. After last night, I don't even know . . . I don't even know if she's here anymore."

"I'm sure she has a busy schedule all her own. You know, places to go, people to haunt." Nolan grins, so I do too.

The doorbell rings, making me jump. I laugh at how easily startled I am. "I'll be right back," I say, walking from the kitchen to the front door. It's the postman, delivering an envelope that was too big to fit in our mailbox. I look at the return address as I take it from him, muttering a barely audible *thank you:* Max's Photo Shop, in Austin.

I reach into my pocket and text Ashley: *Photos arrived—you're the best!!!* Then I spin around—almost tripping in the process. Maybe I do have something to show Nolan after all!

I rip open the envelope and run back into the kitchen. "Look!" I shout, holding the photos up above me like I've just won something.

"Are those the pictures you took?"

I nod, and Nolan reaches out to take them from me. "Let's have a look." Standing side by side, we spread the black-and-white photos out on the kitchen counter.

"Something isn't right." I bite my lip as I lean over to get a closer look. I can't put my finger on it, but something about the photos looks . . . off, somehow.

"Maybe the developers screwed up the film," Nolan suggests, but I shake my head.

"No. I sent the film to Max's for a reason. They're the *best.* And you can tell—nothing is out of focus, none of the film is smudged." Nolan nods, leaning over the counter until our heads are nearly touching. Quickly—trying and no doubt failing to be subtle—I lower my own head closer to the photos, careful to make sure that my face doesn't brush against his.

"Look," I say, pointing to one of the photos of my bedroom. "Do you see it?"

"What?" Nolan says. I can feel his breath on the back of my neck. Being this close to him still doesn't feel right.

Okay, I know I'm thinking about ghosts right now, but there's enough room in my brain to also worry that I'm never going to get a first kiss if I can't handle just standing this close to a boy. A boy I actually *like*, who's being so nice to me—who believes me. But Nolan must sense the way I stiffen, because he slides a few inches down the counter, away from me.

I shake my head. Maybe it's impossible for anything to feel right when you're literally looking at pictures of ghosts.

That'd be a lot easier to believe if I hadn't felt exactly this way when I was brushing glitter off his jacket in our visual arts classroom.

"That shadow," I point to a gray shape in the center of a photo I took of board games scattered across the floor of my room. I'm kind of relieved that the photos are black and white so Nolan can't see that my room is actually bright pink. "There's no object above it, nothing to actually cast a shadow. And yet . . ."

"There it is," Nolan finishes for me.

"There it is," I echo, studying the shadow. From this angle it just kind of looks like a blob. It could be anything.

Nolan says exactly what I'm thinking: "I can't tell what it is." He sounds as frustrated as I feel, shuffling carefully through the pictures. "Maybe you caught it from a different angle in one of the other photos. So we can see what shape it is."

I dig through the photos; everything is all out of sequence. The pictures of the toys in my room are next to pictures of my room when we first arrived, when I hadn't even unpacked my stuffed animals yet. I guess the folks at Max's didn't bother keeping the pictures in order. It's not the kind of thing that was ever important to me before.

"There," I gasp, pointing. Nolan lifts the photo off the counter and holds it up in front of us, at eye level. Or his eye level anyway.

"Wow," he says, and I nod in agreement. My heart is beating so fast now that it feels like it's about to burst from my chest. I'm breathing as hard as if I'd been running. Oscar circles my legs nervously, like he knows something's wrong.

I can't believe it. I mean, it's not like I didn't think I was right about what I was seeing and hearing, but still, I don't know if I ever actually really *believed* I would capture proof. Or at least, not proof like this, not something so clearly visible to the naked eye, something that the person standing next to me can see as easily as I can.

At the center of the photo, in the center of my room, surrounded by board games and stuffed animals, is the very clear, very distinct, utterly undeniable shadow of a little girl.

Before I can stop him Nolan is sprinting up the stairs.

"What are you doing?" I shout as I run after him.

"I want to get a better look!" he shouts back. He throws the door to my room open and practically leaps up onto my desk chair. "This is where you were standing when you took the photo, right?"

I nod. "I thought I'd be able to capture the entire room from there."

"You weren't wrong," Nolan says appraisingly, holding the photo out in front of him.

I shake my head. "Apparently not."

"She was right there." He points to the center of the room.

"You're not going to forget about this in the morning, are you?"

"I'm *never* going to forget about this," Nolan replies solemnly, stepping down from my chair. He looks around the room, blinking. "Geez. That's a lot of pink."

"Really?" I say breathlessly, feigning surprise. "I hadn't noticed." I pretend to look around like I'm seeing it for the first time. But when my gaze falls on my bed, I freeze, no longer worried what Nolan thinks of the pink or Dr. Hoo or my unicorn collection. Instead, I hold up my hand and point at the checkerboard.

Someone has made the next move.

CHAPTER TEN

Kat's Eyes

It's dark by the time Mom gets home, and it's starting to–what else is new?–rain. The combination of the rain and the lower autumn temperatures creates a damp kind of cold I've never felt before, so that even when the thermometer says it's in the fifties, I shiver as though it's below freezing out. At least I'm getting more use out of all my oversized grandpa sweaters; I've been collecting them from thrift shops for years, even though Ashley correctly pointed out that I hardly needed them in Austin. I guess part of me knew I'd have a use for them eventually.

Nolan has long since left to get started on his homework. He asked whether he could take the photos with him, but I shook my head. I needed them, I insisted. I wasn't about to postpone the chance to show Mom my evidence. I lay the pictures out on the kitchen table and waited.

When Mom finally walks in I have to scramble to keep Lex from running out the front door.

"That's strange," Mom says, and I brighten. Maybe this won't actually be that hard. Maybe she's already begun to accept that strange things are going on here.

"I know," I agree enthusiastically. "Lex is an indoor cat. Plus, it's raining, and cats hate the rain. Wonder why he'd want to run away."

Mom's face is wet with rainwater, and the files of papers she always carries with her are completely soaked.

"Did your umbrella break or something?" I ask, and Mom looks surprised by the question. She reaches into her bag and pulls out her umbrella, dry and folded up neatly.

"I guess I forgot I had it," she says absently.

"How could you forget in weather like this?" I ask, but Mom doesn't answer. Instead, she shrugs off her raincoat, letting it fall on the floor. Her straight hair is twisted into a damp ponytail, and her pastel-colored scrubs are wet up to her knees. She kicks off her chunky black clogs, and they land with a thud on top of her raincoat as she makes her way into the kitchen.

I shake my head. She usually rags on *me* for leaving a trail of clothes between the front door and my room when I get home. Maybe it's just because it's so wet and she didn't want to hang it up, where it might . . . what? Dry?

I shake my head. It's the end of a long day, she's tired, and she's soaked, so dropping her coat on the floor is no big deal. Everyone gets lazy from time to time, even someone as neat and organized as Mom.

I turn on all the lights in the kitchen. I've laid the photos out on the table by the window, the one with the little girl's shadow smack in the center of the table, where she can't miss it.

"I have something to show you," I begin.

Mom shakes her head. "Can it wait? I haven't even had anything to eat yet."

I don't mention that I haven't had dinner either; I'd been waiting for her to get home. Instead, I say, "I'll make you something. Anything you want." My voice comes out extra-eager. But it's not dinner I'm excited about.

"Right now I just want a hot bath and an even hotter cup of coffee." Mom heads for the coffeemaker, her eyes half-closed.

"Coffee? At this hour?"

"Yes, Sunshine. At *this* hour. I still have work to do, and I've been exhausted all day."

I sway backward as though I've just been shoved, away from her. I'm not sure she's ever talked to me so curtly. I remind myself that it's not her fault. She doesn't know why she was so tired all day, and I do—we were up half the night, terrified.

Mom fills her mug and heads for the table, the soaking wet papers dripping in her arms. She's about to set them down on the table—it's like she doesn't even see the photos lying there—and I shout, "No!"

Mom spins around. "What is it now?"

I shake my head, imagining my photos stained with a ring of coffee from the bottom of her mug, spattered with water from the edges of her files. They'd be useless then. She'd be able to blame the shadows on the damage.

"You could have ruined my photos," I say, genuinely irritated. She might have destroyed them. I mean, okay, she doesn't know how important they are.

"What?" Mom says, blinking as though she's seeing them for the first time. "Oh, sorry, honey. I didn't see them."

Okay, I know they're black and white, and I know that even

with all the lights on, this room is still pretty dim—which is pathetic, considering that it's the best-lit room in the house, with a fairly tacky chandelier hanging down above the table—but come on! I mean, there's a stack of photos there. How could she not see them?

"Mom, I know you're tired and I know you're busy, but I have something I really want to show you." I walk over to her and take the papers from her, placing them gently on the counter behind us, where they can drip all they want without doing any harm.

"Look," I say, pointing at the photos. "It'll only take a second."

"You took some photos of the house. They're great, honey. And it's so nice to see you embracing our new home like this, finally." She bends her head to sip from her coffee mug. Maybe it's just my imagination, but from here it looks like the coffee is too hot for drinking. I don't mean that it's still steaming; I mean it looks like it's bubbling, boiling.

I shake my head as Mom swallows the coffee smoothly. I must be imagining things.

"Look," I try again, pointing to the photo in the center. The one where the shadow is most distinct. "Look at *that.*"

Mom lifts the photo off the table and holds it up in front of her face. She narrows her eyes.

"Sunshine, your room is a mess," she says finally.

"What?"

"Why are your games and toys scattered everywhere like that? I hope you put everything away."

I shake my head. "Don't look at the toys. Look closer, at the center of the room." I resist the urge to grab the photo and hold it up in front of her. Nolan didn't need me to tell him to look closer. He thought the shadow was every bit as obvious as I did.

"What is it you want me to look at?" Mom asks, sighing impatiently. She lowers the photo out of her eye line.

I pause before answering. Maybe I should wait until tomorrow. Maybe tomorrow Mom will have had a good night's sleep and maybe the sun will be shining so that the light will be better in here and Mom will be able to see.

A clap of thunder sounds in the distance, like maybe the universe is laughing at me for thinking that it might be sunny in the morning.

"Don't you see it?" I ask, surprised at how small my voice sounds. I sound about half my age. "Don't you see the shadow in the center of the room?"

Mom shakes her head. "I don't see anything."

I swallow a gasp, wringing my hands like an old lady who's worried about the weather. I mean, it was one thing all those nights when I heard footsteps and laughter and Mom said it was just the wind, just branches from the Douglas firs hitting the side of the house—that was Mom just being her skeptical self. But this isn't just a little cynicism. It was scary enough when she didn't *remember* what happened this morning, but right now she literally doesn't *see* the same image that Nolan and I saw in the photograph that's right in front of her.

I look up at the ceiling, wondering what the ghost is doing up on our second floor, what kinds of tricks she's played on my mother's brain to blind her like this.

"Mom—" I start, but she cuts me off.

"Please tell me this isn't more ghost nonsense."

"It's not nonsense," I say, still in that small voice.

"It *is* nonsense, Sunshine, and I really wish you'd cut it out." Unlike mine, Mom's voice is anything but small. "I know you're not crazy about Ridgemont, but I am getting sick and tired of your complaining."

"It has nothing to do with whether I like Ridgemont or not," I say, and now my voice sounds even more like a little kid's, and in the worst possible way. I take a deep breath and try to control it. I need to sound calm, to make a compelling argument, using scientific evidence—the photos—the kind of argument that Mom will understand. "I just wanted to show you—"

"Show me what?" Mom says almost shouting and she drops the photo. It flutters down to the floor and I pick it up frantically, scared she might step on it or something, relieved that at least she didn't rip it in half before she let it go.

"Sunshine," Mom says before I can answer. She's not exactly yelling, but she still sounds angry. She puts her mug down on the counter with such a loud bang I'm surprised it doesn't break into a thousand pieces. "I've had just about enough of this. Go to your room."

"Go to my room?" I echo. She's literally never, not once, sent me to my room. "*Seriously?*"

"I need some peace and quiet, and it's quite clear I'm not going to get any with you around. Go to your room," she repeats.

"Fine," I answer. I gather up the photos—who knows what condition they'd be in in the morning if I left them down here with her—and stomp upstairs. I even slam my door behind me.

Alone in my room, I shuffle through the photos, looking at them one after the other. The shadow is still there, clear as daylight, and Mom couldn't see it. And she yelled at me—she's never yelled at me. Anytime we disagreed it always ended in a discussion. And I mean, don't get me wrong, those conversations could get heated, but it never ended with me being sent to my room like a naughty child in a Victorian novel, banished to her room without any supper. This isn't like her. This isn't like *us*.

I put the photos on my desk and turn to face my bed. The checkers game is waiting for me, so I make my next move, sliding a second checker forward, then climb into bed, careful not to disturb the game.

I turn off the lights. Lightning flashes outside again, and this time the thunder follows almost immediately; the storm is practically directly on top of us. In the flash of light I see that the ghost has already made another move: it's my turn again. I press another checker across the board and wait for another flash of lightning. The mildew smell in here is stronger than ever; maybe the rain brings it out.

Or maybe the ghost has something to do with it, I think, remembering the wet bathroom: the soaked tiles and the damp towels, the water dripping from every surface.

A few flashes of lightning go by, but the ghost doesn't make her next move. "Your turn," I say out loud, but another flash of lightning reveals that the checkers haven't moved since my last turn. The mildew smell fades, just a little. Carefully I lower the checkerboard to the floor so I won't disturb it in my sleep. I guess she's done playing.

For now.

CHAPTER ELEVEN
Home Alone

Mom is called back to the hospital for an emergency in the middle of the night. She wakes me up to let me know she's leaving, and I consider begging her to stay, but I kind of think it won't do any good. After all, she doesn't think there's anything worth staying for. And it must be a real emergency, if she's being called back to work at this hour.

"I hope everything will be okay," I call out to her before she leaves. She smiles at me; I guess that means our fight is over, at least for now. I have to concentrate to hear the sound of her car backing out of the driveway and turning on to the street over the thunder, wind, and rain. The thunder and lightning are simultaneous now; the storm has settled on top of us with such force that it feels like it will never stop.

Instead of falling back to sleep, I go over the evening's events in my head: Is Mom really *incapable* of seeing what Nolan and I saw? Does that mean Nolan and I are both crazy and the shadow is some kind of joint hallucination—or is *Mom* crazy, because she can't see it? Or is there something to this magic that you can't perceive it above a certain age or something? Like maybe you have to be young and pure of heart, like in all those movies and fairy tales about children who slip into enchanted worlds without adult supervision?

I shake my head. *No*—a photograph is a photograph, and Nolan and I haven't known each other long enough to have some kind of shared delusion.

Thunder crashes, and Oscar jumps onto my bed, curling himself up beside me the same way he did our first night in this house. "What's the matter, buddy?" I ask, stroking the soft spot between his ears. He loves being petted like this; if he were a cat, he'd be purring right now. But instead, he's shaking, trying to hide his face beneath my arm.

"You never used to be so scared of thunder, big boy," I coo. Oscar is a little dog, but Mom and I both always describe him as big. Suddenly I hear something else, hiding in between crashes of thunder. It's not the thunder that's got Oscar so frightened.

It's the sound of a child crying.

Okay, I know that in, say, a court of law or something, a dog can't exactly testify as a witness. But there's no denying that Oscar is another person—well, you know, another living creature—who *feels* that this house is haunted. He's been scared and jumpy ever since we moved into this house. And Lex literally tried to run out the front door this evening, something he never, ever tried to do in our old house. So that's four of us—Oscar, Lex, me, Nolan—at least one of whom is an impartial third party, may I add—who know *something* is going on here.

"Why are you crying?" I ask my empty room. "Didn't you like playing with me? I thought that was what you wanted."

Oscar nestles under my arm. "Come on, please answer me! Are you the reason this house is so cold and creepy? Can I help you?" I shake my head: what am I doing, asking a ghost if she needs my help? I'm the one who needs help. I'm the one who's stuck in a haunted house, fighting with my mother for the first time in sixteen years.

"Why are you crying?" I plead. I stare at the ceiling like I'm waiting for it to fall down on top of me. "What are you trying to tell me—that you want to play, that you need my help?"

Lightning rips across the sky, illuminating the room once more. What I see makes me scream. Oscar dives down to the ground and under the bed. "I'm sorry, boy," I say, but I'm whispering now instead of shouting, and even with his dog hearing, I doubt he can hear me. Even if he could hear me, I'm pretty sure I wouldn't be able to make him feel any better.

Dr. Hoo is flying around in circles just beneath the ceiling, his wings dripping water as though he were flying through the rain outside—Dr. Hoo, my long-dead, long-since-stuffed owl. His wings make so much noise that I think maybe the entire room is about to levitate.

I reach for the light beside my bed, turn it on, and grab my cell phone. Maybe Mom will be able to see *this*. Maybe Mrs. Soderberg and I were wrong: sure, film can capture things that aren't visible to the naked eye, but when the naked eye can see what I'm seeing now, digital should work just fine.

With my phone's camera trained on the owl, I hit record even though my hands are shaking, so the video will be shaky too. Even though the camera doesn't make a sound—no click, click, click like when I take photos with film—Dr. Hoo seems to sense a change in the air. Abruptly, he stops flying in circles and hovers in place for a heartbeat, his wings still flapping mightily. He looks around, his owl's neck turning almost 360 degrees just like they said on all those nature shows. Finally he looks down, fixing his gaze on me. I shake my head; the owl's eyes aren't real. They're made of glass, long since replaced by the taxidermist. Still, Dr. Hoo seems to perceive me, and he swoops down in my direction.

Oh my gosh, Dr. Hoo is going to kill me! Ashley was right all along. Taxidermied animals are creepy. I should have been grossed out by him.

I scream again—sorry Oscar!—but at the last second Dr. Hoo shifts, and instead of hitting me, he hits the lamp at my bedside, knocking it over and plunging the room into darkness. I drop my phone. I hear it thud against the carpet on the floor, and I tumble out of bed to search for it, but I can't find it. There's no more lightning to illuminate my dark room; the storm has moved on. The sound of flapping wings ceases. Even the falling rain has dwindled into just a slight trickle down the windowpane. Oscar peeks his head out from under the bed and crawls into my lap, panting as though it's hot in here.

But of course, it isn't hot. It's freezing.

I don't know when I fall asleep. To be honest, I don't know *how* I fall asleep, after everything that happened. But the next thing I know, it's morning, and my neck aches from sleeping sitting up with my back against the bed frame. Oscar isn't in my lap anymore, and despite the tree outside my window, enough light is streaming in that I can see that Dr. Hoo is back on his shelf, and my phone is beside me on the ground as though I placed it there for easy access.

"Jeezus Loueezus," I sigh, wrapping my fingers around my phone and standing. I turn my neck from side to side. The air between my bones crackles and pops when I move. "I feel like an old lady," I say out loud.

"What's that?" Mom asks, sticking her head through the door. "When did you get home?"

"Just now. I have exactly three hours to nap before I have to go back in for my next shift."

"But it's Saturday."

"You don't think babies are born on Saturdays?" Mom says, but she's smiling. My whole life Mom has had to work on weekends and holidays, though she tries never to be on duty during Christmas break or my birthday.

"Sorry," I mumble.

"Hey, I wish I had Saturdays off too." She gestures at my phone. "What do you have there?"

I look down. When I picked the phone up, I must have pressed the button to replay the video I shot last night. The sound of thunder and lightning emanates from the phone's tiny speaker. I pause. Let's give this one more try. Maybe the only way Mom will look at this with an open mind is if I don't mention the ghost.

"Ummm," I say slowly. "I shot a video of the storm last night. It must have been right above us. The lightning made everything so bright." I cross the room and hold my phone out in front of me. Mom leans down to look at it.

"Wow," she murmurs.

"Wow?" I echo hopefully. Maybe she sees Dr. Hoo flapping around. Maybe she hears someone crying.

"Looks like it was quite a storm. The thunder must have been deafening."

"Oscar hid under the bed. I thought it was weird because thunder and lightning never used to scare him."

Mom shakes her head, dropping her gaze from the phone. "Oscar's just a big old baby," she says, then pats my shoulder. I practically jump.

"What's the matter?" Mom asks.

"Your hand is freezing," I answer. The back of my T-shirt is moist where she touched me. "Did you just get out of the shower or something?"

"What are you talking about?" she sighs, and I shake my head. I don't want to start this day off with a fight.

"Nothing."

"Why don't we have some breakfast before I hit the hay?"

"Be down in a minute," I say softly as she leaves my room and makes her way downstairs. I sit on the edge of my bed and lift my T-shirt over my head and lay it out flat in front of me.

There's a rusty, wet handprint on the back, the cold water spreading across the shirt's fibers like a stain. Before I know what I'm doing, I've crushed the shirt into a ball and thrown it beneath my bed like I never want to see it again.

I reach for my phone and watch the video once more, straight through from the start. In addition to thunder and lightning, I hear crying and the sound of Dr. Hoo's wings. The owl takes up practically the whole screen, flying circles around my room until he finally plunges straight toward me.

I curl my hands into fists as I head downstairs so Mom won't see the way they're shaking. Something has happened to her, something that's keeping her from seeing what I see and feeling what I feel. She can't even feel that her hand is cold and wet.

Wet with rust-colored water. Just like the water in the bathroom that night.

CHAPTER TWELVE
Extra Credit

"I don't think you should stop recording," Nolan says on Monday.

"Why not?" I say, kicking the ground. It's lunchtime, and Nolan suggested we take a walk rather than talk in the cafeteria. Maybe he was embarrassed to talk about this in front of the rest of the school, the cliques already so firmly established, but Nolan doesn't seem like he cares about that kind of thing. In fact, he's been living in Ridgemont his whole life and doesn't seem to have a crowd the way everyone else does, from the jocks to the misfits. Maybe he preferred his grandfather's company the way I always preferred my mother's.

We're walking in circles on the track behind the school. I take it that Ridgemont High's track team isn't exactly the cream of the crop, because the ground beneath us is muddy and cracked, as though the school doesn't think it's worth keeping it in good shape. It's not raining, but it's misty and there's a chill in the air, making me want to walk ever closer to Nolan, like he's a heat lamp and I'm a fly drawn to his flame. But I don't want to look like the weirdest girl on planet Earth (even if maybe I am), so I settle for just staying in step with him. "My mother can't see anything, no matter what medium I try—photography, video . . . to say nothing of real life."

Nolan shakes his head, his damp, long hair falling across his face. He pushes the sleeves of his leather jacket so they bunch up around his elbows perfectly, like something out of a James Dean movie, even though beneath his jacket he's wearing a flannel button-down and jeans that look like they're at least one size too big, plus a pair of beat-up sneakers that were probably partly white once, which kind of clashes with the James Dean effect of the jacket. "She can't perceive the ghost now. Maybe that will change."

"Doubtful," I mutter, looking at my feet. My Chuck Taylors have been covered in mud and grime since the day we moved here.

"I can tell you're discouraged," Nolan begins, and I laugh.

"Oh really? What gave you that idea?"

"But come on, you should feel good." I raise my eyebrows, and he shrugs. "Okay, maybe not *good*, but better, at least. I mean, you have evidence now. *Proof.* My grandpa spent his whole life talking about ghosts, and he never found proof, not even after ninety years. That's got to count for something, right?"

Nolan isn't entirely wrong: I *thought* I'd feel better if I had proof, but proof seems worthless when my mom can't see it. Or *perceive* it, like Nolan said.

"Why keep recording then? I already have proof, like you said."

"A little more can't hurt. And maybe we'll see something in your videos that you missed in real life."

"Because in real life I'm too busy being terrified to look closely?" I shudder when I remember the way Dr. Hoo flew above me. Part of me did want to hide under the covers until it was over.

Nolan grins. "Exactly."

"Speaking of looking closely . . ." I gesture with my chin to a figure crouched on the decrepit-looking bleachers across the track.

"Is that who I think it is?" Nolan asks. He squints, taking in the long dark hair, the witchy cloak, the pale, pale skin—Ms. Wilde.

"Gosh, that is one creepy lady," I sigh. "What's she doing here?" I fold my arms across my chest and rub them up and down.

Nolan shrugs. "What are we doing here?"

"You're saying she doesn't give you the creeps?"

"Shhh. She might be able to hear us."

I want to roll my eyes, but the truth is, it does kind of look like our art teacher is listening to us. I mean, she doesn't have any of the usual distractions people bring with them to sit all alone: no sandwich to eat, no cell phone to check, no papers to grade, no book to read. She must see us staring at her, because she drops her gaze, her hair falling across her face like a curtain. Nolan and I start walking in the opposite direction, farther away from her—and hopefully out of her earshot.

"What if my mom asks why I'm taking videos around the house?"

"Just tell her it's for a school project or something."

I cock my head to the side, considering. I really don't want to have to keep lying to her. It doesn't feel good—it doesn't feel *natural*, like walking backward or trying to write with the wrong hand. "I guess that's not a total lie," I say slowly. "I mean, you *are* doing an extra-credit project on ghosts of the Northwest. Maybe you could use all this for it?"

"Sure," Nolan says, but he makes a strange sort of face that I can't read. Walking around in circles on a track like this makes me feel like a hamster in a cage, but I pick up my pace a little bit until I'm a few steps ahead of him. "Besides, you said your mom is so busy, she might not even notice, right?"

I nod slowly. "Of course. Good point. Right."

When I showed him the video of Dr. Hoo earlier, Nolan practically threw his arms up over his head. He was actually excited, not horrified, to have more proof of my ghost. Or maybe just of ghosts in general. No wonder he wants me to keep taking videos. They're proof that his grandfather's stories were true—or could have been true, at least. Proof that his grandfather wasn't the crazy old man everyone else thought he was.

"Hey," I slow down so that we're walking in step again. "What if . . . I mean, do you know any experts?"

"Experts?"

"You know, people with experience with this kind of thing. Maybe they could help me or something."

"You mean like the Ghostbusters?" Nolan says, laughing.

"No, I don't mean like the Ghostbusters," I answer, wrinkling my nose just like Mom. "I mean . . . did your grandfather have any friends, people he'd mentioned in some of his stories?"

This time it's Nolan's turn to walk out of step, but instead of speeding up, he slows down. Actually he stops altogether. Now I'm able to read the look on his face, and it's not good. Oops. I shouldn't have brought up his grandfather. I mean, I don't think he's about to cry or anything, but he looks so sad I'm tempted to reach out and hug him. But of course, I don't. Instead, I say, "I'm so sorry, Nolan. I didn't mean to be insensitive."

Nolan shakes his head. "It's not that. I just wish my grandfather were still alive. *He* probably would be able to help us."

"I'm sorry," I repeat.

"Most of his friends are gone. It's really just my grandmother who's left, and she never paid any attention to his ghost stories."

"It was a silly thing to suggest."

"No, it's a good idea. I mean, if you have bugs in your house, you call the exterminator, right?" I nod. "If your sink breaks, you call a plumber," he continues.

"So you're saying it's time to bring in an expert?"

Nolan nods. "We just need to find one first."

I don't think it'll be nearly as easy to find a ghost expert as it is to find an exterminator or a plumber.

"I'll drive to my grandmother's place this weekend. I don't think she touched any of the papers in his desk."

"Papers?" I echo. It's strange to think of Nolan going through his grandfather's desk, like maybe the answers we need will be marked neatly in a file.

Nolan nods. "I know he wrote down some of his stories. You never know what else might be in there."

I'm tempted to ask whether I can come with him, but I can tell from the look on Nolan's face that this is something he'd rather do alone. Besides, how would he explain my presence to his grandmother? *Oh hi, Granny, this is my classmate, Sunshine. I know she never met Gramps, but would you mind if she helped me go through his desk looking for ghost-hints?*

After school I walk into the house holding my phone out in front of me the way cops hold their guns in the movies. But I'm not trying to kill anyone (obviously). I just want to catch them. Mom isn't home (of course); she's at work. There's a note taped to the refrigerator that says, *Don't wait up.* I don't bother taking the note down. I'm pretty sure it'll apply to tomorrow night, and the night after that.

I grab an apple and head upstairs, prepared to capture whatever's on the other side of my bedroom door before I step inside. But with the apple in one hand and my phone in the other, I don't have a hand free to turn the knob, so I pop the apple in my mouth, gripping its flesh with my teeth. Next I reach out, turn the knob, and brace myself.

The checkerboard is right where I left it beside my bed, and I can see that someone has made her countermove: it's my turn. But I guess just checkers isn't enough for her anymore. My Monopoly board is set on the floor with all the pieces in place, the pastel-colored cash neatly distributed for two players.

In my bare feet I step on the little dog from the Monopoly game and let out a shout. I reach down and pick it up, squeezing it in my hand.

"Checkers not enough, huh?" I ask with a smile. I cross the room and roll the dice.

"Double sixes," I shout triumphantly. "Beat that!" I'll play with her if that's what she wants. If it will keep her out of the bathroom, I'll play every game I have. But only until I'm able to figure out who she is and why she's here.

CHAPTER THIRTEEN

The Slip of a Knife

Nolan was right: Mom doesn't question it when I tell her I'm using my phone to record things around the house for a school project.

"A video collage about my life for visual arts class," I say, wishing that Ms. Wilde actually gave out those kinds of assignments instead of lurking all over the school. Mom looks up from her paperwork long enough to smile at me. Maybe she's relieved I'm talking about something other than ghosts for a change. Or maybe she's too busy to care.

I start in my room, recording the movements of the glass unicorns, the board games strewn across my floor, the way Dr. Hoo is facing a different direction every time I open the door. I carry my phone with me everywhere, ready to record at a moment's notice. I skip the bathroom entirely—nothing to see there, not anymore—and head down to the living room, recording the sound of skipping footsteps on the floor above. I race upstairs, trying to capture sight of an actual specter skipping around the hall, but of course, the minute I step foot on the stairs, the footsteps cease. I catch flickering lights and slamming doors. And of course I record our games. We're on our second round of checkers—I won the first game—and we're both busy building real estate empires in Monopoly.

But I think she's cheating. I mean, not cheating exactly, but not quite following the rules either. I came back into the room once and saw that her piece—she picked the shoe—was on Marvin Gardens. But when I looked at her last roll of the dice—five—and counted back from her last spot on the board, it was clear that she should have been on Water Works. So I crouched down beside the board and slid the shoe back one.

But as soon as I lifted my fingers from the shoe, it slid right back to Marvin Gardens.

"Hey!" I shouted. "No cheating." I tried again, and it slid back again. This time the shoe was wet to the touch. "You'd think you'd feel right at home on Water Works," I muttered, sliding it into place once more. I held it there for good measure.

And then, I swear, something—someone—smacked my hand out of the way with such force that I fell backward.

"Geez, have it your way," I said, sitting back up cross-legged in front of the board. I leaned over and studied it. And then it hit me so hard that I felt stupid for not seeing it earlier. She didn't want to be on Water Works, not even for an instant. The symbol for Water Works is a running faucet.

"What are you trying to tell me?" I closed my eyes, remembering the splashing sounds in the bathroom that night.

She didn't answer. I got up and went to my desk and grabbed the fattest black marker I could find. I leaned down over the board and drew all over the Water Works box until it was all but invisible. "There," I said. "We'll play the rest of this game like Water Works doesn't even exist."

Then I did get an answer: the soft sound of a child laughing. And soon I was laughing too, right along with her.

Maybe this was her plan all along. To get me to *like* her. To get me to care.

On Saturday Mom actually has the day off—*hallelujah!*—and we go to the supermarket to gather groceries to cook dinner together, just the way we used to in Austin. (I try not to think about what happened after the last time Mom cooked me dinner.)

"What are we digging into tonight?" I ask eagerly. She printed a new recipe off the Internet and is scanning the list of ingredients.

"Chicken marsala." Mom smiles as she pushes the cart through the produce section, stopping to pick up a carton of mushrooms. She's wearing jeans and a gray sweatshirt; I can't remember the last time I saw her wearing anything but her pastel-colored nurse's scrubs.

"You expect me to eat fungus?" I ask, mock incredulously. Mom knows I love mushrooms.

"And like it," she answers. "We just have to find the wine . . ." She looks up at the signs above each aisle, moving slowly until she finds the right one. She's leaning on the cart in front of her like an elderly person does with a walker. All those long hours and late nights are wearing her out. There are circles under her eyes, and she yawns heavily.

"Why don't I do the cooking tonight?" I volunteer. "You could just put your feet up and rest."

Mom shakes her head. "You know it's more fun when we do it together," she says, and I grin. I wanted to help her and everything, but I was also kind of hoping she'd say that.

At home we unload the groceries and get to work. I feed Oscar and Lex while Mom slips her sweatshirt off, revealing her high school T-shirt underneath.

"Hey!" I shout. "You stole my mustang shirt."

"I most certainly did not. Don't forget it was mine first."

"Prior ownership does not obviate the felony of your theft."

Mom grins. "Sunshine, do you have any idea what you just said?"

I shake my head. "No, but it sounded good," I answer. "I heard something like it on a cop show or something," I add, grinning back. It's all so blissfully ordinary that I'm tempted to lean over and kiss her. But that wouldn't be ordinary, so I don't. Mom begins slicing the mushrooms. She doesn't even bother turning on the kitchen lights before she starts.

"It's too dark in here," I say, flipping the switch, but the room doesn't get any brighter. I turn on the lights over the kitchen table for good measure, but it doesn't make a difference. It takes me a second to realize why.

I mean, of course it's foggy outside—what else is new?—but right now it's foggy *inside.* Mist is snaking its way in from the windows, over the counter and around the stove, above the refrigerator and beneath the table—our own private meteorological phenomenon.

I hesitate before reaching for my phone; I don't want to break up our normal evening. But I guess the stupid fog has already destroyed our brief foray into normalcy, so I go ahead and pull my phone out of the pocket of the jeans I stole from Mom back in August. Mom is so intent on slicing the mushrooms that she doesn't notice it when I hit record and scan the room, walking in an enormous circle around her, recording every last inch of fog. If we were in a movie, this would be the moment when an actual specter would appear. All the mist would gather together, condensing until it was in the shape of a little girl. Maybe she'd open her mouth and say something.

I walk around the counter island, standing across the way from Mom. I focus my camera on the center of the room, waiting. Mom takes up a tiny space in the corner of my screen; the sound of her knife going through the mushrooms is a steady sort of drumbeat, one after another after another.

Suddenly the sound changes, and the corner of my screen turns red.

"Mom!" I shout, dropping my phone with a clatter on the counter. Blood pours out from her left wrist.

"I must have cut myself," she says, stating the obvious. She's much calmer than I would be if I were the one who was bleeding. She *is* a nurse, after all.

"Don't tell me my klutziness is rubbing off on you," I say, but the joke falls flat. Maybe because my voice is shaking as I say it. I grab a wad of paper towels and press them against her left wrist.

"You're shaking, Sunshine," Mom says. "Are you really still that grossed out by the sight of blood?"

I nod, but it's not just the blood. I'm shivering because I'm freezing. The temperature in here seems to have dropped fifty degrees in the last thirty seconds. I gag on the musty smell of mildew in the air.

Her right hand is still wrapped around the knife. She's holding it so tightly that her knuckles are white. "You can put that down," I say, pointing. "Mom?" I prompt. "Put the knife down."

Mom shakes her head. "I'm not finished."

"The mushrooms can wait." I reach for the knife when suddenly–

"Ow!" I shout. Now I'm the one who's bleeding. I hold my left hand out in front of me. There is a gash at the base of my thumb. Tears spring to my eyes.

"Sunshine!" Mom shouts. "What were you thinking?" I shake my head–what *was* I thinking, reaching for the knife like that? They teach you that kind of thing in kindergarten: never grab a knife by the blade.

But I didn't mean to grab the blade. I was reaching for her hand, wrapped around the knife's handle. I must have slipped or something.

"Let me see your hand," Mom says, reaching for me. She doesn't notice that it's so cold that her breath comes out of her mouth as vapor. For a split second I wish I were still holding my phone, recording all of this. No, that's insane. I had to put my phone down to help. The ghost is important and everything, but not nearly as important as the fact that Mom and I are both bleeding.

My blood lands on the counter next to Mom's blood.

Plop, plop. Plop, plop.

Suddenly the room is spinning. My head feels like it's filled with helium and is threatening to pop right off and float away. My cut isn't nearly as bad as Mom's, but still . . . it's just so much blood.

I slide forward, my hand leaving a bloody trail on the counter. For some reason I can't seem to keep my eyes open.

The next thing I know, I'm lying on the couch, with Mom standing over me.

"What happened?"

"You fainted."

"I did?"

"I guess all that blood was too much for you," she says. So much for our normal night.

"I don't think this is very funny," I protest. My hand is bandaged perfectly; so is Mom's. The advantages of living with a medical expert.

"How did I get onto the couch?"

"I carried you."

"You did?" Since when is she strong enough to carry me?

"Dinner's ready," she says.

"You cooked dinner?"

"Of course," she answers, like that's the most obvious thing to do after you've cut both yourself and your daughter and then your daughter passed out. I get up and follow her into the kitchen, still feeling slightly woozy. The mist is completely gone, except for some patches of condensation scattered across the kitchen counter. The room is bright with all the lights on, and Mom is spooning chicken onto two plates.

Maybe it's not too late to salvage this normal evening, I think hopefully. I set my mouth into a smile and force myself to say, "Looks delicious."

But as I cut into the meat, I can see that it's not going to be. "Mom? I don't think this got cooked all the way through."

"What are you talking about?" she answers, reaching across the table and spearing the chicken meat with her fork. The yellowish meat drips water as it crosses to her side of the table, and I try not to gag as she lifts the nearly raw meat to her mouth and chews it with gusto.

"Don't eat that!" I shout. "You'll get sick."

"Don't be ridiculous. It's perfect." Her wound hasn't healed, and blood seeps out of the side of her bandage onto the chicken on her plate. I watch her eat it all: the undercooked meat, the drops of blood. If my phone weren't all the way over on the kitchen counter, I'd record this too. Though it would probably be barely watchable, the way my hands are trembling.

I don't know what this is, but it's certainly not perfect. How can Mom think that anything at all is perfect?

The First Cut

I've always been fond of that human expression: the first cut is the deepest. Of course, I don't actually believe it. The first cut is usually barely enough to cause any real damage. It's the hurts that come later that are the real cause for concern.

Sunshine finally engaged with the child. I'm glad I chose a young spirit for this task: enticing Sunshine with games worked wonders. Sunshine might have gone on for months without interacting, intent only upon what was happening to Katherine.

But clearly this girl has the capacity to care not only about the woman she calls Mom. She cares about the spirit's suffering as well; I could sense her concern when she blacked out the box on the board game that bore the image of a faucet. Sunshine couldn't possibly have fully understood why the picture would be so upsetting to the creature she played with, and yet she knew exactly what to do to soothe the spirit's anxiety.

Empathy can be a powerful tool.

But then empathy is not the only sensation flowing through Sunshine now. I can also feel her fear: I sense it when her pulse quickens, when her hands grow clammy and cold. She doesn't understand what's happening to Katherine. She certainly doesn't yet see that there is something larger at work here, something bigger than the goings-on in her small, damp house.

She is frightened. I am curious: Will she let her fear, or her empathy, determine her next move? Will she take the time to learn more, or will she dive under the covers and hope that one morning she'll awaken to discover that everything has gone back to the way it was before? Surely she longs for the time when her nights with Katherine were full of laughter and affection, not steel and blood. When supernatural *was a word that existed only in stories rather than a reality in her house. When she didn't have to question whether everything she thought she knew about the world had shifted.*

It is almost enough to make me feel sorry for her. She doesn't yet understand that nothing will ever be the way it was before. Perhaps I will send a little help her way, something—or someone—to nudge her in the right direction.

Metaphorically speaking—if not perhaps literally as well—the cuts will only be deeper from here on out.

CHAPTER FOURTEEN
Make New Friends

"Let's start with the most obvious explanation," Nolan says reasonably. "Does your mom have any reason to hurt herself?"

"*That's* the most obvious explanation?" I protest. "How about the knife slipped, and my mom accidentally cut her hand?"

"Followed almost immediately by yours?" Nolan asks incredulously. I finger my bandage—Mom said we didn't need stitches but we do need to keep our wounds clean and dry for a few days.

We're in the library now, cutting Monday's visual arts class. I couldn't stand the idea of having this conversation with Ms. Wilde lurking in the corner of the room, listening. It's my second time ever cutting class, and even though this is an emergency—and the time before was an emergency too—I feel pretty guilty about it. Mentally I lecture myself not to make a habit of this kind of thing. Nolan looks even more nervous than I am about getting caught, even though it was his idea to go to the library in the first place.

"You okay?" I ask.

He nods distractedly. "I've never actually cut a class before," he confides. He looks mildly embarrassed by this admission, like he thinks he's the only junior at Ridgemont High for whom cutting class isn't old hat.

If only he knew.

Nolan must have watched the video I recorded on Saturday night a dozen times. He seems much more interested in Mom's accident—the part I avoid looking at because, *ew, blood*—than he is in the mist I caught on camera.

"She didn't cut my hand," I say now. "It was my fault. I tried to grab the knife."

Nolan shakes his head. "I know you're clumsy, Sunshine, but I really don't think you would grab a blade like that."

"So you think it's more likely that my own mother stabbed herself and then me? Don't be ridiculous."

"Sunshine, are you even *looking* at this?" he asks.

"What are you talking about?"

He holds my camera out in front of us, zooming in on the lower right-hand corner where my mom is chopping mushrooms. "Watch carefully," he instructs.

I see my mother slice one mushroom, and then another. She's every bit as careful and methodical as I imagine she is when she assists on surgeries at the hospital. I never really equated her cooking with her job before, but it occurs to me that maybe she likes recipes—with their clear instructions, their lists of measurements and ingredients—because in a strange way they remind her of her work.

Nolan hits pause. "Pay attention."

"I am," I insist.

"I can tell when your mind is wandering."

"No you can't," I say, but I'm blushing.

"And don't close your eyes when there's blood on the screen."

"I fainted the last time I saw this much blood," I remind him.

"Okay, but this is only a *recording* of blood. There's no actual blood here in the room with you."

"That doesn't make as much difference as you'd think." Even when I'm just watching a hospital show on TV I cover my eyes during the bloody scenes.

"Keep your eyes open," Nolan instructs, pressing play again. I open my eyes wide.

On my phone's small screen I can see that Mom doesn't take her eyes off the knife. With the same care she took in slicing the mushrooms, she lifts the blade and lowers it until it hits her wrist, drawing blood. The surface of her skin is wet, not just with blood, but with water from the mist surrounding her. Her hair is dripping water as though she'd just gotten out of the shower. I didn't even notice that at the time, as though whatever moisture there was in the air, it was touching only her, not me.

"Open your eyes, Sunshine," Nolan reminds me. He hits pause.

"Right," I say. "Sorry."

He presses play again, and I watch as she presses harder, drawing more. Even though she must be in pain, she doesn't stop until I hear my own voice shouting.

That's when I dropped the camera, so there's nothing more to see after that.

"Oh my gosh," I exhale, and Nolan nods.

"What do you think we'd see if you'd been recording when she cut you?"

I shake my head, slouching in my chair. Once, when we were six, Ashley accidentally kicked me in the stomach during a game of Twister, and I still remember the way I curled up into a C-shape, feeling like I would never catch my breath again. Mom said I'd just had the wind knocked out of me, and now I feel like someone has done it again—punched me in the gut, leaving me gasping for my next breath.

Nolan puts my phone down on the table in front of us and scoots his chair closer to me; I concentrate on the sound of the chair scraping against the linoleum floor. Maybe it's leaving a mark and we'll get into trouble for damaging school property on top of whatever trouble we're already in for cutting class.

Before he can put his arms around me I sit up, straightening my spine. Gently he puts his hand on my back, between my shoulder blades. I can feel the heat of his skin through my T-shirt; it's the closest we've ever come to actual skin-on-skin contact. I feel like I might throw up. I take a deep breath and swallow, feeling almost hot.

On top of everything else, the touch of the boy I maybe-kind-of-sort-of like makes me dry heave. *Fantastic.*

"I told you I wasn't good with blood," I say finally, hoping that he'll think that's the reason why I'm practically gagging.

"No one is actually *good* with blood, right?" Nolan answers, shrugging. He drops his hand and inches his chair back across the floor, away from me. The nausea subsides.

"My mom is," I say, biting my bottom lip. For a split second I bite harder, wondering whether this is how my mom felt when the knife touched her skin. When I was a little kid crying from a skinned knee I asked her why it had to hurt so much, and my mom said that pain was actually a good thing, that it's the body's way of warning us that something is wrong, the body's way of saying *Stop.* I press my fingers into my scalp, the tips disappearing beneath my ever-present frizzball.

I shake my head. "She's not the kind of person who would hurt herself. I mean, she gets grouchy sometimes, when work is super busy or whatever. And I know I can irritate her. But she's happy. And . . . look, I don't mean to sound super cheesy or anything, but I know for a fact that she would never, ever hurt me. Not on purpose. Not . . ."

"Not if she was the one in control." Nolan finishes for me.

Suddenly I feel like crying. He must sense it, because he changes the subject. Or at least moves on to the next possibility. "Then we have to consider the less obvious explanation. That the ghost made her do it."

I swallow. "There's more," I say softly. "I mean, something else happened that night. She ate—" Just thinking about it makes me sick to my stomach. "Later that night she still cooked dinner. But she didn't *cook* it. The chicken was practically raw. And she ate it anyway. She said it was *perfect.*" The word tastes sour in my mouth, but Nolan doesn't look disgusted, just really concerned. I continue, "I don't get it. I mean, the little girl always seems so nice. I really thought she just wanted to play with me. Has she just been tricking me into trusting her?"

"It's possible," Nolan considers. "Some kinds of spirits are famous for being tricksters. Or maybe . . . maybe she's not alone."

"What do you mean?"

"You said so yourself—she was begging for her life that night in the bathroom."

"So?"

"So . . . *who* was she begging?"

"I don't know," I answer hopelessly. I play the video one more time, trying to make out a shape in the mist, looking for something—someone?—standing behind my mother, controlling her movements as if she were a mere puppet. But the fog behind her is so thick—growing thicker when she hurts herself—that it's impossible to see anything else.

I'm more confused now than ever. Maybe there are two ghosts in my haunted house? One good, one evil? I fold my arms on the table and drop my head down on top of them, my curls tickling my hands. I didn't even bother trying to pull it back into a ponytail today. What's the point? I'm pretty sure an elastic band wouldn't have a fighting chance against all this.

I can feel Nolan's hand hovering above me, like maybe he wants to rub my back. My muscles stiffen in anticipation, and he moves away. "We'll get to the bottom of this," he promises.

I look up. "Have you had any luck finding an expert who might be able to help us?" I ask hopefully.

"Not exactly. But I've got a lead on one from my grandfather's old files. A professor at the university a couple of towns over."

"What kind of college has a ghost department?"

Nolan shrugs. "We've got to start somewhere, right?"

"I'm scared. What if I'm not there the next time my mom—"

"You *will* be there. Look, you said she's working all the time these days, right?"

I nod.

"So it shouldn't be that hard to be home when she's home so that she's not alone. And if she hurts herself at work, then . . ."

"At least she's already at the hospital," I finish for him. He nods, and I let out a deep breath. I guess it's lucky that my mom is a nurse. What if she were a teacher or a lawyer or something?

Nolan must sense that despite the proximity of medical care, I'm not exactly comforted by the thought of my beloved mother hurting herself at work, so he adds, "Anyway, if it's the house that's haunted—and it's the ghost—"

"Or ghosts," I interrupt.

"Or ghosts," he agrees, "that made her hurt herself, then you don't have to worry about her when she's not home anyway."

I nod just as the bell rings, signaling the end of third period. I push my chair out from under the table, slide my phone in my pants pocket, and pick my backpack up from the floor. "I guess we better get to class."

Nolan nods. "I have chem lab."

"English lit," I answer. Our respective classrooms are on opposite ends of the school, so we each set off in separate directions. The farther I get from him, the colder I feel, until goose bumps are popping up on my arms and legs, all the way down to my feet. I stop at my locker and get out my navy blue peacoat and slip it on. I found it at a vintage shop back in Austin; the original buttons have long since disappeared, and the six buttons that replaced them are totally mismatched, a rainbow of different colors.

How can being close to Nolan feel both so good and so bad? When I'm near him I'm warm. Is that how Mom felt when she held me for the first time? I shake my head—no, because every time Nolan actually touches me, it feels so wrong that I'm tempted to run as far from him as my not-particularly-athletic legs will carry me.

Okay, so maybe I'm not going to get swept up into a life-altering romance like Elizabeth Bennett. It's not like I have time to fall in love anyway, not with everything else that's going on.

What matters is that Nolan is my friend, the first new friend I've made since elementary school. And unlike Ashley, he believes in ghosts and cares about what's going on in my house. He'd watch that video a dozen more times if I asked him to, and I wouldn't be able to get Ashley to watch it once. Nolan doesn't think I'm nuttier than a fruitcake for seeing what I've seen. And because he can see it too, I have proof that I'm not crazy.

To get to English class, I have to pass the visual arts room. When I see Ms. Wilde hovering in the doorway, I brace myself, expecting to be sent to the principal's office for cutting. But instead, as I walk past, the edges of my art teacher's mouth curl up into a subtle, blink-and-you'll-miss-it smile.

Just before I drop into a chair in my English classroom I pick up my phone and send Nolan a text.

What if there's a day when I can't be there with my mom when she's at home?

I don't even have to wait thirty seconds before he sends his reply:

Then I'll be there.

CHAPTER FIFTEEN

Out of Ridgemont and into the Fire?

On Saturday afternoon Nolan sends me a text—no words, just a picture of a wrinkled old article he found among his grandfather's papers. I'm not able to make out much more than the headline: "Local Professor Promises Proof: Ghosts Are Real."

Immediately I write back: *Let's go find him.*

After school a few days later I'm sitting beside Nolan in his enormous beat-up navy blue Chrysler—"Belonged to my grandfather," he says proudly, pushing up the sleeves of his leather jacket.

"Your grandmother just let you have it?"

He shakes his head. "Nah, Gramps gave it to me when he was still alive. My parents took away his license right around the time I got mine." From the sound of Nolan's voice, I guess that his grandfather didn't exactly give up his license willingly. I try to imagine the confrontation: can't let a crazy old man who believes in ghosts behind the wheel. I wonder at what age Nolan's grandfather's belief in the paranormal stopped being something his friends and family called just an odd sort of character quirk and started being dismissed as the ramblings of a nutty old man.

"What was your grandfather's name?" I ask gently.

"Why?"

"I don't know. I feel like he brought us together—" Oh my goodness . . . *brought us together*? What am I saying? We're not together. Not *together*, together anyway. "I just mean . . . I feel like I have him to thank for the fact that you believed me that day in the library. So it feels like I should know his name, that's all."

Nolan nods thoughtfully. "His name was Nolan, actually. I was named after him."

"Well, thank you, Nolan," I say softly, the words heavy with meaning.

I can't imagine an outing more different from the ones Ashley must take in Cory Cooper's convertible. Ashley texted me a selfie she took this morning—the two of them in his car, both wearing sunglasses to shield their eyes even though it's November, on their way to a music festival in downtown Austin. I wrote back: *Looks like fun!* Now I try to imagine how she'd react if I sent her a picture of Nolan and me in his car this morning, heading not to a festival but to a university I've never heard of a couple of towns away where the professor from the article runs the paranormal studies department. She definitely wouldn't write back that it looked like fun.

After a mile or two of silence Nolan says, "You know, if he were here, he'd thank *you*."

"Me?" I squeal. "What for? For dragging his beloved grandson into my mess?"

Nolan cocks his head to the side, considering. "Pretty much," he says finally, and we both burst out laughing.

"So did he ever deliver on his promise?"

"Did who ever deliver on what promise?"

"This professor," I dig the article Nolan found out of the glove compartment. "*Professor Abner Jones promises proof of the paranormal,*" I read. "Think he ever produced said proof?"

Nolan grins. "You feel like you need more evidence?"

"Not for me," I answer quickly. "I mean for everyone else."

"I think we probably would have heard about it if he did. I mean, it'd have been a national news story, not just an article in a local paper that I found stuffed in my grandpa's desk, right?"

I nod. "Right." I finger the article. It was published in 1987, before Nolan or I were born, but it mentions the location of the professor's office on campus: Levis Hall. Nolan tried to find his e-mail address on the university website, but he didn't have any luck. Still, he found a description of one of his classes along with a listing of his office hours. Wednesdays, from two to five.

"Did your grandfather ever meet him, do you think?"

Nolan shrugs. "I don't know. Guess I'll have to add that to our list of questions."

I nod. It's not all that long of a list. It's really just one question: Can you help us? I close my eyes and imagine a bespectacled, gray-haired intellectual type saying, *Of course I can! Easy as pie.*

Okay, maybe he won't exactly say that, but we're about to gain some clarity on everything that's happening, I'm sure of it. That's what experts are for, right?

It's my first time leaving Ridgemont since we moved here, and I actually hold my breath as we cross the county line. I wait for the creepy cold feeling that has saturated my life since moving here—well, not cold right now, since Nolan is close by, but still creepy—to subside.

It doesn't. I stare out the window.

"You worried about your mom?" Nolan asks.

I shake my head. "It's not that, actually. I mean, not right now." Mom is safely at work; she was gone before I woke up this morning and even left me a note saying that she wouldn't be home in time to feed Oscar and Lex their dinner, so I was in charge. Nolan and I have plenty of time.

"What is it then?"

"I'm just so sick of this creepy feeling. You've lived here all your life—do you ever get used to it?"

"Used to what?"

"That *Ridgemont* feeling. Ever since we moved here, nothing feels . . . right. Everything I touch is cold, my hands are always clammy. And the air always feels thin and wet, so that taking a deep breath actually aches."

"Ridgemont doesn't feel like that for me," Nolan shrugs. "I mean, the ghost stuff is creepy and all, but the rest of my life is pretty normal."

"Oh," I answer, surprised. "Even inside my house? You didn't feel like the minute you stepped inside, the temperature dropped about twenty degrees?"

He shakes his head. Maybe those are extra-bonus feelings the ghost is saving just for me.

Or maybe I can feel something that other people can't.

I shake my head. That's just crazy talk.

We wander around the campus for what feels like hours, but we can't find Levis Hall. The college is ringed with towering Douglas firs, just like the streets back in Ridgemont. But unlike my neighborhood, the campus is actually landscaped so there are some wide-open spaces free of trees, where the meager sun (actually, it's not so meager now that we're out of Ridgemont) can get through the clouds. For the first time since we moved to Washington I actually have a reason to dig around in my purse and pull out my electric blue sunglasses. Students are sitting out on the lawns in front of their dorms like they think they might be able to get a tan despite the fact that it's November and about forty degrees outside. A group of boys are tossing around a Frisbee while some girls cheer them on from the sidelines, which looks like a lot less fun than actually playing, if you ask me.

Nolan stops and asks one of the girls for directions to Levis Hall. I'm not standing close enough to hear their exchange, but I can tell from the look on the girl's face that she wonders why we'd bother heading over to that part of the campus. Or maybe, I realize as Nolan pushes his dirty-blond hair off his forehead, it's just that she thinks Nolan is cute. Jealousy makes butterflies flutter in my stomach. Unlike me, she's dressed in normal clothes—nonvintage jeans and a university T-shirt, black sunglasses instead of blue. Her hair is long and straight, hanging flatly past her shoulders, nothing like my frizzball. I wriggle my toes inside my Chuck Taylors and pull the sleeves of my oversized sweater over my wrists, forcing myself to look away, pretending to be fascinated by the Frisbee competition, pretending I don't notice the second Nolan turns from her and back toward me.

"It's all the way on the other side of the campus," he says. We get back into his car and leave the girls and the Frisbee game behind. When we finally pull into Levis Hall's cracked parking lot, Nolan's is the only car there. When I open my door I notice that it looks almost like the asphalt beneath my feet is tread upon so rarely that it's covered not only in fallen leaves but also in a layer of dust.

"Are you sure this is the right place?"

Nolan nods, pointing to a sign outside the enormous red-brick building across the parking lot. "Levis Hall," he reads. "That's where his office is."

I get out of the car and shut my door behind me, eyeing the building in front of us. I can't see a single light coming from any of its windows. "It's like a ghost town over here," I say.

"Pun intended?" Nolan asks.

"Blah, pun most definitely *not* intended!"

Apparently Levis Hall's elevator is out of order, so we climb the stairs. The floor beneath our feet is marble, so our footsteps echo, and the banister is smooth dark wood, cool beneath my fingers. We don't see a single other person, and the fluorescent lights that illuminate the hallway are dim, making everything look abandoned and sad.

"I guess he's not the most popular professor," I whisper. When we reach the fourth floor we're no longer walking on marble but on linoleum, dark green and dust covered enough to make me sneeze.

"I don't think this professor has had anything resembling a line of students waiting for his office hours in a long, long time," Nolan says in agreement.

"If ever," I add.

By the time we knock on the professor's office door—room 4B-04—I'm shivering. Even standing next to Nolan isn't enough to warm me in this cold.

"It must be below freezing in here," I complain, my teeth chattering. Then I remember that Nolan doesn't feel it.

From the other side of the door, someone shouts: "Come in!"

CHAPTER SIXTEEN

Expert Help?

This might just be the messiest room I've ever seen. Nolan has to push extra hard to open the door because there's a stack of papers behind it. And stacks of papers scattered across the floor. And books piled so high they're almost as tall as Nolan, threatening to topple over. I wonder how long the professor has worked here.

"Professor Jones," Nolan says, holding out his hand to a tiny man seated behind the desk. "I'm Nolan Foster." He pauses, hoping to see a flicker of recognition at the name he shares with his grandfather, but there's nothing.

Professor Jones looks like he's about a hundred years old, with glasses as thick as coke bottles on his face, the tiniest wisp of white hair on the top of his mostly bald head, and his skin stained with age spots. No wonder Nolan wasn't able to find his name in the university's e-mail system—I'm not sure the man has ever actually heard of e-mail. He clearly came of age in a time before the Internet existed. There isn't even a computer on his desk.

Instead, his desk is piled high with papers and books, the stacks so tall I have to stand on my tiptoes to see the whole of the professor's face behind them. He's definitely past the age when most people would have retired. He smacks his lips because he's missing a few teeth.

"Have a seat," he says. His voice is dry as paper. It's probably the driest thing in this whole rain-drenched state.

Nolan and I tiptoe between piles of paper to sit on the chairs opposite his desk. Well, not on the chairs themselves, exactly; instead, we perch on the books piled on top of them. I feel paper crinkling beneath my weight, and I sit up straight, trying to make myself lighter so I don't ruin the books beneath me. Not that it looks like they're all that well taken care of, but I still don't want to be rude. I finger what remains of the long, narrow wound on my left hand, curved along the fleshy part between my thumb and forefinger.

"So you're having a ghost problem?" the professor croaks.

"How did you know that?" I ask, folding my arms across my chest, trying to keep warm.

"Why else would you be here?" he answers, a smile playing on the edges of his thin lips. "Whose ghost is it?" The skin on his neck jiggles when he talks.

I shake my head. "I don't know. I mean, I think it's a little girl, but we don't know who it is."

Nolan adds, "I've done research into the deaths that occurred in and around Sunshine's house but couldn't find anyone who matched up with the ghost."

"I think she must be about ten. Because she wants to play with me all the time."

"She wants to play with you?" Professor Jones echoes. A little bit of sparkle breaks through the milkiness of his gray eyes.

I nod. "Checkers, Monopoly, that kind of thing."

"And have you played with her?"

He asks the question so expectantly that I hesitate before answering. Maybe I wasn't supposed to engage with her the way I did. Maybe when I made that very first move on the checkerboard I made an enormous mistake, like by sliding the piece across the board, I was inviting her to stay.

"I thought it might make her happy."

The professor's smile looks like it takes enormous effort: it happens slowly, first his lips widen, then his eyes crinkle, and a few of his yellowed teeth show. He wheezes heavily, as winded as if he'd been lifting weights, not just his own face.

"I thought it would be harmless—" I add softly.

The professor shakes his head. "Few spirits are truly harmless," he says firmly. "Not here on Earth."

Great, that makes me feel so much better. Guess this guy never heard of breaking things gently. My mother would say he has bad bedside manner, like some of the doctors she's worked with over the years.

"Lately, my mom, she's just been acting strange, and the other day—" I reach into my bag for my phone, ready to show him the way my mother cut herself, but the professor starts talking before I can explain.

"Even the friendliest of spirits is dangerous. Because it simply should not be here. It is a fish out of water. A hawk with broken wings. A horse with a broken leg. Do you know what they do to horses with broken legs, child?"

I glance at Nolan. He raises his eyebrows but nods, prompting me to tell my story.

"I think the ghost is doing something to my mother. Or maybe not the little girl ghost. Maybe it's some other ghost we haven't identified yet. But she tried to hurt herself—my mom, I mean. Not the ghost—"

The professor claps his hands and I jump. I wouldn't have thought he'd have the strength to press his hands together hard enough to make such a loud noise.

"Spirits don't belong here," he says hoarsely. I lean forward to hear him better. "Fish out of water. Hawks with broken wings. Horses with broken legs."

I shake my head. "I'm sorry, I don't really understand what you're getting at—"

"They're meant to move on," he says sharply. "They don't belong here."

I glance helplessly at Nolan.

"My grandfather was a fan of yours," Nolan tries, like maybe he thinks the professor will respond to flattery. "His name was Nolan Foster, just like me. I thought he might have sought you out over the years—"

"Never heard of him," Professor Jones interrupts, waving his hand dismissively.

"He wasn't an expert or anything," Nolan explains. "Just a believer."

"Bet they called him crazy," the professor wheezes, coughing in between each word. Nolan nods, and Professor Jones adds, "That's what they called me."

Is that why the university stuck him off in the middle of nowhere in this nearly abandoned building? Maybe he thinks we're here to make fun of him—and, maybe that's why he's speaking in riddles.

"Can you help us?" I ask finally.

"You can help yourself," he answers.

"How?"

The professor's eyelids flutter heavily, like he's falling asleep. "How?" I repeat, my voice high pitched with desperation. Now his eyes close completely and his chin falls against his chest.

"We should go, Sunshine," Nolan says. "I think I may have led us to a dead end."

I shake my head. "I don't have time for dead ends."

"I know." Nolan nods. "I'm sorry." Slowly I stand. We're almost out the door when I hear the professor mumble something behind us.

Nolan turns and steps closer to the desk. "What was that, Professor?"

He says it again, but it just sounds like nonsense to me. I strain to make sense of what he's saying, but it just sounds like "ooooo-each" to me.

"Sorry, I didn't hear that," Nolan says. "Could you tell me again?"

"Loo-seeech," the professor says. Now his eyes are open wide—and locked with mine.

"Nolan," I whisper. "We should go. I don't think he can help us." I don't want to spend another moment in this icy cold room. It makes me feel hopeless. Is this what happens to believers when they get old? Do they sit in lonely little rooms, all their knowledge overlapping until it comes out as nothing more than gibberish? Is this what happened to Nolan's grandfather? What will happen to him? To me?

Nolan goes back and leans over the desk to shake Professor Jones's hand. But instead of pressing his hand into Nolan's, the professor picks up an enormous old book off his desk and holds it out in front of him with trembling hands. There aren't any words on the book's worn leather-bound cover, just faded gold markings, like maybe once there was an elaborate drawing on the cover that had long since worn away.

"Thank you," Nolan says politely.

"Well, that was weird."

Nolan shrugs. "He tried to help us."

"I don't think he *could* help us."

I shudder when I think about Professor Jones all alone in that lonely cold room. When all of this is over, once Mom is safe, I'll go back and visit him. I'll bring him cookies or soup or pudding or whatever you're supposed to bring to an elderly person and spend a whole afternoon listening to his gibberish and pretending to understand it.

"He gave me that." Nolan gestures to the tattered, leather book he placed carefully in the backseat. We're almost back in Ridgemont.

"Did you see all the books in his office? He probably gives one to every visitor."

Nolan smiles. "I don't think he gets many visitors."

"No," I agree. "I don't think he does."

CHAPTER SEVENTEEN
The Luiseach

"I think I've figured out what a luiseach is," Nolan tells me when he walks me home from school a few days later.

Pine needles fall onto my head from the Douglas firs above us. "I thought evergreens didn't shed their leaves in the fall," I complain, brushing the needles from my hair.

"Missed one," Nolan says. Before he can get close enough to take it out for me I flip my hair over and jump up and down.

"What else you hiding in there?" he laughs.

"It's not funny." My hair is so poofy that I could probably use it to smuggle contraband. I pull it into a messy knot at the nape of my neck. "Anyway, what were you saying? You figured out what a *what* is?"

"A luiseach," he answers. "Remember, before we left his office, Professor Jones said it?"

"All I remember is gibberish," I answer honestly.

"I know it sounded like that, but I saw the word in the book he gave me."

"How did you know how to spell it?" Nolan reaches into his backpack and pulls the book out. It looks even more enormous than it did in the back of his car: bound in wrinkled brown leather and so thick that Nolan has to use both hands to hold it. "You've been carrying it around with you all this time?" It must weigh a zillion pounds.

He nods. "I'm reading it every chance I get. It doesn't always make sense—parts of it seem to be written in some kind of code, and parts aren't even in English, but I think I'm finally getting something out of it." He opens to a page he'd marked with a bookmark. "There," he says, pointing to a word in the center of it. I take the book. The paper is yellowed and thin, as translucent as wax paper. The font is so tiny I have to squint to read the word.

Luiseach.

"Louis-each?" I say, trying to ignore the butterflies in my stomach. Who knew that just seeing a word printed on paper could provoke a physical response? "How do you know that's the same word he said?"

"It was the only word in the book that was close to the one the professor said to us."

He didn't say it to *us*, I think but do not say, remembering the way he stared at me as he spoke. He said it to *me*. "You read the whole book already?"

Nolan shrugs like it's no big deal to be able to read a thousand-page tome in a matter of days.

Suddenly a big fat raindrop falls from the sky, landing right in the center of Nolan's new word. Quickly Nolan stuffs the book back into his bag. "Let's make a run for it," he says. "I don't want to risk the book getting wet." He breaks into a sprint, reaching for my hand as he does so.

My fingers wrap around his automatically, as though, unbeknownst to me, all this time they'd just been waiting for a boy's hand to hold. At the same time, my stomach is doing somersaults, high kicks, back flips—whatever a stomach does that makes it feel like it's trying to leap out of its rightful place in your belly and come flying out of your mouth.

So I slide my hand out of Nolan's grasp, put my head down, and sprint. By the time we get to my house I'm panting the way Oscar does when it's ninety degrees outside. Not that I can even remember what those kind of temperatures feel like. My hair is soaked, but for once it's not due entirely to the rain. I'm actually sweating, for what feels like the first time since we moved here.

"Not a runner, huh?" Nolan laughs as I open the door for us. I lead the way into the kitchen, slip off my backpack, and collapse into a chair at the table. Nolan grins, getting us drinks out of the fridge as though this is his house and I'm his guest. Or at least with the same familiarity Ashley used to navigate our kitchen back in Austin. Which is kind of nice.

When I finally catch my breath I say, "Okay, so tell me what you think a luiseach is exactly."

Nolan plops down in the chair beside me and retrieves the book from his bag. I wonder how old it is. It's funny to think of a book like this alongside Nolan's chemistry textbook and math homework. Just another assignment, more research.

Except, instead of an A from the teacher, if we do well, we'll keep my mother from hurting herself again.

"Everything I'm about to say is going to sound crazy," he warns as he hugs the book to his chest.

"I'm not sure how much crazier things can get," I say sadly.

"From what I can tell—and like I said, this book isn't the easiest thing in the world to decipher—luiseach are some kind of paranormal guardians. They're well suited to their task because they can be around the paranormal and yet be perfectly safe—they don't have to worry about being possessed, that kind of thing."

"If only my mom were so lucky," I say wistfully.

"It's not exactly your mom that I have in mind," Nolan mumbles.

"What?"

"I don't want to get ahead of myself," he says quickly, setting the book down on the kitchen table and flipping through its thin pages. He pulls his wire-rimmed glasses from his pocket and puts them on. "According to this, luiseach have been around for centuries and live long lives." He reads aloud from the book: "*Because they can sense older spirits, luiseach are commonly drawn backwards.*" He looks up. "I think that means they like old-fashioned stuff. You know, antiques, cemeteries, stories about the way the world used to be, that kind of thing."

"Sound like my kind of people," I quip, taking a sip of water. "So you're saying we need to find a luiseach to perform an exorcism or something?"

Nolan shakes his head. "Not exactly."

"Why not? It sounds like a luiseach is exactly what we need right now."

"Yeah," Nolan agrees, "It does. I just don't think we need to *find* one exactly."

"Why not? You have a luiseach hiding in your pocket or something?" I reach for his backpack and pretend to rifle through it, like I think I might find a luiseach inside. I guess I picked a bad time to make a joke, because Nolan doesn't even give me a sympathy laugh.

"No," Nolan says slowly, and I take another sip of water. "I'm saying I think *you* are a luiseach."

Water literally shoots up my nose and I spit it out all over the table in front of me. Nolan hunches over the book to protect it from the spray.

"I told you it was going to sound crazy," he says.

I shake my head, pretending not to remember the way Professor Jones looked at me when he said the word. "Okay, but there's crazy, and then there's *crazy*."

"What makes you think that you're *not* a luiseach?" Nolan leans back and folds his arms across his chest.

I don't even know where to begin. "Um, are you kidding? We don't even know if luiseach actually exist outside of the ramblings of a possibly senile old man."

"And this book! It says here that luiseach look like humans and live among humans—they just have certain"—Nolan struggles to find the right word—"*abilities*," he decides finally, "that make them not quite human."

"Just because something is in a book doesn't make it true." With effort, I pick the book up off the table. It's about a million years old. Okay, not that old, but perhaps older than even a first edition of *Pride and Prejudice*. I flip through it, trying to decipher what's so powerful about these pages that they could convince Nolan that I'm something less than human. Or maybe something more.

There's no copyright page, no publisher, no Library of Congress description like there is on a real book. From what I can tell, it doesn't even have a title or an author.

Every book has an author. Maybe this one just didn't want anyone to know who he was.

I put the book down, my hands trembling so much that I practically drop it and it lands on the table with a loud smack. "Let's say—just for the sake of argument—that luiseach are real. I can't possibly be one. You said it yourself, luiseach can be around the paranormal and be perfectly safe. I'm not safe! I'm scared all the time. I feel so creepy everywhere I go."

"Exactly!" Nolan practically shouts.

"Exactly what?"

"You said you've felt weird for months now—cold and strange—everywhere you go."

"So what do you mean?" I ask, though I'm not entirely sure I want to hear his answer.

"I think that creepy feeling is you perceiving the spirits around you. I don't feel it. Your mom doesn't feel it. Only you do. You're capable of perceiving something that the rest of us can't—even though I believe in ghosts, just like you, and can see all the evidence of your haunted house, just like you can."

I shake my head so hard that my neck hurts.

"And you said so yourself, you're *playing* with her. Maybe a normal person wouldn't be able to interact with a ghost like that."

"I wasn't *trying* to interact with her. It just seemed like what she wanted—"

"Okay, but how many normal people would be concerned with—or know—what a ghost wanted?" Nolan counters. "And you love old stuff. My jacket, all those vintage clothes—"

"What, so having a nontraditional sense of style makes me into some kind of paranormal superhero?" I say incredulously, as though just thirty seconds ago I wasn't imagining that luiseach would dress like I do.

"There's just one thing I can't quite figure out," he adds slowly. "The book says that being a luiseach is hereditary. So your mom should be one too. But she's totally been affected by the ghost, or spirit, or demon—whatever's in this house with you." Nolan leans over his book once more, poring over the pages like he believes that if he just looks hard enough, the answer will appear.

Everything that happens next feels like it's going in slow motion. All except for my heart, which is racing. I push my chair out from under the table and slowly stand. Nolan doesn't look up—he's reading every bit as intently as I read Jane Austen. Slowly, like I'm afraid I might trip and fall, I begin to pace the room. Oscar and Lex follow me, questioning looks on their faces, like even they know that something is wrong.

Softly I say, "I'm adopted."

"What?" Nolan asks, still not looking up from his book.

"I'm adopted," I repeat louder, and start pacing at a normal speed.

Now Nolan does look up.

"That doesn't mean I'm a louise, loo—whatever you call it. I mean, plenty of people in the world are adopted. It doesn't mean anything."

"You're right," he nods. "But those tons of people aren't in the situation you're in."

"Tell me more about those things. Louises."

"Loo-seach," Nolan corrects.

"Whatever," I shrug. I know how to pronounce it. I just don't want to.

I continue pacing as Nolan speaks. "*In ancient times luiseach were raised in insular communities, training from childhood to protect humans from the dark side of the paranormal world.*"

"What does that mean? The dark side of the paranormal world?"

A cold breeze blows through the kitchen despite the closed windows. I shiver, but I keep pacing.

"This is where it gets tricky—"

"*This* is where it gets tricky?" I groan. "It hasn't exactly been a piece of cake so far!"

"The books says that there are two sides of the paranormal. Like two sides of a coin."

"Or a magnet," I mumble, but I don't think he hears me.

"The paranormal world is made up of spirits who hang around after they die, waiting to be ushered into the beyond." Before I can ask the most obvious next question, Nolan says, "The book doesn't say anything about what the *beyond* is." He continues. "The light side includes fairly harmless and even helpful ghosts and spirits."

"Few spirits are truly harmless," I recite, recalling the professor's warning.

"Well, maybe not, but this says that most people who die are pretty anxious to move on. It doesn't feel right to stay behind. But every so often a spirit will refuse to move on. And remaining here changes them, makes them turn dark. They're so desperate to cling to life that they begin messing with the living—like poltergeists who can take hold of human bodies, that kind of thing. Over the centuries, in addition to helping the willing spirits move on, luiseach have been protecting humans by forcing dark spirits—the ones who linger too long and become demons—to the other side."

I stop pacing. "So luiseach are kind of like guardian angels for the entire human race?" Definitely not me, I think. I'm too much of a wimp to be anyone's guardian angel.

"Kind of," Nolan nods. "They even exorcise spirits who refuse to be moved, who wreak havoc on humans' lives. The word *luiseach* means 'light-bringer' in Celtic—"

"Celtic?" I echo.

"Old Irish," Nolan explains. "Though I think the word *luiseach* precedes it."

"How can a word be older than a language?"

"If the word was spoken in an even older language first," Nolan supplies, like the answer is obvious. "Anyway, luiseach send good spirits into the light and shed light where spirits are dark. Supposedly they bring a sort of light and joy wherever they go." Nolan looks at me without blinking until I blush. Is he trying to tell me that he feels some kind of light and joy when he's around me?

I don't exactly feel full of light and joy these days.

"I know it sounds crazy," Nolan says. "I know. But you've got to admit there's a lot of evidence here. Like I said, the word literally means light bringer."

"So?" I fold my arms across my chest as though that will somehow slow my speeding heartbeat.

"So . . ." he says, and I swear, I think he's blushing. "Your name *is* Sunshine."

"That's just a name. It doesn't mean anything. It's not like my mom had ever heard of whatchamacallits when she named me."

Nolan doesn't know the story of the first time my mother held me. *With you in my arms, little girl, I felt like I was in a state of perpetual sunshine.* I close my eyes. More than once I'd joked that maybe she felt sunshine the first time she held me because she was living in Texas and it was August and about a million degrees outside, but that particular joke never made her laugh. She always remained serious. *It had nothing to do with the weather*, she'd always insist. I think it was the closest my cynical, scientific mother ever came to believing in magic.

Now Nolan is saying that maybe it *was* magic. Or whatever luiseach call their powers.

Does that mean that when my mother picked me up, that warm, sunshiny feeling she experienced wasn't the joy of a new mother, wasn't just her maternal instinct kicking in like it had for millions of mothers before her? Instead, she felt the way she did because I wasn't entirely *human*?

I shudder—had some other person held me first, maybe they'd have taken me home instead. Maybe I'd be someone else's sunshine. Is this the reason why Mom never needed anyone else—rarely dated, never got serious? Because she had me and my light, whatever that means, so she didn't feel like she needed anything else? Was it some kind of illusion I'd unknowingly cast, a trick I'd unintentionally played?

I squeeze my eyes shut even tighter. Maybe Mom wouldn't have even wanted me if I'd been normal, maybe picking me up wouldn't have felt any different from picking up the dozens of infants she'd probably already held that day.

I shake my head. No. *No.* I am my mother's daughter. I wrinkle my nose like she does and have her same ridiculous sense of humor. Luiseach or not—and probably *not*, I mean, Nolan's evidence is thin, at best—she and I were meant to be together, like she always said.

And I love her so much that I'm not about to let this ghost or demon or poltergeist or dark spirit or whatever is in this house hurt her.

I open my eyes and walk across the kitchen and sink into the chair beside Nolan. "Tell me more," I say softly. He leans over the book and begins reading.

"Should the luiseach fail in their cause, the dark creatures would destroy humanity."

"Well, that's a relief," I say, though it feels like I'm choking. "I was worried it was going to be something serious."

She Is Getting Closer

Sunshine is getting closer. I can sense it each time she awakens a new power, comes to a new understanding.

I sensed it when she first felt the cold. She perceives it as weakness—the strange feeling in her belly, the way her heart quickens, the gooseflesh on her arms—to her, it feels like an illness. But soon—once she has passed—she will learn how to harness that sensation, how to let it wash over her, to welcome it and then release it. Most of us are able to do so intuitively, but so far she hasn't allowed her intuition to take over. When she finally began to understand just what the cold might signify, she forced that understanding away, denied what she was beginning to comprehend. She is fighting this.

And yet, despite her fight, she is making progress. The professor was a lovely trick, if I do say so myself. I'll have to thank Abner for his participation. It took a lot of strength to put him and his office in place, but it was well worth it. And the books were a stroke of brilliance. Just a little bit of help, a nudge to get them onto the correct path.

They didn't notice me driving behind them as they wended their way through the campus's twists and turns. Soon after they left, Abner appeared at my side: She doesn't understand, he said. This is the girl you're counting on to repair what's broken?

But even Abner doesn't know the truth. I don't exactly want to repair anything. And Sunshine could be the reason I don't have to.

How convenient that she found that Nolan so quickly—another way in. If I cared about such things, I would find it touching that Sunshine's journey is bringing him a sense of peace about his own grandfather, one of few humans who truly cared about the paranormal world. In another time, when we congregated with humans, I might have known the man. I might have validated his beliefs. But such times are long past. Such times precede even me, and I am the oldest creature I know.

Nolan was the one to read the book, to find the word and say it out loud first. It is, I suppose, appropriate—considering what he will be to her—that he be the one who puts the pieces together. But this is not about him. It is about her.

It is good to see just how much fight she has in her. Her will is strong, her essence forceful. I wonder how long she will go on fighting before she realizes she must put that fight to better use.

CHAPTER EIGHTEEN
Puzzle Pieces

On the way to school the next day I practice the speech I'm planning to unleash on Nolan the instant I see him: I've decided I'm not one of those guardian angel guys. I mean, we don't even know if anyone is. We just have Professor Jones's book to go on, and it might not even be a real book. He might have his own private printing press hidden in that building, for all we know. It certainly looked like there was plenty of available space. I don't mean to sound cynical, but all of this sounds a little too out of this world to be true.

The last line of the speech is the part that's tripping me up. Because the fact that my house is haunted in the first place is plenty out of this world too. Nolan will be quick to point out that if one out-of-this-world thing can be true, why not another?

And I'm having trouble coming up with any kind of counterargument for that.

It's almost Thanksgiving. I'm finally not the only student bundled up with a hat and scarf every morning. Today I'm wearing a cozy gray cardigan that's at least two sizes too big; the sleeves hang long past my wrists, and I don't even bother trying to roll them up because they're keeping my hands warm. In fact, with such long sleeves, I don't need gloves. Someone in the sweater business should totally try to corner that market: extra-long-sleeved sweaters so you don't need gloves to keep your hands warm! They'd make millions. Or maybe not: everyone else at school is wearing clothes that actually fit them, so it's possible that I'd be the only customer for a product like that.

It's a Thursday, and we don't have visual arts on Thursdays, so my best chance to catch Nolan is in the halls between classes. But he catches me first and starts talking before I can launch into my speech.

"I'm coming over after school today," he declares. "I read something more."

We don't have much time before class, so I try to condense my speech into a single sentence.

"Listen Nolan, I think you might be putting a lot of faith in a tattered old book that a potentially crazy old man gave you." Out of the corner of my eye I see Ms. Wilde leaning against a wall of lockers down the hall. There's no way she can hear us with the sound of kids shouting and laughing, lockers being opened and slammed shut. Still, it feels like she might be listening.

I shake my head. *Get a grip, Sunshine.*

Before I can say anymore Nolan counters, "I'm not just putting faith in a tattered old book. I found more online last night." The bell rings, and he heads to class before I can say that he's totally undermined the rest of my argument.

Later Nolan sits at my kitchen table once more, me across from him. This time, instead of the book laid out in front of him, there's a stack of pages he printed off the Internet.

"What did you do, Google the word *luiseach* and print all the facts off Wikipedia?"

Nolan laughs nervously. "No. I mean, I started by Googling luiseach, but of course nothing came up."

I breathe a teeny, tiny sigh of relief.

"But," he continues and my relief vanishes, "Then I started Googling other words like *dark spirits* and *guardian angels* and *exorcisms* and *possession*. I was getting nowhere and then I Googled *haunted house* along with thc word *guardian*. And I got this." He holds up a densely packed printout covered in words I don't understand.

I push up my sleeves and reach for the paper, trying not to look at the ugly crescent-shaped scar on my left hand. It still looks red and angry, like it doesn't want to heal. Mom probably has a matching mark on her wrist, I just haven't been close enough to her lately to see it.

"What is that, Greek?"

"Latin."

"You speak Latin?"

"Of course not. I just plugged it into a translator." He holds up another printout. "See any words you recognize?"

Well, I see a bunch of words I recognize like *and* and *the* and *age*, but I'm pretty sure the word Nolan's talking about is *luiseach*, which is repeated over and over across the translation.

"Yippee," I say. I'm being sarcastic, but I'm actually really impressed by Nolan's research. I could never have found all of this on my own. Partly because I didn't want to. I mean, I want to save my mother more than I've ever wanted anything, but I also don't want to be an ancient mystical warrior.

The truth is, I Googled the word *luiseach* too. But unlike Nolan, I gave up before I found it.

"Here's something interesting," Nolan begins, pointing about halfway down the third page. "It says that luiseach come of age on their sixteenth birthday. Until then they are unable to perceive ghosts and spirits."

"I turned sixteen a couple weeks before we moved here."

Nolan nods thoughtfully. "It's a weird sort of coincidence, don't you think? That you'd turn sixteen and then almost immediately move into a haunted house."

"But we didn't move here until after my birthday," I say, then quickly wish I could take back the words because they make it sound like I actually agree with Nolan's theory. And I most certainly do not believe that I'm a luiseach. Not . . . not *exactly*.

Nolan scans the pages in front of him. "But you should have felt *something* the instant you turned sixteen, even if it wasn't as powerful as what you feel in this house." He purses his lips like he's trying to figure something out.

The *instant* I turned sixteen is kind of a hard moment to determine because I'm adopted. I don't have a birth mother who can tell me stories of the exact moment I was born, who tells me about the hours of painful contractions and pushing hard until the sound of my cries alerted her to the fact that a new person had just sort of burst into the room. Ashley used to claim that her mom told her she was born precisely at midnight. She claimed that, technically, she had two birthdays, since her birth straddled two days.

The things I know about my own birth are much more

vague. Mom told me that I was found at the hospital in the middle of the night, past midnight on August 15. I was still covered in what she calls amniotic fluid and I call birth goo, though I was swaddled in a soft yellow blanket. They could tell I'd been born only a few hours earlier. So even though I was found on the fifteenth, we always celebrated my birthday as the fourteenth. She was absolutely positive it was the right day, she said, because science doesn't lie.

I can't detect much science in the pages Nolan and I are looking at now. Mom would call them fairy stories, not facts. I wish Mom were here, spouting off scientific explanations to contradict all this insanity. But if Mom were here—the way she's been acting lately—she'd probably confiscate Nolan's papers and send me to my room. *Enough of this ghost nonsense*, she'd say.

"What do you remember about your birthday this year? Was there anything that felt different?"

I shrug. "Nothing out of the ordinary."

"Well, talk me through your day," Nolan tries. He takes off his glasses. "Maybe it will jog your memory."

"I didn't have a Sweet Sixteen party or anything. It was just me, my mom, and Ashley—she's my best friend back in Austin." He nods. "We had dinner and cake." In fact, we did the same thing for my birthday this year that I had since I turned thirteen and convinced Mom she could stop throwing me birthday parties, since I wasn't even friends with most of the classmates on her invite list. I just wanted her and Ashley, and a different kind of cake every year. Thirteen: German chocolate cake. Fourteen: red velvet cake. Fifteen: banana cream pie (not technically cake, I know, but it was delicious). And this year, sixteen, carrot cake with cream cheese frosting (no raisins—why do people put raisins in cookies and cakes, *yuck*). I can't believe how much time I used to spend thinking about what kind of cake to have each year. That seems so unimportant now.

"Mom baked a cake," I say. "She decorated it with candles."

"Sixteen candles." Nolan nods.

"Seventeen, actually. Sixteen plus one to grow on. My mom does that every year." Not that she believes in birthday wishes, of course. She just likes cake and candles.

"Got it. What else?"

"Nothing else! That was it. I blew out the candles and they clapped and then we ate the cake."

"Did you make a wish?"

I hesitate. Every year I always wait until the last second to decide what my wish will be. I don't make up my mind until I'm actually leaning over the cake and taking a deep breath. I like to pick little things—not world peace or winning the lottery. I prefer to make wishes that actually have a chance of coming true. On my thirteenth birthday I wished for Oscar to get over an eye infection that he'd had for months. On my fifteenth I wished to get a good score on my PSATs.

But this year . . . I don't remember. In fact, I don't think I made a wish at all. I've never not made a wish before. I close my eyes, trying to remember. Did something happen to make me forget to pick something?

I picture the evening of my birthday, the three of us sweltering in the Texas heat, because Mom insisted that we open the windows instead of turning on the AC.

"Fresh air is good for you," she'd say, sick and tired of manufactured coolness after another day spent in the hospital's central air conditioning.

The house was a little bit of a disaster area because we'd already started packing. Half our books and clothes were stacked into boxes. Oscar was circling my feet, like he knew that since this year's cake didn't have any chocolate in it—chocolate is poisonous to dogs—we might actually give him a taste.

"Do you hear that?" Nolan asks suddenly. I open my eyes. Footsteps are coming from the floor above us. But not gentle, skipping footsteps. Instead, it sounds like someone is pacing anxiously back and forth.

I look up at the ceiling and say softly, "What are you trying to tell me?"

The steps turn into stomps, like someone jumping up and down.

I stand up and lean over the table. Back in Texas this was the very same table where Mom put my cake, still warm in the middle. I take a deep breath, imitating the way I must have inhaled before I blew out my candles. Now my skin is covered in goose bumps and my heart is pounding. And suddenly I remember: on my birthday I felt exactly the same sensations the instant I inhaled over the cake.

"I did feel something on my sixteenth birthday," I admit. "It's the way I felt when we moved into this house, except it only lasted for a second. Kind of like when you have a fever and your skin is hot to the touch but you still can't stop shivering. And my heart was pounding like I'd just sprinted a mile." I pause. "Not that I know what it feels like to sprint for a mile," I add, and Nolan smiles a little.

Was turning sixteen—and not the move to Ridgemont—the event that jump-started that not-feeling-right sensation that now follows me wherever I go?

"That doesn't mean I'm a luiseach," I add hastily, stepping away from the table. "It could have been a million other things. Maybe I was coming down with something. You have to admit, this is pretty flimsy evidence."

I expect Nolan to argue, but instead he sighs and says, "I know." I sit back down. "This is like trying to put together a puzzle with a million pieces and no picture of the end result to guide you." He flips through his pages. "It also says here that luiseach are never alone. They're aided by a protector and a mentor. And according to this, your mentor should have presented himself or herself to you by now. They're supposed to show up to begin your training when you turn sixteen." He runs his fingers through his fine hair. "But maybe that goes back to when luiseach lived in insular communities, and things are different now? I can't figure it out."

"What about their protector?" I ask. I prefer the sound of a protector to a mentor, anyway. Some protection would come in handy right about now. "Does it say anything about when a protector shows up?"

"There's even less in here about protectors." Nolan shoves the papers across the table. "And you'd think now would be the time the *protector* at least would show up," he adds, echoing my thoughts. "You could use some protection, with your mom in danger."

CHAPTER NINETEEN
Caught in a Web

The sound of keys rattling in the front door makes both of us jump.

"Mom is never home this early." I push my chair from the table and start stacking all of Nolan's papers on top of each other so quickly that it's a miracle I don't give myself a paper cut.

I'm feeling something that I've never, ever felt before: nervous that my mother is about to walk into the room.

"Hi Mom!" I say a bit too loudly. If Nolan notices my false cheer, he keeps it to himself. Maybe he's just curious to finally get a look at my mother in real life, this person he's heard so much about, this person he's watched hurt herself over and over again in the video on my phone, but has never actually met.

"Hi," Mom answers absently, drifting through the kitchen, her eyes on a patient file in her hand. She doesn't look up at us. I don't think she even realizes that another person is in the room with us.

"Mom, this is my . . ." I hesitate, searching for the right thing to call Nolan. He's not my boyfriend, obviously. But he feels like more than just a regular friend too. My goodness, could I be more of a *girl* right now? Seriously, with everything that's going on, you'd think I wouldn't exactly have time to worry about semantics. "This is Nolan," I say finally. "We're in the same art class."

Nolan stands up, his chair squeaking against the tile. "Hello, Mrs. Griffith," he says, sticking out his hand for her to shake. He's so adorably polite that I have to bite my lip to keep from grinning.

But Mom doesn't take his hand. Instead, she says, "It's Ms."

"I'm sorry?" Nolan blinks.

"*Mizzzz* Griffith," she replies, exaggerating the word. "Not Mrs."

Mom has never asked any of my friends to call her Miss or Ms. or Mrs. anything. She's always just been Kat.

"Nolan and I were just studying–"

"For art class?" Mom interrupts, her voice thick with mockery. She drops her file onto the kitchen counter with a *smack.* "Have to study to make the best collage?"

I open my mouth to say *of course not*, but before I can get the words out, Nolan asks, "How did you know we were working on collages in class?"

Mom shrugs as though she couldn't care less. "Sunshine must have mentioned it."

I turn to Nolan and shake my head from side to side. I haven't mentioned it. She hasn't even asked about school in weeks. In fact, this might be the most we've talked since the night she cut herself. I glance around the kitchen: at the counter where she bled, at the butcher block that holds our knives, including the one she hurt herself with.

"So what *are* you studying?" Mom sighs finally, stepping toward the table.

"Nothing," I say quickly. Too quickly. Mom raises her eyebrows, suddenly interested.

"I certainly hope you weren't studying nothing. I know what happens when you study *nothing*."

I blush pinker than I've blushed in my entire life, horrified that Mom is implying that Nolan and I were . . . blah, I can't even think it! If only she knew how it felt when Nolan got too close.

"Nolan was just leaving—"

"No, I wasn't," he says firmly. He shoots me a look that says, *I'm not leaving you alone like this.*

I try to shoot one back that says, *Don't be ridiculous, she's my mother*, but I'm pretty sure it's unconvincing. How could I convince him when I can't even convince myself? I glance at the wound on my left hand, a reminder that my mother did kind of sort of stab me. I mean, we don't know for sure that it wasn't an accident. I didn't manage to record that part.

"Maybe you should leave, Nolan," Mom says, a strange sort of brightness in her voice. "Sunshine and I never really get to spend any time together these days. I've been working such long hours, you see."

"I understand, ma'am, but Sunshine and I have a lot more reading to get through," he gestures to the stacks of papers on the kitchen table.

"I'm sure that can wait. Schoolwork isn't nearly as important as family time." Mom crosses the room and brushes the papers

Nolan worked so hard to gather onto the floor. I crouch down immediately to retrieve them, crawling through her shadow to get to them. A shadow that's much, much bigger than it should be, as if she's twice as tall as she used to be.

"Mom?" I ask softly. "Are you okay?"

"Get up off the floor, Sunshine," she says harshly.

"Let me just get these together for Nolan so he can take them home with him." The pages are moist in my hands, as though they landed in a puddle on the ground instead of on our dry kitchen floor. Nolan crouches down beside me, grabbing as many of the pages as he can.

"Suit yourself," Mom practically spits. She spins on her heel and leaves the room, her enormous shadow trailing behind her.

"She's not usually like that," I say quickly.

"No need to explain," Nolan answers.

A few of the papers landed clear across the kitchen and I crawl toward the kitchen sink to retrieve them.

And then I scream.

"What is it?" Nolan scrambles across the tile floor, but I'm frozen with fear, unable to answer him. I just point. On top of one of Nolan's pages—perhaps right on top of the word *luiseach*—is the biggest daddy longlegs spider I've ever seen.

Nolan carefully slides a paper underneath the spider and opens the window above the sink, releasing it back into the wild. I stay perfectly still all the while, staring at the place on the page where the enormous spider was seconds ago: now all that remains is a large rust-colored damp spot.

Nolan closes the window quickly and crouches on the floor beside me.

"Spiders, blood—you sure are a wimpy luiseach." Nolan tries to grin, but I shake my head, too scared to argue about what I might or might not be. I know he's trying to get me to laugh, but I'm not sure anything will ever be funny to me again.

But it's funny to someone. Because I swear I can hear the sound of my mother laughing in the other room.

You okay? Nolan texts a few hours later. I'm in my room with the lights off and the door locked.

Fine, I answer, though we both know it's a lie.

What happened after I left?

Nothing, I reply. *Mom stayed in her room. Guess all that family-time stuff was just talk.*

She was trying to get rid of me, Nolan answers.

Why?

I don't know.

I tell him I'm going to sleep and put my phone down, but I doubt I'll get much sleep tonight. I close my eyes and listen for the sound of my mother moving around in the next room. I imagine her getting ready for bed, brushing her teeth, pulling her hair into a ponytail. But the thought of dozens of spiders crawling down from the ceiling quickly overtakes those images.

I open my eyes and turn on the light. No spiders in sight.

"Do you know why this is happening to her?" I say out loud, even though I can't believe I'm asking a ghost for help. "I'll play with you forever if you just tell me what's going on." I gesture to the checkerboard beside my bed: last night she beat me, and this morning I woke up to a freshly arranged board, all set for another game. "I thought we were getting to be friends," I say sadly.

Somehow, much to my surprise, I fall asleep. Instead of nightmares about spiders, I dream about the little girl in the tattered dress, the one I dreamt of on our first night here. Tonight her dress is dripping with water, as though she just went for a swim. She's running down a long hallway, her tiny feet leaving wet footprints on the carpet beneath them, gesturing for me to follow her. I sprint after her, but no matter how hard I try, I can't catch up to her. She's always one step ahead.

But she always glances back to make sure I'm still there.

CHAPTER TWENTY

A Rift

At school the next day Nolan grabs me before first period. "I went back to my grandfather's last night. I'm coming over after school again."

"I don't know if that's such a good idea–"

"If your mom freaks out on us again, we'll go someplace else," Nolan cuts me off. "But I want to do this at your place."

"Why?"

"Because I want to see how your ghost reacts." He raises his eyebrows.

By 3:45 we're back at my kitchen table, and Nolan is rifling through stacks of paper once more. "So I saw something when I was looking online the other night . . ." he begins, searching. "In one of these articles. I didn't get a chance to read it carefully–"

"What do you mean?" I ask, mock incredulous. "Did you actually *skim* something instead of poring over it carefully?"

Nolan grins. "It was three in the morning by the time I figured out the whole Google haunted house and guardian combination. I fell asleep before I could read everything I found."

"Wow," I say, genuinely touched. "You stayed up till three in the morning for me? I mean," I add hastily, gesturing at the papers strewn across the table, "for all this?" Nolan doesn't answer right away, so I keep talking, rambling the way I did when we first met. I'd hoped I'd gotten over those Nolan-specific nerves, but apparently not. "But what were you saying? There was something else, right? In one of these articles? I could help you find it." I reach for the papers on the table in front of Nolan and start flipping through them, like I'll be able to find what he's looking for without knowing what it is in the first place.

Nolan furrows his brow. "You okay?"

"I'm fine. I mean . . ." I take a deep breath. "This is all just a lot to take in." And it is. I don't just mean the luiseach stuff. I slide the pages back across the table, careful not to brush my hands against his. "Maybe you should handle this part. I don't even know what you're looking for."

Nolan nods, flipping through the papers. "I saw something about luiseach birth rates in here somewhere."

The house seems to shudder, like we're caught in our own private wind tunnel.

"Golly," I breathe, planting my hands firmly on the table like I think I can steady the whole house that way.

"Wow," Nolan says, looking at the ceiling above us. He slides his glasses up over his forehead. A sudden breeze makes the overhead light swing back and forth like a pendulum.

I try to ignore the way I'm shivering. "Maybe the house

doesn't want me to come up with some kind of crack about luiseach birth rates."

"Maybe luiseach just aren't getting it on often enough," Nolan suggests. If Ashley were here, she'd make a naughty joke, but all I can do is blush. Anyway, like Mom, Ashley would be no help if she were actually here. She'd roll her eyes at this whole conversation, insisting that finding articles on the Internet hardly amounts to proof. *You can find almost anything on the Internet—photos of the Loch Ness monster, of mermaids, of unicorns*, she'd say. *That doesn't mean they're real.*

I swallow a sigh. I know that when I text Ashley later, I won't mention any of this to her.

Maybe I won't text her later after all.

The house stills, and Lex leaps up on top of Nolan's papers.

"Scat," I say to my cat, but he lies down and starts licking his paws. Nolan slides his stack out from under him.

"Here it is!" he shouts. He pats Lex. "Thanks for the help, buddy." Lex jumps off the table, like it's his way of saying: *You're welcome. My work here is done.*

"It says that luiseach live longer than the average human. But I couldn't find anything about how often they're born, their childhoods, that kind of thing. So last night I drove to my grandparents' again and searched through Gramps's desk."

"You drove all the way to your grandmother's?" I ask.

Nolan shrugs. "It's just a couple of hours. And this was too important to wait for." He produces an enormous file folder, yellowed with age. "Gramps had stacks and stacks of articles." He picks up a paper and reads aloud: "*There are whispers that it's been decades, perhaps centuries since the last luiseach was born.*"

"Your grandfather knew about luiseach?" I ask incredulously.

Nolan grins. "Guess he got sick and tired of being called crazy. It looks like he'd been researching for years, trying to find solid evidence of the ghosts he'd always believed in."

"That's why he saved that article about Professor Jones," I say, remembering the headline that promised proof. "And now you do have proof."

"I know," Nolan nods, a sad sort of smile playing on the edges of his lips. "I just wish I could have found it before he died. It'd have been so amazing to . . . I don't know, share this with him, I guess."

"I think he probably knows what you found. If the last few months have taught me anything . . ." I trail off meaningfully, the words I don't say hanging in the air between us: Nolan's grandfather could be watching us, right now, cheering us on.

Nolan nods and refocuses his attention on the article in front of him. He reads aloud once more: "*Some say it's been a thousand years. Rumor has it that this is the source of a rift within the luiseach community.*"

On the stove behind us the teakettle begins to whistle, even though it's empty and there's no flame lit beneath it. Nolan and I exchange a look with a capital L.

"Why would low birth rates cause a rift?"

Nolan shakes his head. "I don't know. Maybe they're just scared."

"Shouldn't being scared draw them closer together? You said they lived in super-close-knit communities, right?"

"Sometimes fear makes people turn against each other."

I nod. I mean, Mom and I have always been so close, but now that I'm scared a ghost or a demon or a dark spirit or whatever might be possessing her, we have no relationship. Our own private rift.

"So what?" I have to shout to be heard over the kettle's whine. "You're saying that you think I'm the first luiseach to be born in a century or something?"

"Maybe," Nolan answers solemnly. The bulb above us—still swinging back and forth—dims as he adds, "but more than that—I think I'm saying that you're the *last* luiseach to be born."

I'm about to tell Nolan that's crazy when the bulb above us brightens, so bright that it's blinding, like someone set it on fire from the inside. Suddenly it bursts, sending shards of glass down from the ceiling like rain.

I scream, jumping up from my chair so that it falls with a crash on the floor behind me. Oscar dives under the table like he's ducking for cover. He's got the right idea, because glass continues to rain down, far more glass than a single bulb could possibly contain.

Covering my head with my hands, I glance over at Nolan. He's still seated in his chair, and he hasn't so much as gasped. I feel like a total wimp for screaming.

But then I see that he's holding his hands out in front of him; his left palm is covered in blood.

"Oh my gosh!" I shout.

Blood is dripping from his hand onto the papers beneath, rendering them illegible. "What are you doing?" I shout at the ceiling, certain that the ghost can hear me.

In answer, the storm of glass stops as abruptly as it began, the teakettle stops whistling, and the light stops swinging back and forth.

"Come here," I say frantically to Nolan. He stands up and walks to the island in the center of the kitchen while I reach for the first aid kit under the kitchen sink, the same one I used when my mother cut herself.

I press a fistful of gauze into Nolan's palm, careful not to let my skin touch his, keeping my arm straight so we're not standing too close. "Our cuts almost match," I say, holding up my left hand, the angry red scar between my thumb and forefinger. If Nolan's cut leaves a scar, it will be almost in the center of his palm.

"I thought you weren't good with blood."

"I'm not." I press harder. Mom says you're supposed to apply pressure when someone is bleeding, to help staunch the flow.

"You seem okay."

Blood is still dripping from his wound. "You might need stitches," I say worriedly. Without warning, Nolan places his undamaged right hand on top of mine, applying more pressure.

I take a deep breath and concentrate so I can swallow the feeling that follows. The sensation is overwhelming: the muscles in my legs are demanding that I take a step backward, away from him. The bones in my fingers want to drop the gauze and slide out from under his grip. And my throat—this is something beyond nausea. It's not quite that I want to throw up; it's more that I want to expel Nolan's scent from my nostrils. He's wearing his grandfather's leather jacket, just as he does almost every day, and my arms want to rip it from his body and tear it to shreds, just to get rid of the scent of it.

And yet . . . somehow I ignore all the signals my body is sending me and I don't move. I *won't* move. My friend is in trouble. My friend—maybe the only friend I have left, with Mom in outer space and Ashley oblivious—is bleeding, and I have to help him. Mom once said I should spend the day at the hospital to get over my fear of blood—you know, immersion therapy or something. Maybe I can immersion therapy away this weird feeling I get when I touch Nolan.

So instead of letting go of his hand, I press harder, ignoring my nausea, silently screaming at my muscles to stop trying to move in the opposite direction. I concentrate on the feeling of the callus in his right palm, pressing against the back of my hand. I stare at the creases in his leather jacket, butter-soft after so many years of use. And all the while—even though it doesn't exactly feel *good,* being so close to him—there's also a pleasant flutter of butterflies flapping around my stomach. I feel warmer than I have in months, a warmth coming from the center of my body and spreading out to my extremities.

Part of me, at least, likes Nolan's touch.

"I think it's stopped bleeding," he says, lifting his hand off of mine. I remove the gauze and take a look. What had been gushing blood has slowed into a trickle. The wound is ugly and wide, but not deep.

"Guess you don't need stitches."

"Guess not." Nolan steps away from me, turning toward the kitchen sink, rinsing the blood from his hand. He holds it out for me to bandage, then grabs a paper towel and wipes away the blood that dripped onto the kitchen counter.

A rush of cold air fills the space he used to take up beside me, and I shiver.

"Where do you keep your broom?" he asks, and I gesture to a long, skinny cabinet beside the sink. He sweeps up the glass on the floor around the table. Next he finds a fresh lightbulb and climbs onto the table to replace the one that broke.

"How can you be so calm?" I ask.

"I don't know," he shrugs. "Maybe because I grew up believing in ghosts. For you, this is all still pretty new."

"It's new for you. You may have believed in ghosts, but you

said so yourself–you never had any actual evidence that they existed before."

"True," Nolan agrees, screwing in the lightbulb.

"Was this the reaction you had in mind when you said you wanted to do this here?" I ask, gesturing at the ceiling.

"I didn't have anything in mind, really. I just had a hunch."

"A hunch that what?" I ask, gesturing to the ruined pages on the kitchen table.

Nolan hops down off the table. He runs his undamaged hand through his hair, brushing it away from his face. "I thought maybe someone would be really excited that we've found out this much."

"Excited?" I echo. "She practically cut your hand off."

"Not even close," Nolan counters. "Anyway, I don't think she was trying to hurt either of us. She was just trying to make sure we were paying attention."

CHAPTER TWENTY-ONE

The Professor's Disappearing Act

Nolan and I run out the front door to his car, sitting idly in the driveway. I don't even stop long enough to put my peacoat on over my (two-sizes-too-big) gray sweater.

"Professor Jones must know something more!" I practically shout as Nolan speeds out of Ridgemont toward the university. I was so anxious to get out the door that I forgot to leave dinner for Oscar and Lex. I'll make it up for them when I get home.

"Even if he doesn't know anything, those books in his office . . ." Nolan trails off hopefully, his eyes practically glowing in anticipation of getting his hands on all that research material. "One of them will tell us something about what luiseach actually *do* to get rid of dark spirits."

He thinks we'll find instructions or something, a step-by-step guide that's simple to follow, just like the recipes Mom likes to print off the Internet. She always said that if you could read, you could cook. Nolan seems to believe that if you can read, you can exorcise.

"I'll spend all night digging through them if I have to."

"Me too," I nod, but the truth is, I don't feel nearly as confident as Nolan sounds. There must have been hundreds of books in Professor Jones's office. It would take longer than a single night to read them all, even with both of us there. It could take months, especially since we don't really know exactly what we're looking for. I close my eyes, and an image of my mother's bleeding wrist blossoms up behind my eyelids.

I don't know if we *have* months.

"Can we talk about something else?" I ask suddenly. "Please? I just need a break from all of this." I lift my hands and gesture to the air in front of me, like that's where the ghost is hiding. Which–what do I know?–maybe she is.

"Sure." Nolan smiles. "What do you want to talk about?"

"Anything. Something. Actually . . ." I smile back. "I know exactly what I want to talk about."

"What's that?"

"You."

"Me?"

"You know all about my life and my dramas, and now you think that I'm not even technically *human*, and I barely know anything about you."

"What do you want to know?"

I purse my lips, trying to remember what I already know about Nolan. He's lived in Ridgemont his whole life, and his family has been in the Northwest for generations. His grandfather was his favorite person in the whole world.

"So your grandfather was your dad's dad?"

"Technically, I had one of each," Nolan answers with a smile. "But, yes, the grandfather you're thinking about was my dad's dad."

"Do you have any brothers or sisters?"

"Nope. Only child."

"Me too."

"I know."

"I know you know."

"Well then, why did you say so?"

I shrug. "I don't know. Just making conversation."

"Anything else?"

"Have you ever gotten a grade below a B-plus?"

Nolan furrows his brow mock-seriously, as though he's mentally reviewing all the grades he's ever gotten. "Nah," he answers finally, "though all this ghost hunting did cut into my study time this semester."

I laugh out loud. I'm practically sleepwalking through finals myself. "Hope I didn't mess with your GPA."

"If my grandfather were still alive, he'd have told me that grades weren't nearly as important as helping a damsel in distress—especially when that distress is paranormal."

"Hey!" I protest. "I'm not just some helpless damsel."

"No," Nolan nods in agreement, "you're not."

By the time we get to Levis Hall I know that Nolan always wished he had a little brother, but his parents didn't have any luck getting pregnant after him. I know he loves dogs but never had one of his own, though he did grow up with a pet rabbit. ("Not the same thing," I said, and he agreed.) He actually likes

Ridgemont, and the lack of sunlight doesn't bother him in the slightest, though he can understand that it might bother someone who hadn't grown up here.

We sprint through the parking lot and up the stairs to the professor's office. Once again there's no other person in sight, but I don't care. I don't even care if Professor Jones is there or not; we'll pick his lock if we have to—not that I know how to pick a lock, but that seems beside the point. We just need to get our hands on his books.

Or Nolan's hands on them, anyway. Thank goodness the one believer I happened to befriend since we moved to Ridgemont also happens to be an honor student with a gift for research. What are the odds of such a lucky coincidence? Maybe one day—when we're not sprinting upstairs and I'm able to actually catch my breath long enough to say more than a syllable at a time—I'll ask Nolan and he'll actually want to do the math to calculate the odds.

Ashley would think it was nerdy, but I think it's *wonderful.*

As we race down the hall I get a bad feeling. I mean, a *worse* feeling. (I was already pretty saturated in bad feelings to begin with.) It's cold, but it was cold the last time we were here. But something about this cold feels different.

My heart is pounding, but we did just run up the stairs and down the hall, and anyway, my heart pounds all the time these days.

Maybe it's a luiseach thing. Maybe our—*their*—temperatures drop and their hearts pound when something paranormal is about to happen?

A cold gust of wind slams the door to Professor Jones's office just as we're about to step inside.

"So now the ghost professor's office is haunted?" I say nervously, trying to make a joke, but Nolan doesn't crack a smile. Instead, he leans his weight against the door and pushes it open.

Professor Jones's office is empty. I don't mean he's not there. I don't even mean that his books and papers aren't there, or that maybe he just up and retired since we saw him last. I mean this place is *empty*.

The desk is gone, the chairs are gone. There are dark wood built-in bookshelves behind the place where his desk used to be, but they're covered in dust like no one's actually placed a book on them in years. It's dark out—past six—so no light from outside streams in. I try turning on the light switch by the door, but there's isn't even a bulb in the fixture overhead. The windows are open, and air from the outside is making the curtains wave and billow so that they look kind of like little kids dressed up in sheets on Halloween.

It's so cold in here that every breath I take is painful, sending icy air into my lungs until I think my throat will freeze.

"Dammit!" Nolan shouts, kicking the ground. I shake my head; just a few days ago books and papers would have gone flying had he swung his leg out like that.

"This isn't possible," I say slowly, my teeth chattering as I slam the windows shut. Nolan shrugs his leather jacket off and puts it on my shoulders. "You look like you need this more than I do," he says. He's only wearing a black sweatshirt underneath but doesn't seem nearly as cold as I am.

Nolan reaches into his jeans pocket for his phone. "I'm going to call him."

"We don't know his phone number," I protest, but that doesn't stop him. He Googles "Professor Abner Jones" over and over again until he finds a home address—just a few miles away from the university—and a phone number.

My breath catches when I hear someone on the other line picking up.

"Is Professor Jones there?" he asks. I can't quite make out what the person on the other end is saying, and I look at Nolan desperately.

"I'm sorry?" he says, his voice dropping lower. "I'm not sure I heard you correctly . . . could you just—please—say that again?"

Moving more quickly than maybe I've ever moved before, I reach out and grab Nolan's phone and hit speaker just in time to hear the person on the other end reply, "My husband died seven years ago."

"Your husband was Professor Abner Jones?" I ask. My voice is high and squeaky.

"Yes," the woman on the other end of the line answers. She sounds tired—too tired to ask who we are and why we're looking for her late husband.

"I'm so sorry we disturbed you," I say quickly and press *end* before Nolan can stop me. I back away from him and his phone, almost crashing into the empty bookshelves.

"Okay, let's start with the most obvious explanation," my voice trembles, echoing what Nolan said when I first showed him the video of my mother cutting herself. "Someone else was pretending to be Professor Jones, just to mess with us."

"No one knew when we were coming here or even that we were coming here at all. Sunshine," he adds softly, "I think the most obvious explanation is actually that—"

"Don't say it!" I moan. "I mean, I know you have to say it, but can you just wait a second first?" I sit down on the dusty ground and take a deep breath, wrapping his leather jacket around myself, soaking up its warmth.

"Has it been long enough yet?" Nolan asks finally.

I sink into a slouch. "Okay, fine."

"I think the most obvious explanation is that Professor Jones was a ghost."

I nod. "This place had everything—the creepy feeling, the cold." I pause and bite my lip. "It didn't have the smell, though."

"The smell?"

I nod. "Yeah, the moldy-dampy-musty-smell that saturates my house and only gets stronger when the ghost is near." I run my fingers along the floor, expecting moisture, but instead it's completely dry.

"Just when I think I've figured something out," I look around, perplexed. "Anyway, why would a ghost help us?" I say finally. "We're trying to get rid of a ghost."

Nolan lowers himself into a crouch beside me. He runs his fingers through his hair, the gesture I've come to recognize as a sign that he's working something out. "We don't know exactly what we're trying to do. Or who exactly we're trying to get rid of."

Before I can answer—or protest, or burst into tears, or scream in frustration—a splitting sound fills the air. I scream, and Nolan shifts so his body is covering mine.

Because a wooden beam in the ceiling above us is splitting open.

"What is it with ceilings today?" I wail, crawling as fast as I can toward the door, sliding across the dusty floor. Nolan follows behind me as the splitting sound gets louder and louder, until it turns into a booming sound like the sky is falling.

Just before Nolan slams the office door shut behind us I turn around just in time to see the entire room collapsing in a cloud of dust.

"Let's get out of here!" he shouts. Dust makes my eyes sting, and Nolan can't stop coughing. We sprint toward the stairs; even though we're running and covered in sweat, I don't think I've ever felt so cold. The splitting sound just gets louder and louder: it can't just be the professor's office that's collapsing. But there's no time to turn around and look.

We run through the parking lot to Nolan's car, which he kicks into gear like a race car driver.

"Wait!" I shout, before he can pull out of the parking lot.

"Are you crazy?" he answers. I turn around and look at the building we just ran from. It looks like Levis Hall is letting out an enormous breath, its windows blowing out, its doors falling off their hinges.

"It just looks like some dilapidated old building now," Nolan gasps. "A place frat boys sneak into on a dare or something."

I stare out the window as we drive through the campus. No one else seems to notice the explosion that took place just seconds before. I remember the look that girl gave us when we asked for directions to Levis Hall.

"Maybe it was always just some dilapidated old building," I suggest. "Maybe we just couldn't see it that way until now."

"But how?" Nolan asks, and I shake my head.

"I don't know," I answer.

Somehow the ride home from the university feels shorter than the ride there. I lean forward in my seat and play with the radio, but I can't find anything I want to listen to, so I switch it off.

Silence fills the car. I'm still wearing Nolan's jacket, and I slouch so that the shoulders are up around my ears. I breathe in the scent of the old leather: soft as butter, warm as wool, and speckled in dust from Levis Hall. I pull the sleeves down over my wrists, longer even than my oversized sweater. Still, nothing has ever felt like it fit quite so perfectly. I wish I had a mirror so I could see how it looks, but I settle for eyeing my reflection in the window. This jacket is the coolest thing I've ever worn. I wish I could enjoy it.

"Something has been bugging me," I say finally.

"Just one thing?" Nolan asks, keeping his eyes on the road.

"You said that luiseach birth rates were low, right?"

He nods.

"And you think I'm the last luiseach to be born, and even if you're right, clearly I don't have a clue how to do whatever it is that luiseach do, right?"

He nods again.

"Okay, but if no luiseach are being born, then wouldn't, like, dark spirits or demons or whatever they're called be taking over the planet by now?"

Nolan doesn't answer right away. He turns the steering wheel, leaning into the curves that will bring us back into Ridgemont.

"I don't know," he answers finally, lifting a hand from the wheel to brush his hair back from his forehead. "Maybe there are fewer dark spirits than there used to be?" We both know it's a weak guess.

"Maybe the dark spirits started winning," I say.

"What do you mean?"

"Maybe that's why this is happening to my mom. There's no luiseach to protect people like her because the luiseach are dying out, being defeated by dark spirits left and right. Maybe that's why no luiseach are being born—because there aren't enough luiseach left to procreate. The dark spirits are killing them."

The idea is terrifying. I mean, if everything we've read is true, then luiseach are kind of essential to the survival of the human race. I slouch lower, wrapping the jacket around myself like a blanket.

Nolan shakes his head. "No. That can't be it."

"Why not?"

"Because every article I read, in every language, agreed on one thing."

"What's that?"

"A luiseach's spirit—its soul, its essence, or whatever you want to call it—has an advantage over a mere mortal's."

"What's that?"

"It cannot be taken, damaged, or destroyed by a ghost or a demon."

CHAPTER TWENTY-TWO

What Are We Fighting For?

"Snow weather," Nolan says as he pulls into my driveway, rolling down his window to point at the clouds above us. They hang heavy and low, but somehow the evening sky is bright. I nod in agreement, even though the truth is I have no idea what constitutes snow weather—it never snowed in Austin.

"Do you want me to come in?"

I shake my head. "What for? You already know what's going on inside." It comes out sounding nastier than I'd intended. I attempt a smile, but the muscles in my mouth refuse to cooperate, like they're reminding me that I don't exactly have anything to smile about.

"I know, but I could stick around. Maybe keep you company till your mom comes home."

I shake my head, thinking of the way she behaved the last time she came home and found Nolan in the house, the long shadow that followed her from one room into the next, and the spider on the kitchen floor. I shudder.

"What's the point?" Now my cranky mouth muscles aren't just preventing me from smiling; they're also making me say cranky things. "There's nothing you can do to help her. We didn't find any more answers today."

Just more questions, I think, but don't say. I rest my elbows on my knees and drop my face into my hands.

"I'll keep searching," Nolan promises. "There's got to be more online. Or maybe . . ."

I look up. "Maybe what?"

He presses his lips together like he knows I won't like what he's about to say. "Maybe your powers will just kind of . . . I don't know, kick in or something."

I unclick my seat belt and twist to face him. "My powers?" I ask, a lump rising in my throat. I swallow it down. I'm not much of a crier. I didn't cry in third grade when I fell off a seesaw and broke my nose. Not in eighth grade when I overheard some not-nice boy in class refer to me as a weirdo. Not in tenth grade when I tripped in gym class and sprained my ankle and had to walk around with crutches for two weeks. Mom says I didn't even cry much as a baby.

But then I've never felt quite this hopeless before. "How can you still be so sure that I'm a loos, louise, loony–blah, whatever you call it!"

"Luiseach," Nolan says quietly. We both know full well that I know how to pronounce it by now.

"Whatever," I answer. "I'm not one. I can't be."

"Why not?"

"Because a luiseach would know what to do in a situation like this, and I most decidedly do not." Jane Austen–speak, kind of. "All I am is a girl who's terrified about what's happening to her mother. And who doesn't have the slightest clue how to save her."

The lump in my throat refuses to disappear. Hot tears spring to my eyes. Mom will be home soon, and I don't even want to see her. For the first time in my life I'm the kind of kid who wishes her parents would stay out later so she could have the house to herself.

But I'm pretty sure there isn't another kid on the planet who has the same reasons for wanting to be alone that I do.

I'm tired. I'm *so* tired. I've been keeping such a close watch on her, staring at her across the dinner table to be sure her knife doesn't slice into her skin instead of into her steak or chicken or whatever we're eating. (Or not eating, as the case may be. I haven't exactly had the greatest appetite lately.)

And I'm tired because I haven't slept through the night in months. Lately it's not ghostly noises that wake me but my own anxiety: two, three, ten times a night I slip from my bedroom to hover in Mom's doorway, listening to the steady rhythm of her breathing, in and out, in and out, in and out. I watch her chest rise and fall in the darkness, like I think that it's going to stop at any moment.

And I'm tired because I miss my best friend. Not Ashley and not Nolan, but my *mom*. I miss watching movies together and eating pizza together and the way she makes fun of me. I miss taking Oscar on long walks together, and I miss her scolding me when she catches me raiding her closet for the zillionth time. We barely even talk anymore. We just sit in the house in silence. I don't think she even notices the way I stare at her. It feels like she hardly notices me at all.

And I'm too tired to explain any of this to Nolan. In fact,

suddenly his involvement in all of this feels all wrong, as mysterious and illogical as the rest of it.

"What do you care, anyway?" I say suddenly. "You didn't even know me three months ago. You can't possibly be that concerned about the fate of a girl you barely even know."

"I don't barely know you—" he begins, but I cut him off.

"Haven't you already gotten everything you need?"

"What do you mean?"

The stupid, stubborn lump in my throat has turned into stupid, stubborn tears shaking in the corners of my eyes. "For your extra-credit project! I would hate to be the reason your perfect GPA didn't hold up." My voice sounds different from how it usually sounds.

Further proof that I can't be a luiseach. They're full of light—isn't that what Nolan said? I have literally never felt so dark.

"I told you, I don't care about that—"

"So you were just in it for your grandfather? Well, now you have your proof, so you don't need me anymore."

"Proof?" Nolan echoes.

"The proof your grandfather spent his life searching for? You can show it to your dad, your mom, your grandmother, the whole world—show them that your grandfather wasn't just some crazy old man like they all thought." I don't think I've ever said anything so mean in my entire life.

Nolan responds, his voice calm and even. Nothing like mine. "Look, Sunshine, I'm not going to lie to you. It means a lot to me to know that my grandfather was right, that even now, months after his death, his research helped us." He locks his eyes with mine. I blink, and a few tears fall out of my eyes and onto my cheeks, shockingly cold. Nolan and I are nowhere near touching, but that wrong-end-of-the-magnet feeling starts to take hold. I lean back, pressing myself against the door behind me, trying to increase the distance between us.

"And yes," he continues, "there's a part of me that wants to show everything we've found to every single person who ever dismissed my grandfather as a nutty old man. I mean, you and I sat across a desk from a real, live ghost!"

Another time, another place, I'd make fun of him for referring to a ghost as *live.* But now I just mutter, "Glad it was so exciting for you."

Nolan continues as though I haven't said a thing. "And maybe my grandfather is the reason I got involved in all this to begin with–" His hair falls across his amber eyes, but for once he doesn't brush it away. "But do you really think he's the reason I'm still here?"

"I don't know why you're here," I say hoarsely. "But I think it's time for you to leave."

"What are you talking about? I'm trying to help you. Like I said, I'll do more research–"

"Where has your research gotten us? Chasing phantom professors and dead ends! I don't have *time* for dead ends. My mother could be in serious danger." Butterflies tap dance across my belly.

"I know that–"

"And you think you can help us by reading some more old books?" My mouth has a mind of its own, and I feel powerless to stop it from saying these mean things. "I don't need your help," I lie. For someone who never so much as fibbed about finishing her vegetables a few months ago, I'm getting pretty good at lying. "I'm not some helpless *damsel in distress* who needs a boy to help her."

"I never thought you were."

"Then I'll ask you again, what do you care, anyway?" I press my chin into my shoulder, feeling the leather of Nolan's jacket pressing back.

"I care about *you!* I don't want anything to happen to you." Nolan's words hang thickly in the air between us. Softly, he adds, "Or to your mom. Look, I know you're feeling threatened right now. I understand that you feel like you have to—I don't know, lash out, pick a fight with me or something."

"Don't tell me how I feel."

"Okay, I won't."

"Like I said, I think it's time for you to leave." I slip off his jacket and hold it out for him to take, careful not to let his hands brush against mine when he finally does.

"I'll be gone a few days," he says, shrugging the jacket on.

"What?" I answer, beginning to shiver. Despite the fact that I'm practically forcing him to go, the prospect of his prolonged absence sends another pack of butterflies flying through my stomach. I guess this is what people mean when they talk about being on an emotional roller coaster.

"My parents and I are going to visit my grandmother. I know she's just a couple of towns away, but we always stay with her for the holidays."

"The holidays?" I echo dumbly.

"Tomorrow is Christmas Eve."

"Oh," I answer blankly. Then I get out of the car and slam the door shut behind me. I stand and watch him back out and drive away. Through the fog I can make out green and red lights someone tossed messily onto the lower branches of the tree in the yard of the house across from ours. It's an evergreen, but it doesn't look anything like a Christmas tree.

Tomorrow is Christmas Eve. School is out for winter break. People are headed home to their families' houses, gathering around pine trees, basting turkeys, wrapping presents.

I'd honestly forgotten.

Lex and Oscar run to greet me as I walk in the door. I fill their bowls with food, apologizing for the way I left them a few hours earlier. They rub against my legs gratefully, but their presence doesn't make the house feel any less empty.

For the first time in my whole life we don't have a Christmas tree. We didn't strap it to the top of our car and struggle to carry it through the front door and bicker over whether I was holding it straight while Mom crouched on the floor, trying to secure it in our rusty tree stand. We didn't stay up late drinking eggnog (a drink neither of us actually enjoy, but both of us still insist upon), while we decorated our too-tall tree with lights and silly ornaments I'd made in nursery school—a clay one in the shape of my handprint, a stick-figure Santa Claus made out of popsicle sticks.

I never actually believed in Santa Claus. When I was little Mom told me to write him a letter and tell him what I wanted, but somehow I always knew *she* was the one fulfilling my Christmas wishes. After all, I never asked Santa for a glass unicorn, but when I was five years old there was one waiting for me under the tree on Christmas morning, just as there would be every Christmas afterward.

Until now. There's no way my mother remembered to get me a new unicorn this year. A few months ago I thought about asking her for one of the UV lamps that combat seasonal affective disorder. Now I don't think anything could brighten my mood. Not even actual sunshine.

I stomp through the house, up the stairs, and into my room. I sit on my bed, still wearing my boots, my hair still damp from the air outside and covered in Levis Hall dust. I feel the absence of the weight of Nolan's jacket on my shoulders. My steps have tracked mud through the house, but I don't think Mom will notice. Still, I know I'll retrace my steps with carpet cleaner before she gets home. I don't want her to get into trouble with our landlord. Though I wouldn't feel that bad since he's the one who rented us a haunted house.

I can't remember the last time I had an actual conversation with Ashley. It's been texts only over the past few months, as it became obvious that I was less interested in Cory Cooper than I was in ghosts—and as she became interested in nothing but Cory Cooper. We just kind of stopped calling each other. The last text I got from her said *Cory let me drive his car.* That was two days ago, and I haven't written back yet. I wasn't sure how I was supposed to react. I guess that's some kind of big step in their relationship. But I couldn't seem to make myself get excited about it, even for Ashley. I had more important things going on, things that Ashley couldn't possibly understand.

I wish I knew *who* it was in this house with us. Maybe if I knew the name of the little girl I heard begging for her life in the bathroom—if I knew her story—I'd be able to figure out why this was happening. Or maybe if I knew who she was begging, I'd understand just what kind of threat we're up against.

But I sent away the one person who wanted to help me find out.

I flop back against the bed, and (of course) instead of hitting the pillows like I intended, I thwack my head against the wall behind me. Probably right on top of an enormous pink flower. "Still klutzy," I say with a sigh. "I guess some things never change." I just wish some of the *good* things hadn't changed.

Before he backed out of the driveway Nolan rolled his window down to say one last thing to me. "You believe in *ghosts*, Sunshine," he said. "Why can't you believe in *this*–in what *you* are? In what you're capable of?"

"But that's just the thing," I say out loud now, even though he's not around to hear me. "I haven't the slightest clue what I'm capable of."

I'm Growing Concerned

I knew she'd be resistant—after a human childhood she couldn't immediately understand all of this—but I expected she'd have made more progress by now. She was so quick to recognize the foreign presence in her house, but in the months that have passed since I moved them to Ridgemont she's been fighting against the next logical conclusion.

She doesn't even recognize her instincts for what they are. She has been comforting the innocent spirit in the house, whether she understands it or not, in ways that a human never could.

But I need her strengths to lie not just in comfort but in the fight. My plan is destined for failure if she doesn't have the strength I need. And what will become of our kind then? Not just our kind—what will become of humans, without luiseach on Earth to protect them? Unless my theory proves correct . . .

The boy was not part of the plan. Such helpmates often don't materialize until much later in a luiseach's life. And the last thing I want is for her to get caught up in a distraction. I made express precautions against such things years ago. And my precautions do seem to be working. I see them in the way she reacts when he touches her. Her body stiffens and she moves away. She swallows hard, as though trying not to gag.

Still, their connection is strong. The measures I set in place don't seem to be keeping him away—or keeping her away from him. This was most definitely not part of the plan.

But perhaps the time has come to alter the plan.

CHAPTER TWENTY-THREE

New Clues

The little girl in the tattered dress is in my dreams again. This time she's crouched in the corner of the bathroom, crying quietly, water dripping from her hem onto the floor beneath her. *Plop, plop. Plop, plop.* I crawl across the tiles to get to her, but she's always just out of my reach, eluding my touch. The scent of mildew is heavy in the air, and she won't look at me, only at the tiles beneath her small bare feet.

"Why are you crying?" I whisper, but she doesn't answer. "Can I help you?" I ask, but there's no response. She just sits there, her tears falling on the floor so rapidly that once more it reminds me of that part of *Alice in Wonderland* when Alice nearly drowns in her own tears.

Is this the same girl who paced above Nolan and me, who got so excited that the lightbulb exploded above us? She must be. And she wants me to figure this out. At least Nolan thinks so.

So finally I ask, "Can you help me?" Abruptly her tears stop. She looks up, and I can see that her eyes are dark brown, nearly black. She opens her mouth, but if any sound comes out, I can't hear it.

"What?" I ask her. "I'm sorry—I couldn't hear you."

She opens her mouth again. There's the murmur of whispers, but I can't make out any words.

"What?" I ask again, and she whispers her answer, but I still can't hear it. "Please!" I say desperately. Now I'm near tears.

She whispers more, but I still can't make it out. The girl looks nearly as frustrated as I feel. I try again to get closer to her, to put my ear close to her lips, but she slips ever farther away, until I'm left alone in the bathroom, the water from her tears seeping into my pajamas.

I wake up with a gasp.

My pajamas are dotted with droplets of cold water. I roll over and see the blinking light of my alarm clock: 2:07 a.m. I press my eyes shut, but I know I'm not going back to sleep. Not for a while at least.

I get up. On my way to Mom's room I stop and peer into the bathroom. I can't believe I'm actually hoping to see a crying girl with a tattered dress crouched in the corner, just as she was in my dream. What kind of freak *hopes* to see a ghost?

But the bathroom is empty, except for Lex perched on top of the toilet, his new favorite place to sleep.

"You'd tell me if you saw a ghost, wouldn't you, Lex?" I ask, but he doesn't answer. Instead, he opens his eyes and yawns, as if to say, *This is my room. Please go away.*

"Some help you are," I mumble. He blinks his green eyes. Ashley was right—my eyes do look kind of like his. "Maybe I'm part cat," I whisper. "I mean, that can't be any crazier than what Nolan thinks I am."

I tiptoe down the hallway and open Mom's door slowly, listening for the steady sounds of her breath. She didn't get home until ten o'clock tonight. She must have forgotten that it's Christmas-time, just like I did.

She's sleeping in her scrubs, pastel peach with dancing teddy bears on the edges of her short sleeves, the kind she used to refuse to wear. She'd always complained that it's difficult for neonatal nurses to be taken seriously when they're wearing scrubs covered in kittens and teddy bears. (The same types of patterns I choose to sleep in, but that's beside the point.) She'd insist on wearing solid-colored scrubs. Why is she wearing these now? Maybe the hospital was out of plain scrubs. Or maybe she doesn't remember that she used to care about things like that.

Her straight auburn hair is spread out messily on the pillow beneath her head. Her breath is kind of ragged, like maybe she's coming down with a cold or something.

I tiptoe into her room and lean over the bed. I expect her eyes to snap open, expect her to say, *What on earth are you doing?* I wouldn't be able to come up with an answer that would satisfy her. *I'd hoped you'd gotten over all that ghost stuff*, she'd sigh, her voice heavy with disappointment.

No, I'd answer. *I haven't gotten over it. I just found someone else to talk to about it.*

Then I'd tell her all about Nolan, about this boy who is so nice and so smart and who laughs at my jokes and doesn't seem to mind that I'm a total klutz. I would tell her that when I first saw him I thought he was very cute, with a nerdy, eighties-movie kind of quality about him. Mom would laugh, and we'd end up talking about all the silly movies we rented on Saturday nights when I was growing up. But after that, Mom would turn serious and suggest that I call Nolan to apologize. And I'd make a face, but I'd know she was right.

I close my eyes. Wow, is this what I've been reduced to? *Imagining* conversations with my mother instead of actually *having* them?

I don't think I've actually ever felt lonely before. I've heard other people complain about loneliness, I've read about it in books and watched it on TV shows, but I never actually *felt* it myself. It just didn't seem to apply to me. I mean, of course I spent plenty of time by myself, even back when we lived in Austin. As soon as I was old enough not to need a babysitter I became a latchkey kid: letting myself into the house after school, making my own snacks while Mom worked, cooking dinner when she had to work late, dutifully doing my homework without a parent to tell me so.

But all that time I never felt lonely. Even with my mother at work, I never once doubted that she'd come home if I needed her. That she'd always, always be there for me, no matter what.

Now, here she is, just inches away from me, and I've never felt so alone.

My mother grunts in her sleep, and I jump away, my heart pounding. I shake my head; plenty of people make noises in their sleep. I should just go back to my own room, climb under my covers, and get some much-needed sleep.

And I'm about to go do all that—well, try to do all that—when my mother makes another noise. And then another. And another.

Suddenly she sits up in her bed. I jump away in surprise, expecting her to yell at me. But her eyes are closed, her muscles stiff. Her back is straight, her fingers are curled into tightly clenched fists, and her mouth is open. Ugly, awful sounds start to come out of it. Her voice doesn't sound anything like her voice at all.

I don't think they're just noises. I think they're *words.* But words I don't recognize. Words in a language I've never heard, a language my mother doesn't speak. A language that–from the guttural, hacking, horrible sound of it–doesn't resemble any other language that any other person on the planet speaks.

"Mom?" I say softly and take a step closer to the bed. I should wait. She'll lie back onto her pillows eventually, right? She's probably just having a bad dream or something. Plenty of people make noises when they have bad dreams.

But the strange words coming from her mouth are only getting louder. They sound like gibberish, but angry gibberish–shouts and protestations. She stretches her arms out in front of her and points her finger at something across the room that I can't see. Oscar and Lex are hovering in the doorway, wondering what happened to their friend Kat.

Then she lets out a howl, a scream that makes my flesh crawl.

"Mom!" I scream. I pounce onto the bed and reach for her, ready to grab her arms and wrestle if I have to, ready to slap her across the face if that's what it takes to wake her. But the instant my fingers touch her arm, her body goes slack. The horrible sounds stop coming from her mouth, and instead she lets out a sleepy sort of sigh as she lies back onto her pillows.

"Is that you, Sunshine?" she asks sleepily. Her voice is back to normal now.

"It's me," I answer.

"My Sunshine," she says.

"I think you were having a bad dream."

"I think I was," she agrees groggily. "But my Sunshine made it go away." Her eyelids flutter like she's trying to wake up to talk to me, but sleep has too deep a hold on her.

"Don't try to wake up," I say, reaching out to brush her hair off her forehead. She rolls over onto her side, curling up like a cat. I wait until her breath is smooth and even—not ragged like it was before—and then I get up off the bed and tiptoe back to my room.

Did I do that? I mean, not the scary, guttural-speaking part—I don't know who or what did that—but the nice, peaceful, falling back to sleep part? *My Sunshine made it go away.* Did my touch somehow—I don't know—startle the words out of her throat, ease her muscles into relaxing?

Nolan would say that I did. Because I'm a luiseach. I was bringing light, or whatever it is that we—*they*—do. He would say that my powers were kicking in, just like he'd hoped they would.

But Nolan isn't here to say anything at all.

Oscar beats me back to my room, using my absence from the bed as his chance to lie down on my pillow, taking up all the space my head previously occupied. Curling around him, I slide back under the covers. I wonder whether I'll dream of the girl again, whispering words I can't hear. Nothing like Mom's shouts.

"Too bad I can't bring you into my dream with me," I murmur to Oscar. "Maybe you'd be able to hear that little girl with your supersonic dog hearing. Not that it would do me much good, since I don't speak dog and you don't speak English."

But then I hear whispers once more, the same muffled sounds from my dream. I pinch myself to make sure I'm still awake.

"That wasn't you, was it, Oscar?" I'm only half kidding. If he suddenly opened his mouth and started lecturing me in a tony British accent, I'm not sure I'd even find it surprising anymore.

The whispers continue.

"I'm sorry," I say to the darkness, "I still can't hear you."

I lean over and turn on my bedside light, as though I think that illumination will magically enable me to hear better.

There, peeking out from beneath my worn copy of *Pride and Prejudice*, is a stack of the black-and-white pictures I took back in August. (Wowza, that feels like a million years ago now.) I glance at my camera perched on the bookshelves above my bed. I haven't touched it in ages, just left it all alone, dust collecting in its gears; after the way my mom acted, it felt like all my pictures of this house were worthless.

I push the book aside and gaze at the photo on top of the stack: a picture of this room that I must have taken from the bed. It's a picture of my desk and the window, the shelf with my unicorn collection. I could never forget this picture. Because when I took it the unicorn with the broken horn had been in the back, hidden behind the ones that remained intact. But when I saw the developed photograph, there he was again, this time standing front and center.

"How'd you pull that off?" I say out loud, picking the picture up and studying it. "You know how to work Photoshop or something?" Did her magical ghost powers follow the film to Austin? Did they seep into the machines when the people at Max's developed it?

There's no answer. The nonsense whispers stop.

In my hands the picture grows cold, like it's made of ice instead of paper. I almost drop it, but I grip it harder and lean forward to take a closer look. Beads of water sprout along its edges, like someone with wet fingers is holding it alongside me.

I lean over to place the photo beneath my bedside lamp. The hairs on the back of my neck start to prick and tickle. "What is it? What did you do?"

There. There are words scrawled across my desk. No, not words. A name. I squint, wishing I had one of those magnifying glasses that fit in the crook of my eye like jewelers wear to inspect diamonds for flaws.

I stand up and walk across the room and switch on my desk lamp. As I suspected, the words are traced out of water here in 3-D too. The muscles in my mouth finally, finally allow me the tiniest little bit of a smile.

"Anna Wilde," I read out loud, and the shelf that holds my unicorns begins to shake. "Anna Wilde," I say again, louder this time, and Oscar stands up on the bed behind me, wagging his tiny tail back and forth frantically, as though he'd been waiting for me to say that name all this time.

Maybe he could hear her after all.

CHAPTER TWENTY-FOUR

Anna Wilde

I sit down at my desk and open my laptop. I Google "Anna Wilde," being careful not to smudge the wet letters on my desk.

Hundreds of matches come up. This must be the opposite of how Nolan felt when he Googled "luiseach" for the first time.

I reach for my phone. It's the middle of the night, but I don't think Nolan will mind being woken up when I have such a big development to share—

No. I shake my head. For a second there I forgot that we fought earlier. Forgot that maybe he'll never want to hear from me again. Forgot that I was the meanest version of myself that I've ever been, after he'd never been anything but nice to me.

Forgot that I'm on my own now.

I scroll down through the results on my screen. Apparently there's more than one Anna Wilde in the world. I try to narrow it down. I search again, this time typing the words "Ridgemont, Washington" after Anna's name. Fewer results come up, but there's still plenty to choose from.

I click on a link for the *Ridgemont Herald*. I blink at the bold headline scrawled across my computer screen: "Man Discovers Drowned Daughter, Dies from Shock."

I read that two years ago, a ten-year-old girl named Anna Wilde drowned in the bathtub of her family's house somewhere in Ridgemont. When her father discovered her lifeless body, he had a heart attack and died on the spot. The man's wife and girl's mother, back home from a business trip, discovered their bodies later. A lump rises in my throat as I think about what happened to this poor family, to the little girl who's been my playmate for months now.

I turn around and look at my bedroom door, knowing that the bathroom is just outside. I shiver as I remember the sound of the girl–Anna–begging for her life, splashing against someone's hold.

I turn back to the article. It says that no foul play was suspected. It was just a terrible accident. A family tragedy. I shake my head. What I heard in the bathroom that night was no accident.

I scroll down. There is a picture of an empty bathtub. I lean closer to my computer.

And the lump in my throat shifts. Oh my gosh, I'm going to throw up. Literally.

I get up so fast that I knock my chair over, and the *thump* of it hitting the carpet makes Oscar jump off my bed and hide beneath it. I barely make it to the bathroom in time. It's been hours since I ate anything, so I don't actually have much in me to throw up. Still, my body manages to empty itself, the muscles in my belly spasming and clenching until everything aches.

I crouch beside the toilet and rest my head on the cool porcelain. For the first time in months–outside of Nolan's presence—I'm warm. Not just warm. I'm *hot.* My face is covered in a sheen of sweat.

I close my eyes.

I've felt nauseated every time Nolan came too close, but that's nothing compared to this. With Nolan I could usually swallow my gags, and I never actually threw up. Most of all, with him I could just take a step away and the feeling would subside.

I wipe my mouth and flush the toilet. I lean over the sink and splash some cold water on my face. When Anna's ghost was locked in this bathroom, was she reenacting the night of her death? Was she somehow forced to relive it? Just the thought makes me shudder with horror.

No foul play was suspected. How did the police come to that conclusion? Maybe the police—just like my mother the next day—*couldn't* see what I see now.

I take a deep breath before I step back inside my bedroom. I pull my laptop from my desk and bring it to bed with me, slide under the covers, and prop the computer on my lap. I can hear Oscar's breath coming from under the bed, steady and comforting.

I look again.

In the photos of the bathtub where Anna drowned, there are dozens—no, hundreds—of tiny scratches spread out across the tile. It's hard to imagine that a young girl could make those marks, but I guess we find hidden stores of strength we never knew we had when we're fighting for our lives. Anna's death wasn't just a terrible accident—a girl left alone too long. Someone held her down. And she struggled with all her might against that hold.

I think of the sounds I heard in my mother's bedroom tonight. Not the words, but before that—the way her breath sounded labored, like she was congested somehow. Like her lungs were *wet*.

I continue reading. There's a picture of Anna and one of her father—I imagine the police taking them from the living room fireplace's mantle, where they'd been displayed for anyone to see. I study Anna's photo, trying to see whether she resembles the little girl from my dreams. I can make out her dark hair, her pale skin, the eyes that are almost black.

Tears spring to my eyes. It's not like I didn't know she was dead. I mean, she's a *ghost*, after all. But somehow, reading all of this—knowing her name, seeing her face—the weight of it feels heavier somehow: a little girl is dead. So is her father.

I study his picture. He looks nothing like her; she must resemble her mother. He's freckled, blond, tan, handsome. He looks like the picture of health. Hardly the person you'd expect to have a heart attack. Perhaps his heart simply broke when he saw his daughter was gone.

Even though the house is silent, my ears ring with the memory of the little girl in the bathroom, begging for her life behind a locked door.

According to the article, Anna's father had been a devoted family man. Friends and neighbors were devastated but not completely surprised that the loss of his daughter destroyed him. He'd been a doting father—never missed a dance recital, coached the softball team, taught her to ride a two-wheeler in their driveway.

The last paragraph of the article says that Anna's mother had her daughter and husband cremated.

Anna's mother. Who was her mother? My gosh, that poor woman lost everything. Does she have any idea about what really happened to her daughter? I scan the article once more. Brief mentions are sprinkled throughout the article.

The girl's mother was out of town on business.

Her mother had her body cremated.

She had been married to her husband for fifteen years.

It's not until the final sentence that Anna's mother's name is revealed: *The child's mother, Victoria Wilde, could not be reached for comment.*

Victoria Wilde?

As in, *I'm Victoria Wilde, let's make some art, shall we?*

As in *All that death, good work, Nolan?*

As in lurking, skulking, spying Victoria Wilde?

Could it be *that* Victoria Wilde?

"Victoria Wilde?" I say out loud, almost as though I expect her to answer. It's so cold that when I speak, I can see my breath. I hadn't even noticed the drop in the temperature—maybe I'm getting used to it.

"Victoria Wilde," I repeat slowly, concentrating on the way my lips purse on the *O* and the *W*. Her name feels heavy in my mouth, a solid, certain thing. I shut the computer and swing my legs off the bed, planting my feet firmly on the floor.

"Victoria Wilde," I say once more. Maybe there's a reason she's always been nearby, listening, watching. Maybe she knows exactly what went on in her house while she was "out of town on business."

Maybe she knows everything.

She Found Victoria

I was wondering how long it would take, how much time would pass before Sunshine would confront the strange teacher who'd been eavesdropping on her conversations and discover that she'd found an elder luiseach. I am pleased she put the pieces together herself, without the boy.

No, not herself—Anna helped her. Anna guided her seamlessly. Anna wants Sunshine to succeed not just for her own sake but for Sunshine's sake too. Anna cares about her—a human feeling, to be sure, but it's useful in this instance.

After all, it is a human feeling—fear that she might lose Katherine forever—that will motivate Sunshine now. Clearly the girl needed to know what was at stake—learning that she was the only creature with the power to save her mother, to save Anna, to help Victoria—in order to accept what she really is.

Perhaps she has lived among humans too long. If she passes her test, I will help her gain some distance from that. However motivating they might be, human emotions are a weakness. We don't have room for weakness. Our work is too important. A rift to repair. A future to restore.

Soon she will learn that there is so much more at risk than the life of one woman, the memory of one little girl.

Soon she will understand that this test is actually quite small, quite simple, compared to the work she has yet to do. The rift must be addressed. The future of our race must be resolved.

There is so much work yet to be done.

CHAPTER TWENTY-FIVE
Victoria Wilde

I left Mom home alone. I decided it was worth the risk after I looked up Victoria's address and discovered that she lives only a ten-minute walk from our house. There are a couple of inches of snow on the ground—Nolan was right about snow weather. It fell overnight, and Ridgemont woke to a white almost-Christmas.

It turns out that ten minutes is a long time when you're alone with your thoughts. You realize that it's seven in the morning on Christmas Eve, and you don't exactly know what your weird teacher's sleeping habits are. You realize you're about to pound on practically a stranger's door and tell her that you know her daughter is dead, and you don't think her death was an accident, like the police said. You wonder how she'll react to the fact that you're not here to comfort her or even offer sympathy. Instead, you're here because you think her daughter is a spirit caught between two worlds, trapped inside your house.

You realize that, odds are, this woman is going to slam the door in your face and kick you out of her classroom when school starts again in January.

Following a map on my phone, I turn onto Ms. Wilde's street, then immediately decide that I've made a big mistake. I don't mean in seeking out Ms. Wilde, I mean *literally* I think I made a wrong turn. No way does anyone live on this street. It's so desolate that it makes our neighborhood look chipper and friendly and crowded.

There are no houses to be seen here, only trees. Enormous, towering evergreens that make me feel as tiny as an ant. I glance down at my phone; Victoria's address is number three Pinecone Drive, and the map insists that I'm on Pinecone Drive—there are enough pinecones littered across the ground to justify the name—though there's no street sign to confirm my location.

Slowly I walk down the street, and it's like walking on a path through a forest. The branches are so thick that some of them touch overhead, like I'm walking through a tunnel. Under other circumstances I would probably find this place beautiful; I can't hear a single car from the nearby streets or see any planes flying overhead. These trees have probably been here, growing tall and strong, for a hundred years or more. But I'm too worried about finding Ms. Wilde's house to enjoy any of it. Finally I see a driveway on my right. If her house is number three, there ought to be at least a number one and a number two, but there are no other driveways, no other homes peering out from between the trees.

I turn onto the driveway, and what I see is almost funny. Because Victoria Wilde's house is, well . . . Victorian. The house itself is narrow, with a set of disproportionately wide stairs that lead to an enormous front porch. The second floor has a big wrap-around terrace, and the third floor—the attic, maybe—is literally a sloped, pointy turret, like the house is a teeny tiny little castle. It looks kind of like a wedding cake, but, surrounded by a dark forest of trees, it doesn't look the least bit festive. It almost resembles a witch's cottage, the way it's set deep in the woods. I swallow as I walk up the driveway—here's hoping she's not planning on cooking me or something. I didn't exactly leave myself a trail of breadcrumbs so I could find my way back home.

My hand is shaking when I knock on Ms. Wilde's door. I tell myself that's the cold—not the nerves—but, seriously, who do I think I'm kidding?

Ms. Wilde—or Mrs., I guess now—answers quickly, as though she'd been expecting someone to arrive. I don't have to say anything; she just invites me inside.

"I'm sorry about the hour—" I begin, but stop myself. Ms. Wilde is fully dressed in her long, flowing, witchy clothes. No pajamas here, but instead a charcoal gray skirt that's so long it touches the ground around her feet. She's wearing a black knitted shawl with an open weave so that it looks like it's made of lace instead of wool over a loose-fitting black top. Another black shawl is wrapped around her neck like a scarf. I suddenly feel very underdressed in my jeans and puffy ski jacket. Her long dark hair hangs like a curtain almost all the way down to her waist. Another time, another place, I'd be jealous of how straight it is. Almost like my mom's, but much longer and much darker.

She smiles. Her eyes are dark brown—almost black—just like Anna's. "Let's have a seat in the living room." She leads the way down a hall and into a brightly lit room decorated in creams and peaches. The exact opposite of the dark clothes she wears.

Is this the house where Anna was killed? This cozy, cheerful home?

"I'm sorry—were you expecting me?" I say to her back, but she doesn't answer. There's something strange about this house, but it takes me a second to put my finger on it.

Oh my gosh. It's warm. Not just warm, but *bright,* as though windows are flooded with sunlight instead of fog and mist.

"You have a beautiful home," I say dumbly, because I don't know how else to begin. The inside looks nothing like the outside. Victoria gestures for me to sit down on a fluffy couch covered in tiny pink flowers. (A pretty kind of pink, by the way. Nothing like the ghastly—that's right, *ghastly,* I can't help it if the perfect word also happens to be a Jane Austen word—pink in my bedroom.)

"Would you like some tea?" she offers, sitting down in an overstuffed white chair across from me. Between us is an ottoman topped with a tray holding a full tea set. Under other circumstances I'd probably love it; it's very old fashioned, the kind of set I imagine Elizabeth Bennett sipped her tea from. But I don't think I can stomach anything right now, not even tea, so I shake my head. Ms. Wilde pours herself a drink.

"Ms. Wilde," I begin, but she holds up her hand to stop me.

"Victoria," she says. "Please."

I'm pretty sure I'm not supposed to call my teacher by her first name, but I'm probably not supposed to show up on her doorstep either, so I guess it doesn't matter. "Okay," I start again. "Victoria, I need to ask you something." She raises her eyebrows expectantly. Now more than ever, she looks like a teacher, waiting for her student to ask the right question. But I don't quite know what to say.

So instead I look around the room. My eyes land on a stuffed white owl—not stuffed like Dr. Hoo is stuffed, but stuffed like a toy. Other than that, it looks exactly like Dr. Hoo.

"Nice owl," I say awkwardly.

Victoria nods. "It was my daughter's favorite."

"That explains a lot," I say breathlessly. I can't remember the last time I walked into my room and found Dr. Hoo in the same position he'd been in when I left.

"Does it?" Victoria asks, her dark eyes bright and open wide.

"Anna Wilde was your daughter," I begin slowly. "I think . . ." I pause, trying to figure out the right way to say it. I should have come here with more of a plan, a rehearsed speech, something. "I think she might be . . . I mean, there's no easy way to say this, but . . ." I scratch my head, pressing my frizzball down as smoothly as possible, like I think messy hair is somehow disrespectful.

"I think she's been visiting—I mean, not visiting, obviously, but staying—no, that's not the right word. Ummm, she's living—" Oh geez, did I just say she's *living?* Golly, I'm doing this all wrong. The girl is dead. Her ghost might be inhabiting my house, but that's not the same thing as *living* there. My gosh, what's the right word for it? Maybe in all those books that disappeared from the professor's office there was something that could help with this, an etiquette guide for ghostly conversations or something.

But then Victoria says it, the most obvious word of all: "My daughter is haunting you."

"Not me, exactly. I mean, not just me. My mom too." All of a sudden, I wish I had taken some tea. Then at least I'd have something to do with my hands. Now all I can do is press them onto my jeans. "How did you know?"

Victoria puts her teacup down on the tufted ottoman between us. She smiles sadly. "I knew it was you. Your eyes—"

I shake my head. "I don't understand what my eyes have to do with anything," I interrupt quietly.

"At first I thought maybe it was your boyfriend, Nolan—"

"He's not my boyfriend," I say quickly. For some reason, even now—especially now—it seems important to make that distinction.

"But then I saw your eyes, and it all made sense," she continues, as though I hadn't spoken.

"I'm sorry, but *what* makes sense?" I shake my head. If you ask me, nothing about any of this makes anything even resembling sense.

"I'm sure this is confusing for you. In the old days we lived together. We knew what to expect when we turned sixteen."

"We?" I echo. A single butterfly takes flight in my belly, but it's enough to make my hands shake in my lap. I resist the urge to sit on top of them. "What do you mean, *we*?"

She pauses and then says the word that sounded like gibberish not too long ago: "Luiseach."

Holy majoly. I found one. A real-life luiseach. Is that why she saw death in even the most cheerful of art projects? Why she was always lurking and listening? Because she is a luiseach?

Or was it more than that? Maybe she was looking for something. For someone.

For me?

"Are you my mentor?" *My* mentor. It just came out, this tacit acknowledgment that I know I am what Nolan says I am. If I didn't believe that I was a luiseach, I wouldn't expect to have a mentor.

"No." She smiles that same sad smile. "But your mentor has been watching you for a long time."

Well, that's creepy. I mean, the idea of someone watching me. Wait—it's more than just creepy. It's *awful.* "Well if she's—or he's—watching, why hasn't he or she done anything to help? Why won't he or she jump in and help my mom before things get worse?" Instead of husky and dry, now my voice sounds high pitched and shrill.

Victoria's voice is perfectly calm when she answers. In fact, her voice has been calm since the instant I showed up on her doorstep, soft and almost melodic. "Your mentor is incredibly powerful, Sunshine, but he will not intercede at this time." *He.* Now at least I know something about my mentor: he's a man. "You see," Victoria continues, "luiseach are kind of like guardian angels—"

"I know," I interrupt, my voice trembling. "They protect humans from dark spirits," I say it like I've said it a million times before. Like I haven't denied that they exist, let alone that I might be one. "They all have a mentor and a protector, and they come of age at sixteen."

For the first time today Victoria actually looks surprised, her eyes wide and her brow furrowed. "You know more than I expected," she says slowly.

"Nolan. He's been helping me. He's good at research, that kind of thing."

A knowing sort of smile crosses her face as she sits silently.

Okay, I know I'm in the middle of something here, but I have to just stop and complain for a second. I hate—*hate*—when grownups look at teenagers like that, like they think we're involved in some kind of puppy love, and isn't that the most adorable thing?

"He's not my boyfriend," I say again, quietly this time.

"I believe you," Victoria answers. She leans back in her chair. "Did Nolan's research also reveal that all luiseach are tested by their mentors at sixteen? They can only begin their training once they've passed their tests."

"Are you saying that this—everything that's happening in my house—is some kind of test I'm supposed to pass?"

"Yes."

I wrinkle my nose, just like Mom. "And my mentor won't help me, because he wants to see how I'm going to handle this myself, right?" She nods. "Well then, can *you* help me, please?"

"It's your test, Sunshine, not mine."

"I promise I don't care if your help means that I fail the test." Doesn't she understand that my mother is so much more important than whether or not I get to start luiseach training? "Can't you just—I don't know—throw your best luiseach magic at my mom?" I take a deep breath, trying to gather my thoughts. "It's my *mom.* And she's already hurt herself once. Just tell me what Anna wants. Please."

"It's not my daughter who's causing your problems," Victoria cuts in. "Well, not exactly."

"What do you mean?"

She takes a sip of her tea, swallowing slowly. "I made a deal," she says softly, gazing into her teacup. "A deal to help my daughter move on."

"I don't understand. If you're a luiseach, can't *you* help her? I mean, isn't that what luiseach do—usher spirits to the other side?"

Victoria shakes her head. "I failed her. She needed a stronger luiseach than me. So I gave up my powers. That was the price he required, and I was more than happy to oblige."

"The price who required?" I ask.

Instead of answering, Victoria says, "First, I have to tell you how my daughter died."

"You don't have to," I say softly. I interlace my fingers and rest them on my lap. I don't want to make this poor woman relive what must have been the worst day of her life.

"Yes, I do," Victoria holds up her hand. "You need to know that both Anna and my husband were murdered."

CHAPTER TWENTY-SIX

Possession

"I thought your husband had a heart attack." I imagine how shocked he must have been when he saw his daughter, lifeless in her bathtub. It'd be enough to stop any parent's heart from beating.

"It can look like a heart attack," Victoria concedes.

"How can *murder* look like a heart attack?"

"Let me explain," she says in her soft, melodic voice. "It's complicated."

"I'll say," I sigh, and Victoria smiles sadly once more. She pours some tea into a porcelain cup and hands it to me. I take a sip and listen to her story.

"I knew what I was from the moment I was born," Victoria begins. "I looked forward to my sixteenth birthday. The instant I turned sixteen, I became aware of the spirits around me. I could sense them as no mortal could, interact with them as no mortal could. I couldn't wait to pass my test and begin the job of helping them move on."

I can't imagine looking forward to a test like this.

Maybe just once there was a luiseach who said, *No, thank you. I'd rather not spend my life helping spirits and exorcising demons. I'd like to go to college, get a normal nine-to-five job, have health insurance and a 401K.*

Maybe just once over the centuries, one luiseach said, *No.*

Victoria continues, "I passed my test with flying colors and began work with my mentor immediately. He started me out slow," she explains. "At first I was just helping light spirits move on."

"How could you tell if a spirit was light or not?"

"Spirits are drawn to us. The instant they leave their mortal bodies, a light spirit will seek us out, anxious to move on."

"What if there isn't a luiseach nearby when they die?"

"Distance isn't quite the same thing in the spirit world as it is here in the physical one. A light spirit a thousand miles away would have been able to sense me back then, had I been the nearest luiseach. It would have been drawn to me as a moth to a flame." She smiles, as though the memory of all the spirits she helped to move on is comforting to her.

"How do you do it—help them move on?"

Victoria cocks her head to the side. "It's difficult to explain," she begins. "You just sort of . . . *feel* it." She pauses, then asks, "Tell me, Sunshine, have you spent most of your life among humans feeling somehow different, something other?"

"Not exactly," I answer. "I mean, my mom and I are really close. I've gone to school just like everyone else, made friends." Well, two friends, Ashley and then Nolan.

"Yes, but haven't you ever felt like this life didn't quite fit?"

I close my eyes, considering. I never fit *in*, if that's what Victoria means. I don't dress quite like everyone else, don't read quite the same books or share quite the same hobbies. But lots of kids don't fit in, right? Suddenly I think of Mom's voice: *You could trip over your own two feet.* Is this why I was always such a klutz? Not because I was born clumsy, but because I simply didn't *fit* in the day-to-day world?

I open my eyes. Victoria's gaze is focused on my face, waiting patiently for me to answer.

"Maybe," I admit finally, my voice not quite steady.

"Luiseach are meant to work with spirits. We can manage in the human world, even form powerful bonds with human friends and family, but the truth is, nothing will ever come quite as *naturally* to us as helping a spirit move from this world to the next. Just as a light spirit is drawn to you, you are compelled to receive it. Just as it longs to move on, you will feel an urge to help it on its journey."

You don't know what I will feel, I think but do not say. "What about dark spirits?"

"Dark spirits are a different story. Often they're spirits that were taken too soon, lives that were snuffed out unexpectedly. They deny their natural instincts, fight against the pull toward the nearest luiseach. Instead, they hide from us. After a few years of training, after I'd helped thousands of light spirits move on, my mentor judged me ready for the next level of luiseach work—seeking out resistant spirits and forcing them to move on before they turned ever darker."

"What do you mean darker?"

Softly, Victoria answers, "A spirit that lingers on Earth too long changes. It spends so much time fighting against its instincts that it shifts into something else entirely, bearing no resemblance to the human it once was. The spirit of the kindest human you ever met can turn into an evil creature over time. Such spirits endanger human lives, and it is a luiseach's sacred mission to prevent this danger. These spirits are consumed by one thing and one thing only: gathering the strength they need to stay by any means necessary."

"What does that mean?" I ask hoarsely, not entirely certain I want to know the answer.

Victoria shakes her head. "I'm getting ahead of myself." She stops to sip some tea. "I have to finish telling you my own story. I excelled at my work," she explains, a sad sort of pride in her voice. "It was what I was born to do. I was so good that my mentor finally decided to let me in on his *real* work–his secret undertaking. It required working long hours, travel, being away from my family, but it was thrilling."

"What do you mean his real work? I thought helping spirits move on was what luiseach did."

"It is what we do," Victoria nods. "But in order for us to keep doing it, a balance needs to be restored. My mentor was investigating how to restore that balance."

"Why was that a secret?"

"Not everyone in the luiseach community would have agreed with his theories on restoration."

I try to remember everything Nolan told me about luiseach. It's hereditary. They have mentors and protectors. They used to live in insular communities. Nothing about a balance. Unless . . .

"Wait," I say suddenly. "Did your work have something to do with the rift? With the fact that fewer luiseach are being born?"

"Yes."

"Nolan thinks that I'm the last luiseach to have been born."

Victoria's eyes widen. "Nolan is a smart boy."

I bite my lip. Is she saying that Nolan is right—that no luiseach have been born since me? And if the rift is really about the low birth rates . . . "Wait—are you saying that I'm connected to the rift somehow?"

"All will be revealed in time," Victoria responds and resumes her story. "Years after we began our work together my mentor and I had a falling out."

"Why?"

"First, I fell in love with a human. I wasn't the first luiseach to marry a mortal—with numbers dwindling, it was inevitable that it would happen from time to time. We settled here in Ridgemont, his hometown. After my daughter was born I had to beg my mentor to allow me to resume the work I'd been doing before."

"Why? If you were so good at it, didn't he want you back?"

"Well, this was the reason for our falling out. I'd promised him that I wouldn't have a child."

"Why not?"

"Any child I had with my husband would be human. It takes two luiseach parents to have a luiseach baby."

"Lucky me," I whisper to myself.

"But finally I convinced him to take me back. The work we'd been doing was too important for him to hold a grudge."

"Did your husband know what you were?"

Victoria shakes her head, almost smiling at the memory. "No. He thought I was something of a traveling salesman. I didn't lie, not exactly. I'd told him I traveled the world saving lives. He took it to mean I sold pharmaceutical products. I never corrected him. He wouldn't have believed me if I had. He was a chemistry teacher. He believed in science, not in spirits."

I nod with understanding. I know what it's like to live with a nonbeliever.

"The winter my family was killed followed an autumn of record rains. Our street flooded; our neighbors' home was destroyed. It wasn't difficult for the demon to get inside—just follow the flow of the water and drift into our basement, then crawl up the rusty pipes and into our rooms."

"The demon?" I echo. I know I shouldn't be surprised that a demon is involved in all of this, but it still sends a flutter of butterflies through my belly.

Victoria nods. "A water demon."

"There are different kinds of demons?" I ask, but even as I say it I know it makes sense: the mildewy smell in our house, the wet fingerprints on my checkers, the damp carpet beneath my feet.

We must have a water demon too.

"They're not all that uncommon in this part of the world, though it's believed they originated in the South American rain forest. They thrive in moist climates. It must have been living here for months before it decided it would use my husband to take my daughter's life."

Victoria pauses, taking a deep breath. I can tell she's trying to swallow a lump in her throat. I lean forward and put my hand on her knee. This part of the story, at least, I understand completely. I know about the ways mothers and daughters love each other.

"The demon drove my husband to drown our daughter."

"Your husband drowned Anna?" My voice is no louder than a whisper. I'm suddenly very glad that I blacked out the Water Works box on my Monopoly board. I wish I'd done it sooner.

"No," Victoria answers firmly. "The *demon* drowned Anna. It just used my husband's body to do it, as it is using your mother's body now."

I shake my head. I mean, my mother hasn't exactly been herself lately—she's been angry and distant—but I've never actually been *scared* of her. Whatever is doing this to her, I can't believe it's strong enough to compel her to kill me.

But then I remember, according to Nolan, a luiseach is safe from dark spirits. So if it's a dark spirit that's controlling my mother, it's powerless to make her kill me.

"The police couldn't detect signs of a struggle—the scratches on the tile around the tub, the bruises on her arms and neck were invisible to them."

I close my eyes, imagining Anna's neck ringed with a dark purple bruise.

I open them as Victoria says, "But that's not the worst part."

I can't really imagine something worse than a demon forcing a loving parent to harm his own child. I'm not sure I want to hear what's next, but I guess I don't have a choice.

"When a human's life is taken by a demon, his or her spirit is trapped in a world of anguish."

"That's why Anna can't move on?"

"She'll continue to be tormented until the demon is fully exorcised, ushered by a luiseach into the beyond. The demon follows her everywhere, always just a few steps behind."

Wait, does that mean that the other spirit in my house is *this* demon, the creature who killed Anna and her father? I remember the sounds I heard coming from my mother's mouth last night. It's not just my *house* the demon is inhabiting.

"It's *inside* my mother?" I can barely get the words out.

Slowly Victoria nods.

"And it's my test to destroy it before it does to my mother what it did to your husband?" The words I don't say are stuck in my throat, choking me: . . . *before it kills her too.*

Suddenly Victoria's role in all of this becomes clear.

"And you made a deal with my mentor to make Anna's demon my test? Because it needs to be fully exorcised before her spirit can move on?"

This time when Victoria nods, it looks like her head weighs a thousand pounds, like she can only move it with great effort. "It was hardly a coincidence that your mother was offered her dream job in a town with one of the wettest climates in the country."

"My mentor got my mother her job?" I ask incredulously. "How long has this been going on?"

"He's been putting the pieces of your test in place for months. I've been helping as much as I could."

"How?" I ask breathlessly.

"Luiseach can guide spirits, but they cannot move them, not without great strength. When I relinquished my powers, it gave off the energy he needed to set the test in motion—to put Anna in your house. Then I just had to wait until you revealed yourself to me."

"Are you even an art teacher?"

"No," she answers, smiling. "He arranged that job. All he told me was that one of my students would be the young luiseach living with my daughter."

"That explains a lot," I say softly.

"It does?" Victoria asks, weary but almost laughing. "Was I really that bad?"

"*Let's make some art, shall we?* You weren't exactly teacher of the year." I force myself to smile in the midst of all this anguish, and Victoria does too.

I shouldn't be smiling at her. I should be *angry* at her—this test has put my mom's life in danger—but I can't. Even through her smile Victoria's pain is written clearly on her face. She's a mother trying to save her daughter.

"Why can't my mom hear Anna, perceive that we're living in a haunted house?"

"The demon has grown clever." Victoria presses her lips into a straight line. "He must have blocked your mother's ability to perceive spirits in order to cause strife between you, to make it that much more difficult for you to protect her."

I'm finally beginning to understand. When we first moved to our new house Anna was happy—laughing, begging to play, whispering good night. The demon was a few steps behind—just like Victoria said—but he hadn't quite arrived yet. But then, that horrible night when the bathroom door was locked, when Mom and I heard Anna's voice pleading for mercy—that was when Anna's demon arrived. Nolan was right again: there was more than one spirit in the house. Even Victoria sensed its arrival; I remember the next morning she told us she'd had nightmares and barely slept.

Almost immediately after that night Mom went from denying that the noises I heard were paranormal—*There's no such thing as ghosts, Sunshine*—to being unable to hear the noises at all. She went from busy and tired to so distant that sometimes it felt like she wasn't there at all.

Somehow, even with the demon in our house—in *Mom*—Anna found the strength to reach out to me. She wanted to make sure

I knew she was still there, that I wasn't alone. No wonder the house was shaking when Nolan and I finally began to put the pieces together, no wonder the lightbulb burst above our heads. Nolan was right. Anna was *excited.* Maybe she understood this was my test all along. Maybe she was trying to help me, the only way she could.

And no wonder the demon tried to stop us when Mom came home and it saw what we were up to. Gosh, does the demon have access to Mom's thoughts and memories? Did it go through her brain, discover that I'm scared of spiders, and plant that daddy longlegs there just for me?

"I think it's obvious by now that I'm not cut out to pass this test, right?" I rub my hands together anxiously. If my mentor's been watching me like Victoria says he has, surely he can see that. "So can't you just tell my mentor to come out of the shadows or wherever he's hiding, do his best luiseach sorcery, and get rid of the demon and save my mom?"

"That's not how it works," Victoria answers sadly.

"How does it work?"

"You have to exorcise the demon yourself."

"What if I can't? I mean, my mentor will swoop in to save the day, right?" My palms are moist with sweat.

Victoria doesn't answer.

"What happens then?" My voice is so small that I don't know if she can hear me. "Will my mom's spirit be unsettled, the way Anna's is?" I can barely say the word *spirit.* Those two tiny syllables feel like saying that Mom will die.

"Anna wasn't possessed by the demon herself. Rather, she was a victim of its possession of my husband. Tormented though she is, her spirit survived. The same cannot be said for the poor souls the demon actually inhabits. As it inhabited my husband."

The warmth of Victoria's house shifts from cozy to oppressive. I yank at the neck of my sweater as though it's choking me and brush my hair from my forehead, the sweat on my palms making them sticky. My throat feels dry, so I reach for the tea Victoria poured for me and sip it, even though the cup threatens to slip through my sweating fingers. The liquid is so hot that it scalds me. I swear it wasn't that hot a few minutes ago.

"How did the demon make your husband's death look like a heart attack?" I ask hoarsely.

"When a water demon—or any demon, really—is finished possessing another person, that body becomes nothing more than dead weight to them. They want to rid themselves of it as quickly as possible."

A lump rises in my throat, choking me as she continues. "Possession means that the demon is literally living inside another body, and within that body it can move freely. This demon had one goal in possessing my husband—use his body to drown my daughter."

"Why?" I whisper, the tiny word struggling to fit around the lump in my throat.

"I told you that once a spirit turns wholly dark—once it becomes a demon—it will do whatever it takes to remain strong enough to stay on Earth. Releasing a spirit from a mortal body makes a demon stronger."

Releasing a spirit. "You mean killing someone?"

She nods. "If it had been a fire demon, it would have burned Anna to death. An earth demon often buries its victims alive. And a water demon drowns them."

I shake my head, thinking about the little girl who's determined to beat me at Monopoly. How could someone hurt her?

"After Anna was dead the demon had no more use for my husband. So it reached its watery demon hand inside my husband's chest, squeezing his heart until it simply stopped beating."

I close my eyes, trying not to imagine a cold, wet hand hovering near my mother's heart, just waiting to take hold. Tears start streaming down my face.

"And his spirit?" I manage to whisper. "What happens to the souls of the people the demon inhabits?"

Victoria looks away from a moment, taking a deep breath before she turns back and says, "Those spirits do not survive. The demon destroys them completely."

CHAPTER TWENTY-SEVEN

The Long Way Home

"What does that mean?"

"It means they do not move on. They simply . . . cease to exist."

"I don't understand." The lump in my throat is so big, I'm surprised I can get any words out at all.

"Slowly, over time, every single person whose lives they touched will begin to forget them. Until no one can remember having known them at all."

"But you still remember your husband."

"I do. But it's only a matter of time." Victoria shifts her weight uncomfortably, as though she's sitting on a hard wooden chair, not a plush one. "Already I cannot recall just how we met, how he asked me to marry him, the color of his eyes."

"You have pictures of him," I try.

"Yes, but someday I'll simply throw those pictures away, wondering why there are photographs of a stranger in my house."

I think about my mother—the inside jokes and shared clothes, the way she laughs, her perfectly straight auburn hair and freckled skin. I could never forget all that.

Could I?

I stand up and start for the door. "I should go." I grab my coat from the twisted wooden rack by the door, trying to ignore the fact that beneath my own jacket there's a smaller one that must have belonged to Anna before she died. I wonder what other relics of her remain in this house. I wonder whether the turreted top floor was her favorite place to play. Did she play there with her father? Will Anna's ghost remember him even after Victoria's memories vanish? Maybe it would be better if Anna forgot him—forgot that his body drowned her, even if it was just carrying out the demon's will. Did he know what he was doing as it was happening? I close my eyes and press the heel of my hand to my forehead, overwhelmed.

I spin around on my heel. "How can you sound so casual about forgetting your husband? How can you be so *resigned* to it? If it were me, I'd paper my house with blown-up photographs. I'd write down all my memories so I could remember every detail."

Victoria puts her hands on my shoulders, her voice still frustratingly calm. "I'm afraid it wouldn't make a difference, Sunshine. Eventually you'd throw them all away, wondering how they got there in the first place. Believe me. I've seen it happen." I can feel the warmth of her palms through my T-shirt, my sweater, my jacket.

I twist myself from her grasp. "Well, it's not going to happen to me. I'm going home to my mother. I should never have left her alone." Hot tears overflow from my eyes and roll down my cheeks. "She's already hurt herself once." I finger the scar at the base of my left thumb.

Victoria looks directly into my eyes. "But not seriously, right?"

The lump in my throat is getting bigger by the second. "She sliced her wrist open with a knife. Then she turned the knife on me," I add. "It looked plenty serious to me."

"I know this must be overwhelming, Sunshine, but I need you to listen to me now. Think about it. Your mother is a *nurse.* She has medical expertise. If she wanted to cause any real damage, she'd know how. The demon only made her do that to get your attention—not to inflict any real damage."

"Why did the demon want my attention?"

"For a demon, that's part of the fun—wreaking havoc, frightening people, destroying their lives. It knew that the surest way to scare you was to make you worry about your mother's safety, to drive a wedge between two people who'd always been so close."

How does Victoria know so much about us? Maybe she's been lying to me all this time. Maybe she *is* my mentor. Maybe this is part of my test.

"How do I know you're telling the truth?" My voice shakes as an even more awful thought occurs to me. "How do I know you're not possessed by the demon too? Maybe you're just keeping me here so I can't get home in time to save my mom!" I open the front door, grateful for the gust of cool air that blows in from outside. I step onto the front porch and begin sprinting down the stairs and across the front yard.

"You have until New Year's Eve!" she shouts, speaking quickly to get the words out before I'm out of reach.

I spin around. "Why New Year's Eve?"

"That's when he killed my family—at midnight on New Year's Eve last year. The demon has tormented its share of people in the year that's passed, but hasn't destroyed one since. It draws strength from the turn of one year into the next. The strength it needs to actually take a life."

New Year's Eve. One week from today. I press the heels of my sneakers into Victoria's snow-spattered yard. Without looking up I say, "So I have some time to figure out how to save her?"

"You do." She nods. "I promise you that she will be safe until then. But there is one more thing," Victoria adds softly, and now I do look up. "Once a full year has passed since Anna's death without the demon's exorcism, her spirit . . ." She pauses. Now I think she's the one who's going to burst into tears. But she swallows her tears and sets her mouth into a straight line long enough to say, "Anna's spirit will be destroyed too. I will forget–"

"I understand," I say quickly so she doesn't have to say it out loud: *I will forget that I ever had a family. That I ever was a mother.*

"I can help you," Victoria begins, but I shake my head.

"I thought you said it was my test, not yours."

"It is. But I'm allowed to help, now that you've found me."

I nod. "I'll come back," I promise. I need all the help I can get.

Even though I'm longing to see our house filled with Mom's knickknacks, her clothes, her fingerprints–all that proof that she is a real, solid person and not a fading memory–I walk home slowly, going over in my mind everything that Victoria just told me. She said I had time, so I may as well take it. I'm about halfway home when I reach into my pocket for my phone and begin typing.

You'll never believe what I found out.

Delete.

I have so much to tell you!

Delete.

You were right and I was wrong.

Delete.

It's impossible to find the right thing to say to Nolan. I draft and discard a dozen text messages on the walk from Victoria's house to my own. Finally I type *I'm sorry* and hit send. The tiniest little bit of snow is falling, just a flurry. I dig a hat out of my jacket pocket and shove it on my head, but it doesn't make a bit of difference. I'm still cold, colder maybe than I've ever been in my entire life. And that's saying something, because I've spent most of the past few months freezing.

I'm tempted to resend the text a dozen times, but I settle for once. And then I wait. I must have checked my phone twenty times before I turn onto our street. I'm so busy looking down that I trip and fall nearly flat on my face in front of someone's driveway.

"Ow," I say out loud, even though there's no one around to hear me. It's still early, and for once the fog isn't blindingly thick. I think it's too cold for fog, like the deep freeze has made everything crystal clear.

I'm a luiseach. A guardian angel. A supernatural warrior. A light bringer. Just like Nolan said I was. And it's up to me to save my mother.

Not just my mother. And not just Anna's spirit and Victoria's memories. It's up to me to save *myself.* Because who will I be if I don't have Mom? If I can't even *remember* that I used to have her? She's the only family I have.

Though I can't help wondering whether Victoria knows who my real parents are. The two luiseach who gave me up. Maybe she knows why.

I shake my head. I don't care whether Victoria knows. I don't care whether she offers to bring me to them. They aren't my parents. Mom is all the parent I'll ever need. The only one I want.

Still on my knees, snow melting into my jeans, I glance around to make sure there's no one around and try saying it out loud, like I just want to know what the sentence will feel like: "I'm a luiseach."

Butterflies flutter in my stomach, but otherwise nothing happens. I say it again, louder this time: "I'm a luiseach."

Still nothing, not even a bird or a squirrel to startle with the sound of my voice. Almost as if I wasn't saying something earth shattering, something that—just a few months ago, back in Austin, when Ashley and I were arguing over which movie to see, which boy was cutest, which ice cream flavor best—would have sounded unbelievable, incredible, even to a weirdo like me.

Ashley would say that I'd lost my mind. She'd say Mom probably just needs therapy—and me too, for believing all this. Her response would be so utterly *normal.* I wipe the dirt and pine needles and snow from my palms and stand up. The knees of my jeans are wet from my fall, and the right leg is ripped open. I guess texting and walking is almost as bad an idea as texting and driving. I sigh. All the words Victoria spoke are dancing around in my head, twisting and turning over one another, forming an enormous ball of anguish.

For just a few minutes I want to think about something else, anything else. Something that's a little bit easier to wrap my head around. Even the most seasoned luiseach probably has to take a break once in a while, right? Standing still, I send another text, this one to Ashley.

Merry Christmas, I write. *I miss you.*

It's the truth. Last year at this time Ashley and I were texting each other pictures of our Christmas trees, arguing over which of us had done a better job stringing the lights, and giggling over the ornaments we'd made for each other out of popsicle sticks back when we were six.

Ashley responds right away. *Merry Christmas! I miss you too. How are things with Cory Cooper?*

So amazing. I can't believe I'm actually going to have someone to kiss at midnight on New Year's Eve for once!

I almost laugh out loud at the difference between Ashley's and my New Year's Eve plans. Ashley's still living the life of a normal teenager, still trying to get me to be normal with her, just like she has for years—telling me to shop at normal stores, to wear normal clothes, to try normal hobbies. At least now I know that it wasn't entirely my fault that I was never any good at being normal. I wasn't born normal. Apparently I wasn't even born *human.*

I couldn't help it that I love taxidermied animals and vintage clothes and books written two centuries ago. But the truth is, although I never cared about fitting in, I do miss the normal things Ashley and I used to do together. Just *regular* stuff like going to the movies or to a party. Lying out around the pool in her backyard. Listening to music. Studying SAT words. Eating pizza while we watched TV.

Ashley writes, *How are you? How's Kat?*

So much for thinking about something else. I have no idea how to answer that question. I could tell Ashley that my mom is sick. She would care—she loves my mom. When we were growing up she and I spent as much time at each other's houses as we did at our own. She'd probably offer to beg her parents for a plane ticket so she could fly up here and help me take care of Mom. Of course, she'd probably think that care involved making soup and picking up prescriptions at the pharmacy, not evil spirits and exorcisms.

I shake my head. How will it work—this forgetting? Will I remember Ashley, but not the fact that she loved my mom? But how can I remember Ashley without remembering Mom and our life in Austin—all those things are tied up together so tightly. Does that mean I'll forget my life in Austin too? I'll only remember my haunted life here in Ridgemont?

How long will it take for me to forget? Victoria hasn't forgotten her husband yet, not completely, and he died only a year ago. Maybe it will happen slowly. At first I'll just wonder where my favorite mustang T-shirt came from, but eventually I won't know who raised me until, finally, I'll believe that no one raised me at all. That I never was a part of a family, even a small one that was only made up of two people.

My phone buzzes with another text from Ashley: *Hello? Earth to Sunshine?* So I write back, *We're fine*, hoping that in a few days it will be the truth. Maybe that way it's not technically a lie.

Make any progress with that hot guy?

We had a fight, I type honestly.

Oh no! Think you can work it out?

I'm not sure.

Well, keep me posted.

I will.

And let me know if you want to talk about it.

I smile a tiny, sad sort of smile. I can't talk about it without talking about a dozen other things Ashley won't believe or understand. The truth is, even though Ashley and I have been close since elementary school, we've never actually had all that much in common, and now—with so much distance between us, going to different schools, living in climates so different we may as well be on different planets—we have even less to talk about. The two thousand miles between Austin, Texas, and Ridgemont, Washington, did come between us in the end. Now it feels absurd that we ever thought our friendship was stronger than that.

I stuff my phone back into my pocket and resume the walk home. Even after the desolation of Victoria's street, our neighborhood looks even more deserted than usual today. The decorative lights outside the house across from ours aren't lit. It looks like no one is home. This isn't the kind of neighborhood people come home to for the holidays. It's the kind of place people leave.

CHAPTER TWENTY-EIGHT

Apologies and Thank Yous

Mom is in the kitchen sipping coffee when I walk in. She's still dressed in the scrubs she slept in, her auburn hair mussed and knotted down her back. She probably asked to have today off months ago, long before the demon moved in, back when she still cared about holidays and vacation. She doesn't look surprised to see me, doesn't ask what I was up to at this hour on the first day of winter vacation, doesn't ask how my jeans ended up dirty and ripped.

"I was just taking a walk," I say. Even if she's not asking, I feel the need to make up some kind of excuse.

If I stared long enough and hard enough, would I be able to see the demon beneath her skin? I narrow my eyes, remembering the shadow that trailed behind her from one room to the next, so much bigger than her shadow should have been. Was that the demon's shadow I saw?

I take a deep breath, tasting the mildewy-ness that saturates our house. I take off my hat, gloves, and jacket, then put them dutifully away in the coat closet by the front door. I run my fingers through my frizzball and knead my scalp with my fingertips the way Mom did when I was little and couldn't sleep.

If I fail, I guess I won't remember that. Maybe I'll rub my scalp and wonder why it's so comforting.

I trudge upstairs to shower and change. I pull my phone from my jeans pocket, impressed that I had enough willpower to keep from looking for nearly five whole minutes. Still no word from Nolan.

Maybe I should text him again.

Maybe he was somewhere without a signal and my message got lost somewhere in the cyber-ether and he's just walking around in the woods somewhere, totally oblivious to my apology.

Or maybe he's just so angry at me that an apology wasn't enough. I force myself to put my phone away.

In my room not even one item is out of place—no toys strewn across the floor, no unicorns facing the wrong way. The checkerboard is exactly how I left it: Anna hasn't made her next move. Even Dr. Hoo is still and dry on his perch.

"Anna Wilde," I say out loud. The walls shudder in response. "I talked to your mother. She misses you. And I know how much you miss her."

I bite my lip. I sure miss mine.

"I'm sorry for all the times I wanted you gone," I add softly. "I know it's not your fault you're still here. That none of this is your fault."

It's my fault. Because I was born different.

After a shower I change into pj's—no feet, but Christmas colored, red and green with white kittens dancing across my shoulders like the Rockettes. I pull my computer onto my lap and search for exorcisms and demons and luiseach until the words all bleed into each other. I can't make heads or tails of any of it. Having another week won't do me any good if I can't make more progress than this. *What am I going to do?* Miraculously, I fall asleep eventually, my hand still on the mouse.

I don't know how much later it is when I wake to the sound of knocking on my door.

"Come in, Mom," I call, slamming my laptop shut.

"It's not your mom," a male voice answers. A voice I know well. I pull myself to sit up and try to straighten my pajamas and flatten my hair as Nolan steps into my room. Despite the fact that it's much colder out now than it was the day I met him, he's still wearing his leather jacket, though now there's a gray scarf wrapped around his neck and a black knit hat pulled down tightly over his ears, his blond hair peeking out from under it.

"I got your text," he says. He slips off his hat and sits on the edge of the bed, the mattress dipping beneath his weight. I feel a rush of warmth in his presence—not the oppressive heat I felt in Victoria's house, and certainly not the bitter cold I felt on the walk home. Not to sound like Goldilocks or anything, but this warmth is just right.

"I wasn't sure. You didn't write back."

"I couldn't," he replies. "I was driving."

"Where?"

"Here."

"Won't your parents be mad at you for missing Christmas with your grandmother?"

Nolan shrugs like he knows that they might be, but it wasn't enough to make him stay. "I couldn't stay away. Not when I knew you needed me."

Ashley was wrong. Neither the pink nor the taxidermied bird will make Nolan turn tail and run away as fast as his legs will carry him. Not if he came back after everything else that happened.

If this were a movie, now would be when he leaned in to kiss me. Or maybe he'd just take my hand, and the warmth of his skin against mine would make my heart flutter and maybe our lips would fit together like they were meant for each other.

But this isn't a movie, and even though I like how close to me he's sitting, I still feel strange. I wonder whether Nolan can feel it too. Maybe this haunting—maybe Anna and the demon—are the reason for it. Maybe the feeling will dissipate if I defeat the demon and save Anna and my mom. Which I *must* do. I *have* to. I *will.*

Or anyway, I'll try.

"You were right," I say.

"About what?"

"About everything," I sigh. "But mostly, about me." I take a deep breath and say, "I'm a luiseach."

"Oh, you know how to pronounce it now?" Nolan smiles, but I know he's serious.

"Shut up," I say shoving him gently away, careful to make sure that my palm presses against his jacket and not his skin. A gagging fit would really ruin this moment.

"I did a little research of my own. And I found some new evidence." I tell him all about Anna Wilde, about running to Victoria's house at the crack of dawn. About the fact that Victoria confirmed what Nolan already believed: I'm a luiseach.

"There's something else," I add urgently. I explain what will happen to my mother's spirit—and Anna's too—if we fail. I swallow the lump in my throat. I don't want to cry anymore. I can cry all I want once all this is over, but right now I have to stay focused.

"But we only have a week," I add urgently. "And I have so much to learn before then."

"I know." Nolan nods. "But I'll help you. And Ms. Wilde can help too. Good thing you found a luiseach, right?"

"I left that part out. She's not anymore. She had to give up her powers in order to put the test in motion."

"You can stop being a luiseach?" Nolan asks. "I thought it was a lifelong kind of thing."

"Apparently not." I try to sound nonchalant, but the truth is, I want to know more about what Victoria did. So that when all this is over—when my mom is safe—I'll be able to do it too. Give up my powers and go back to being a normal sixteen-year-old. Well, as normal as I ever was.

"Okay, but she *used* to be a luiseach, at least. She must remember what to do, right?"

"I hope so," I say, and I smile. "I'm sorry."

"You already apologized."

"Over text doesn't count. I needed to say it out loud."

"Apology accepted."

"Are you sure?" I smile again. "I mean, you're in a position of power here. You could probably make me grovel a little bit more. No need to waste this opportunity."

Nolan cocks his head to the side as though he's weighing his options. "Nah," he says finally.

"You sure are letting me off easy."

"It's not your fault. You couldn't fight with a demon, so you picked a fight with me. I understand."

"You sure understand a lot more than I do."

"I picked a lot of fights with my parents after my grandfather died." He pauses, running his fingers back and forth over my comforter like it's a keyboard. "Can I tell you something?"

"Of course."

"I was telling the truth when I said I came back here to help you, but I also came back because I hate being at my grandparents' cabin without him there."

Nolan swallows hard, his Adam's apple bouncing up and down. He glances around the room, his eyes landing on the checkerboard and the Monopoly game.

"Are these the games you're playing with Anna?" he asks, and I nod. He leans down over the board. "Are you red or black?"

"Red," I answer. He starts to slide one of my checkers across the board, right next to one of Anna's. When he lifts his hand, the checker slides right back.

"Weird," he says, sliding it again. And again, it slides back.

"Maybe she doesn't want to play with you," I say, attempting a joke, but I'm actually mesmerized.

"Maybe," Nolan says, brushing his hands though his hair. "Or maybe I *can't* play with her."

"What do you mean?"

"I'm not a luiseach. So I can't interact with ghosts like you can."

"It's a checkerboard, not a Ouija board," I protest, but I know he's right. "I'm glad you came back."

"Me too."

I bite my lip. "I owe you more than just an apology."

"You do?" Nolan drops his gaze, his hair falling across his face.

"I owe you a thank you. I mean, I owe you about ten thousand thank yous. For all your research and your help. For believing me. For believing *in* me, even when I didn't."

I pull my sleeve down over my wrist so that my palm is covered, and I rest my hand on top of Nolan's on the bed, squeezing gently. He turns his own hand over and wraps his fingers around mine. Despite the strangeness, it does feel like our hands fit together.

"You said I couldn't fight a demon so I fought with you instead?"

"Yeah?"

"Turns out I *can* fight a demon. I *have* to. I just have to figure out how."

CHAPTER TWENTY-NINE

A Wise and Trusted Teacher

The day after Christmas Nolan and I walk together from my house to Victoria's. Unlike my last visit, this one takes place at a reasonable hour, almost noon.

"The last time we got expert help it didn't go all that well," I say as we walk down Victoria's woodsy street, cringing at the memory of Professor Jones's freezing empty office, the building that threatened to fall down around us.

"Sure it did," Nolan counters. "We never would have learned the word *luiseach.* We never would have figured out what you are."

I nod aimlessly as I walk beside him through the cold. The snow has turned to ice, and it crunches beneath our feet. It feels like we're breaking something with every step we take.

Nolan is wearing his grandfather's leather jacket, and a wool hat covers his dirty-blond hair. My own frizzball is tucked into an old gray hat of my mother's, with a matching scarf wrapped around my neck. When we get to Victoria's house I keep the scarf on. It smells like Mom.

Victoria is smiling when she opens the door. "Welcome back," she says; then turning to Nolan, she adds, "Welcome." I guess she expected he'd be coming with me.

Victoria's dark clothes stand out against her brightly decorated house. I wonder whether she dressed like this before Anna died or whether she wears the dark clothes as a sign of mourning.

"You said you could help," I begin eagerly as she leads us into the living room. I don't sit down like Nolan does when Victoria gestures to her couch. Instead, I take a deep breath and make the request I've been practicing for the past twenty-four hours. "I need you to teach me everything you know about how to exorcise a demon. Will you be my mentor?" When she doesn't answer immediately, I add a desperate, "Please?"

Victoria shakes her head. "I'm sorry, Sunshine. It doesn't work that way. You already have a mentor."

"No, I don't!" I'm tempted to stomp my foot like a little kid, but Victoria's carpet is so plush that it would barely make a sound. Instead, I lift my hands desperately, begging for help. "If I had a mentor, then he'd be here, helping me, teaching me. Isn't that what mentors do?"

I looked up the word mentor in the dictionary this morning: *a wise and trusted counselor or teacher.* Victoria might not be a qualified art teacher, but she's still the closest thing I have to that definition.

"He *is* helping you," Victoria insists.

"How?"

"The professor," Nolan says softly, and I turn around to face him. He looks so out of place in this room—Victoria's plush furniture seems to swallow up his long arms and legs. "Your mentor must have brought him back to help us."

Nolan has a point: someone must have put that specter of a professor there for us to find. "So my mentor hacked into the university's computer system with a listing of a long-dead professor's office hours? Furnished an empty office in an abandoned building that he somehow magicked into looking only slightly less abandoned?"

"Maybe he even planted the article about him in my grandfather's papers," he thinks aloud, his voice intense.

I bite my bottom lip. Okay, fine, that's *some* help. But it's not nearly *enough* help. Not when my mother's life is at stake.

"He will appear, Sunshine. You just have to wait." Victoria brings her long white fingers to her mouth, as though she's said too much. I feel like she's barely saying anything at all.

"But I *can* help you," she offers slowly, her soft voice melodic as she stands and disappears into the kitchen.

"Why don't you sit down?" Nolan suggests gently, and I sit on the couch beside him, but not too close. I don't actually need his warmth, not in this house.

I expect Victoria to return with a tray full of tea, but instead she comes back holding a handkerchief wrapped around something. "Here," she says, holding the package out to me.

I unwrap the item and immediately drop it into my lap.

"A rusty old knife?" It's not even a big knife. I mean, it's not, like, a butter knife or anything, but it's not exactly a sword or an axe either. It's the kind of knife Mom uses to chop onions or carrots or celery. The sort of knife you'd find in most any kitchen.

"It's not a rusty old knife," Victoria counters. "Can't you see what it really is?"

I shake my head. "What's it supposed to look like?"

"It's a weapon," she says breathlessly. "A weapon that only a luiseach can wield. Concentrate. Don't you see it?"

"See what?"

"See something more than just an ordinary knife?"

I pick up the knife and hold it up in front of me, turning it over in my hands. I squint and stare at it, then I squeeze it tight. I drop it to the floor with a hollow *thump* against the carpet. All the while it stays an ordinary old knife.

"What do you see when you look at it?" I ask.

"It doesn't matter what I see," Victoria replies. "The weapon manifests itself differently for each of us, based on our strength and our needs—and based on the strength and power of the demon we're using it against, of course."

"What do you mean by strength and power? Are you saying that on midnight on New Year's Eve my mother will be as strong as Superman?"

"Not exactly. Your mother will be incapacitated, but her body—possessed by the demon—will be powerful."

"But if her body is going to have superhuman strength, how am I supposed to overpower it? You said you couldn't destroy this demon, and you've been doing this for a lot longer than I have. It's only been a few months since my sixteenth birthday." Tears spring to my eyes. If she couldn't destroy this demon, how am I supposed to? What kind of a mentor gives his mentee a task that even a seasoned luiseach couldn't overcome? I feel like I'm destined to fail.

"It's been fifty-one years since I turned sixteen," Victoria says.

"But–" Nolan does the math automatically, "That would make you sixty-seven years old."

Victoria nods, and I lean forward, studying her face. There is barely a line on her forehead. Her eyes are ringed with dark circles—guess she doesn't sleep much, just like me—but there aren't crow's feet peeking out at the corners. She smiles, and I see that her lips are full and thick, her teeth bright white. Either Victoria has the world's greatest plastic surgeon, or . . . I think back to some of Nolan's earlier research. *Luiseach live long lives.* They—we—must age at a different rate too.

"It's true that I couldn't defeat this demon, but it wasn't just because I wasn't strong enough. I was away for my work when the demon murdered my family." She pauses. "I should have been there." Her words are tight and clipped. "In the months prior to the murders Anna had been complaining that her father was distant. I thought she was just upset that I'd been traveling so much and was trying to get me to spend more time at home. I promised I'd make it up to her when my work was done." Victoria swallows; the pain of making a promise to her daughter that she couldn't keep is written on her face. Suddenly I'm able to see each of her sixty-seven years etched on her skin.

"Distant how?" Nolan asks.

"It's hard to explain. At first it was small. Little things that only Anna or I would have been able to recognize. He still went to work, did his job, picked Anna up after school, bought groceries, made sure there was dinner on the table. Anna said he just seemed, somehow . . ." She trails off, searching for the right word.

"Absent," I supply.

"Yes." Victoria nods sadly. "Anna complained of missing him when he was right there with her."

"Just like my mom."

"Just like your mom," Victoria agrees.

"But couldn't you—I mean, luiseach can feel spirits, can't they? Couldn't you feel there was a demon in the house? I mean, when you were home?"

"So many spirits followed me everywhere. My mentor had trained me to tune them out—let another luiseach help them move on—so I could concentrate on our work."

Victoria stands up and turns so that her back is to us. She takes a shallow, ragged breath, like she's trying not to cry. I glance at Nolan. Maybe all these questions are too much for her. We're practically forcing her to relive her family's murder.

"I'm sorry—" I begin, but Victoria holds up her hand, cutting me off.

She turns around to face us, her pale face flushed with color. "You're stronger than the demon. I promise you that."

I shake my head. I've never felt strong. I get winded walking up a couple of flights of stairs. I've been picked last for every team in every gym class I've been in since kindergarten. "I can't even kill a spider," I insist, shuddering. "Believe me, I'm kind of a weakling."

"You're stronger than you know," Victoria says, and it sounds like a command. "Your parents—" She pauses. "You are descended from two of the most powerful luiseach in history."

Now it's my turn to stand and turn my back on everyone else. Victoria does know who my birth parents are after all! Maybe all luiseach know, if my birth parents are two such powerful and important pillars of the community.

"Who are they?" I'm not sure I want to know, but I have to ask. Butterflies flutter in my belly, and I hold my breath as I wait for an answer.

"I can't tell you that."

I exhale. "Did you know they abandoned me?"

"It's complicated–"

"Actually it's not complicated. You don't abandon a helpless baby."

"One day you will understand. Your father–"

"I don't have a father," I say firmly, biting my lip to keep from crying. "I have a mother–*one* mother–and her name is Katherine Griffith. She's the *only* mother I want. Believe me, I'm not interested in meeting the mother who left me all alone to be found at my mom's hospital."

"It wasn't your mother who left you. Your father–he was trying to protect you." She says it like it's perfectly reasonable.

"That's a pretty pathetic way to protect a baby." Stubbornly, I brush away the tears streaming down my face.

I hear Nolan stand up behind me. I step away before he can try to put his arms around me. Still I can feel the heat of his body, just inches away from mine. Not as comforting as a hug, but it still feels good. Well, not actually *good*–nothing feels good right now–but better, somehow.

"I'm sorry," Victoria says, "It will all become clear–"

"When?" I answer, turning around, my tears splashing hotly against my cheeks and chin. But I'm not sad anymore. I'm angry. "When will it be clear? Once the demon is exorcised using some kind of magical luiseach weapon that I can't see? Once my mentor finally comes out of the shadows and reveals himself and explains why the test he set up for me put the only family I have–the only family I *want,* the person who would *never* choose to abandon me–in danger?"

Once more the warmth of Victoria's house feels oppressive.

I pull my hair into a ponytail and unwrap Mom's scarf from around my neck. I walk to the window, throwing it open. The curtains blow back and I stand there, letting the wind wash over me.

"I'm beginning to think that luiseach—luiseaches, *blah*, whatever the plural is—are the bad guys. They *desert* their children. They place *innocent* people in jeopardy." It actually feels good when the breeze makes goose bumps blossom on my arms and legs. I turn around to face Victoria, the wind at my back. "I don't want anything to do with any of this," I sniff, swallowing the lump in my throat and pressing the heel of my hand against my forehead.

"I know this is difficult," Victoria says quietly. "There are so many questions I can't answer."

"*Won't* answer," I mumble, wiping away my remaining tears with my sleeve.

"But I can tell you that the first step toward clarity will come with freeing your mother from the demon's hold—and even if you don't want anything to do with any of this, I know that more than anything you want to save her."

She's right. Maybe my mentor designed it this way on purpose. You can't exactly skip a test when the results are so important to you. I lower my hand from my forehead so that I'm covering my eyes.

I take a deep breath and drop my hands, shut the window, and walk back to the couch. I lift the knife off the floor and stare at it once more.

Still, all I see is a rusty old knife.

CHAPTER THIRTY

Heavy Metal

"Maybe it needs to be activated for Sunshine to see it," Nolan offers.

"What do you mean, activated?" I don't think it has an on-off switch.

He shrugs. "Maybe since . . . I don't know. Maybe since you haven't passed the test yet, you're not able to see it."

"But how can I pass the test if I can't see the weapon I need in order to pass the test?" I ask wearily.

"Maybe it will show itself when you need it."

I look at Victoria, who nods intently. "He could be right," she says slowly. "Perhaps when the demon confronts you—with all of its strength and power—you will find the motivation you need to see the weapon."

"Is that how you saw it?"

"It was given to me in a time of great need. I saw it immediately—but then, I needed it immediately."

"And you've been able to see it since then, whether you need it or not?"

"I always see it in the form it was in the last time I used it."

"But then can't you use it on my mother? I mean, I know you're not supposed to be a luiseach anymore, but if you can see the weapon–"

"It doesn't work that way." Victoria shakes her head. "It's not my test to pass. Anyway, it would be useless to try right now."

"What do you mean?"

"Confronting her now would be useless. You need to wait until the demon takes full possession of her."

"Midnight on New Year's Eve," Nolan says slowly.

Victoria nods. "At any other time it will just be your mother you're attacking, not the demon."

"What does the weapon look like for you?" Nolan asks Victoria.

Victoria hesitates before answering, like she's not sure whether she's supposed to share that piece of information. Finally she responds. "It's a rope."

"A rope?" I echo. "That doesn't sound particularly supernatural."

Victoria smiles almost wistfully, as though she's remembering the days she wielded the rope with pleasure. "It wasn't just any rope. It was a rope that was stronger than iron. Once bound by it, it was impossible to break free. It was a rope with edges as sharp as steel, so that even the slightest touch was like being cut by a knife."

"Did you cut a lot of people doing luiseach work?" I ask, queasy at the thought of all that blood–another reason to give up my powers when this is all over.

"Just one," she answers softly. "My husband."

I loosen my grip on the knife the tiniest bit. "What?"

"By the time I arrived home it was too late." Her usually melodic voice loses some of its music as she continues. "My husband and my daughter were already dead. Still, I grabbed my weapon and tied it around my husband, tighter and tighter. I thought I could squeeze the demon out, strangle him out. But a postmortem attack proved to be useless. The demon was already gone, and he'd taken my daughter's spirit with him."

"I'm sorry," I whisper, blinking back tears. I imagine Victoria opening her front door, slipping off her coat, calling for her family and wondering why they weren't answering. I imagine her walking up the stairs, never thinking for a second of the horrors that were waiting for her in her daughter's bathroom. Maybe Anna's body was floating in the bathtub, her cheeks still pink with life; perhaps her husband's flesh was still warm when she wound her rope around it. I envision my graceful, composed art teacher wailing with grief. I can't imagine anything more terrible. It makes me want to drop this knife and never pick it up again.

Instead, I force myself to tighten my grip.

"What if it doesn't—" I pause, struggling to remember the word Victoria used earlier. "*manifest* for me in time?"

"It will," Nolan says firmly.

"How do you know?"

"Because you'll be ready to fight. You won't be scared, and you won't be weak. People find all kinds of hidden stores of strength when they're fighting for their lives. They do things they never knew they were capable of."

I shake my head. "But the demon can't kill me, remember?"

"I know," Nolan nods. "But it can kill me."

"What do you mean?"

"At midnight on New Year's Eve I'll be standing right beside you. The demon will attack me—a human—the same way it attacked Anna, right?" He looks at Victoria for confirmation. She bows her head solemnly.

"When your mother tries to hurt me," he continues, "the weapon will manifest. Because you'll need it to protect me."

"You don't know that for sure. I can't ask you to take that kind of risk."

"It's not a risk. Think about it. What more motivation could you possibly have? You'll be saving your mother's life—and mine. Two people you—" Nolan stops abruptly. "Two people you care about," he finishes softly. "Anna's spirit too. That's three. Plus you'll know exactly when the demon takes full possession of Kat, because that's when she'll try to hurt me. It could work." He looks up at Victoria, his dirty-blond hair mussed like a little kid's. "Ms. Wilde, what do you think?"

Nolan didn't ask what I think, but if he had, I'd say that if this is what my mentor had planned, then whoever and wherever he is, he is a big fat sicko.

"Please call me Victoria, Nolan." She sits down in the chair across from us. "It's not ideal. But," she adds slowly, "Nolan does have a point. Perhaps you're the kind of person whose strengths manifest only when faced with the proper motivation."

"Perhaps," I echo. "But we don't know for sure."

"No," Victoria agrees. "We don't."

CHAPTER THIRTY-ONE
Happy New Year

The morning of New Year's Eve I have trouble getting dressed. I know, I know—it's the silliest of all possible problems I could have, considering the circumstances. Still, it's really frustrating me that there doesn't seem to be anything in my closet that's appropriate to wear to an exorcism.

Not that I have any clue what a person is actually *supposed* to wear to an exorcism—I don't think there's an etiquette guide to cover this particular event—but all my clothes are so brightly colored, and it seems like the kind of thing you should wear dark colors to. Like you're going to a funeral. Or robbing a house.

Or walking into battle.

I wish I had armor or camouflage, but I finally settle on the Levis I stole from Mom back in August and a navy blue top I found at my favorite thrift shop in Austin. It has tiny little white flowers embroidered on the cuffs of its long sleeves, but other than that, I think it is literally the darkest, plainest thing I own. Which feels like a kind of camouflage.

I slide Victoria's knife from its hiding place beneath Dr. Hoo's platform. Victoria made me take it home with me, just in case we were wrong about the whole midnight-on-New-Year's-Eve thing. But it still hasn't manifested itself into a powerful weapon that only a luiseach can wield. It's still just a knife.

Now I walk around my room with the knife in my hand, holding it out in front of me like it's a sword and I'm a master fencer. "En garde!" I shout to no one in particular.

I must look like a crazy person, swishing around the room with a knife. If Mom were to come in right now, surely she'd have me institutionalized.

But I know Mom won't come in. She hasn't stepped foot inside my room in weeks. Maybe she's forgotten that I live here.

I jab the knife once more, and I swear I hear a giggle coming from the air above me. "You better not be laughing at me!" I whisper up to Anna, but I can't help smiling a tiny smile myself. This morning we finished both our checkers game (she won) and our Monopoly game (I won).

Now that the fun is over, I say to her, "Let's hope your mom knows what she's talking about."

Nolan comes over at 8 p.m., cradling a long, slim paper-bag-wrapped package in his arms. "For you." He holds it out in front of him.

I peek inside. "Fireworks?"

"It *is* New Year's Eve," he answers, a mix of nerves and hope in his voice. "If all goes well, we're going to have more than one reason to celebrate after midnight."

I try to smile back at him, but my mouth won't cooperate.

Maybe after tonight I'll never actually smile again. If I fail, what would I have to smile about, with my mother gone and forgotten?

"That's awfully optimistic of you," I finally manage to say.

"What can I say? I believe in you."

I blush under his gaze, and he follows me into the kitchen, where I place the fireworks gingerly on the counter.

"And one more thing—" he adds, taking off his grandfather's jacket. "For luck." He slips his arms from the sleeves. He's wearing a dark green, long-sleeved shirt underneath, jeans, and beat-up brown boots. He holds the jacket out to me, and when I don't take it, he lifts it onto my shoulders. It feels so right that suddenly I know why I had so much trouble getting dressed this morning: I was waiting to put this on.

"For luck," I agree, sliding my arms into the sleeves. The jacket feels familiar, like I'm the one who's been wearing it every day for the past nine months, not Nolan.

"Here," Nolan says, reaching over to roll the cuffs past my wrists. "We wouldn't want to risk—" He cuts himself off.

"Risk what? That my hands would get lost in the too-long sleeves and I wouldn't be able to wield my mystical magical weapon like I'm supposed to?"

Nolan doesn't answer, intent on pushing the sleeves up my arms. There are already so many unpleasant sensations floating around my body—knots in my stomach, dry mouth, sweaty palms—that for once his touch hardly makes much difference.

"Aren't you scared?" I ask softly.

"Of course," Nolan answers.

"You don't look scared."

Nolan looks up at me and smiles. "I've got a pretty good poker face."

I shake my head. If I fail, Nolan could end up like Anna—not just dead, but his spirit tethered to the demon, trapped in a world of torment, at risk of being forgotten forever.

I take a deep breath and say, "Promise me you'll run, if things start to look bad. If it looks like I'm going to fail, just get out of here, as quickly as you can. Before the demon can—" The lump in my throat makes it impossible to say the word *kill.* Instead, I say, "Before it can hurt you."

"I'm not going to leave you—"

"Just promise. Please."

"Okay," Nolan finally says, nodding. "I promise."

He follows me into the living room, where Mom is sitting in a chair across from the TV like a zombie. (I wonder if zombies are real too. I'll have to ask Victoria when all of this is over.) Mom barely acknowledges Nolan's presence, though he politely says, "Hello Ms. Griffith." I wonder whether she even remembers that she told him to call her that. She's wearing black jeans and a charcoal gray sweater, like maybe I'm not the only one who thought dark colors were the most appropriate wardrobe for tonight.

Victoria arrives at nine, dressed in her usual dark, long witchy clothes. When I open the door to let her in, I hear thunder rumbling in the distance. Still, I think it might actually be warmer outside than it is inside. At least for mc.

"We're just sitting in the living room, watching the clock." I gesture for her to follow me into the next room. But when I turn around, Mom is standing behind us, blocking the way. She barely moved when Nolan got here. Why does she care now that Victoria is here?

"Mom," I say, trying to sound like this isn't the single weirdest night of my life, "This is my . . ." I don't know what to call her. My friend? My teacher? My nonmentor? Finally I say, "This is Victoria Wilde. She's from our school."

Another rumble of thunder. Rain begins splashing against the windows and the roof.

Mom narrows her eyes. "Have we met?" she asks, holding her hand out to shake Victoria's.

"Not exactly," Victoria answers with a trembling smile. It takes me a second to understand what she means. My mother has never met Victoria, but the demon living inside of her has.

Victoria takes my mother's hand and pumps it up and down enthusiastically. When she finally releases her I see that the edges of her long-sleeved sweater are wet where my mother touched it.

Where the demon touched it.

Mom leads the way back into the living room. On TV the ball is dropping in New York City; there, it's already midnight.

Here the seconds tick by. I sit in the center of the sofa, Nolan and Victoria on either side of me, like I'm the meat in the middle of a luiseach sandwich. I'm sitting on the knife. Whenever whatever is going to happen begins, I'll reach for it and hope it does whatever it's supposed to do.

"How will we know when it's time?" I whisper to Victoria, my mouth so dry that I can barely get the words out. I cough.

"Believe me," Victoria says. She reaches for my hand and squeezes it. "You'll know."

I can feel the cold of the blade through my jeans.

At 11:48 p.m. Mom stands. In unison, like we're performing some kind of carefully choreographed dance, Nolan, Victoria, and I stand and turn. We watch her go into the next room.

"Should I follow her?" I whisper. Victoria nods anxiously. I slip the knife into my back pocket, blade down, so that the end is sticking halfway out, and I follow my mother into the kitchen.

"Whatcha doing?" I ask, trying to sound casual.

"I thought I'd make some popcorn for you and your friends," Mom says brightly. She doesn't bother turning on the lights as she reaches into the pantry.

"That's nice," I answer. Mom walks around the countertop island in the center of the kitchen and puts a packet of popcorn into the microwave; the machine lights up and hums when she turns it on. The sound of kernels popping fills the room.

Pop-pop. Pop-pop.

"Why don't you go sit down with your friends?" Mom says. "I'll bring it out when it's ready."

"It's okay, I don't mind waiting." A fake sort of buttery smell wafts from the microwave. Normally it'd make my mouth water, but tonight my throat is dry.

Pop-pop. Pop-pop.

"Sunshine, really, don't be silly. Go into the other room." Mom leans back against the kitchen sink and the water begins running. The sink doesn't drain; instead, it fills up. Like a small steel bathtub. "Your friend Nolan can help me," she adds, her eyes gazing past me, focusing on something behind me.

I turn around and see Victoria and Nolan, hovering in the doorway between the kitchen and the living room, watching us. Hanging on every word. Mom locks eyes with Nolan, the demon's intended victim.

Victoria shakes her head slowly, keeping her eyes focused on Mom. Her way of telling me: *Don't take your eyes off her.*

The microwave beeps. The popcorn is finished. But neither Mom nor I make a move to get it out. The machine beeps again, reminding us that our food is ready. The buttery smell shifts; now it smells like something is burning. Water begins flowing over the edge of the sink.

What happens next, happens so fast that later, I won't be sure how it happens at all.

Nolan is next to my mother on the other side of the counter. Mom's arms are wrapped around him. Her eyes don't look like her eyes at all; instead of almost gray, they're dark black, so that the iris is indistinguishable from the pupils. Her hair is suddenly completely soaking wet.

Nolan is several inches taller than Mom, but she's holding him from behind with just one arm. He's struggling against her, but he can't seem to get free. She presses his head toward the sink, his face hovering just inches above the water.

I guess this is what Victoria meant when she said I'd know when it started.

I reach for the knife, but my hands are shaking so hard that I can barely wrap my fingers around it. My muscles are about as useful as a bowl of Jell-O. I manage to hold the blade out in front of me, but it still looks like just a rusty old knife. Mom lowers Nolan's face into the sink. He struggles against her hold, water splashing up and drenching the countertop, but he's no match for her strength.

"Come on!" I shout at the ceiling, at the luiseach gods or my mentor or whoever is in charge of all this. I stare at the knife and beg, "Manifest already!" My hand is shaking so hard that I'm scared I'm going to drop it.

"Don't let go, Sunshine!" Victoria shouts from the doorway. Mom turns her eyes from me to Victoria, like she's noticing the other woman's presence in our house for the first time.

Mom smiles, but her smile doesn't look like any smile I've ever seen on her face before. In fact, it doesn't look like a smile at all; smiles are warm, friendly, joyous—this is something else entirely. Her teeth are inhumanly white, practically glowing in the dark of the kitchen. Water drips out of her open mouth. Her eyes have turned an eerie sort of blue, like they're not eyes at all but rather tiny swimming pools.

She lifts Nolan's head from the sink and smashes his skull against the counter. She releases him and he falls to the ground, unconscious. The mildew smell is so strong that I think I will choke on it.

"Nolan!" I scream. I drop to the floor and crawl around the island, crouch over his body. Oscar appears at my side and starts licking Nolan's face, a dog's version of CPR. I can hear Lex mewing from the countertop above us.

I put the knife down beside Nolan and lean down over my friend. I can feel his breath on my face—at least he's still breathing. For once, being this close to him doesn't make my skin crawl. Blood pours out of a gash in his forehead. He couldn't run away now if he wanted to.

Oh no, what if proximity to Nolan doesn't bother me because he's dying? What if whatever it is that made the awful wrong-end-of-the-magnet feeling kick in is fading away?

Suddenly a terrible cracking sound makes the house shake. The ceiling above us is ripping away, as easily as if it were made of cloth. I scream as the second floor disappears and a blast of freezing air blows into the house. The rain from the storm outside—there's no outside anymore, we're all outside now—is drenching us. Oscar and Lex dash toward the living room, hoping to get away from this mess. I try to position myself over

Nolan like an umbrella, but it's useless. I shiver like a leaf; right now, being close to him isn't making me any warmer.

Across the room I hear a voice that sounds nothing like my mother's say, "I didn't expect to see you here." She's talking to Victoria, not me. I wait to hear Victoria answer her, but there's nothing: only the sound of the wind and the rain, then a horrible laugh coming from my mother's mouth. Then a splash as Victoria's body falls to the ground.

Another crack, and the wall between us and the driveway vanishes; more water rushes in. Nolan is lying in at least three inches of it, rising steadily around us. I turn his head, trying to angle his mouth and nose above the water line, scared that he might drown.

At once I'm aware of the weight of a shadow hanging over me. I look up. There's my mother with her strange liquid eyes, staring at me.

"Young love torn asunder," she says, but in a voice much lower, meaner, and uglier than her own. How strange to hear someone else's voice coming out of her mouth. "What a tragedy." She clucks her tongue.

"What did you do to Victoria?" I ask desperately. I can't see her from my place on the floor, behind the kitchen island. The demon just laughs in response, and I know that whatever it did, Victoria can't help me now. I shiver, as drenched as if I'd just taken a shower.

Nolan is unconscious.

He can't help me either.

And my mother is absent, trapped somewhere inside her own body. Does she even know what's happening? Is she watching this from somewhere beneath the demon, screaming to be set free?

I'm all alone. It's just me and the demon and our broken-down, roofless house. Pellets of rain crash against my face and stream into my eyes, until my mother's body standing above me is nothing more than a blur. I'm so cold that my teeth are chattering, banging against each other angrily.

I'm not even holding the knife anymore. It lies uselessly beside Nolan's body. So much for a weapon that's supposed to manifest itself when you need it.

With her superhuman demon strength, my mother reaches down and flips Nolan over with just her left arm. I try to crawl out of the way, try to grab the knife once more, but I slip and fall on my back beneath the weight of Nolan's body, now pinned on top of mine, the knife digging into my back beneath us. At least I still feel Nolan's breath against my cheek.

I try to arch my back so I can slide my arm beneath it to reach for the knife. But I can barely reach it with my fingertips. I open my mouth to scream but water rushes in, choking me.

Oh gosh, Victoria and Nolan were both wrong.

I'm not the kind of person who finds hidden stores of strength when she's faced with a crisis.

I'm the type of person who flails around on the ground, splashing in demon rainwater.

"Somebody help us!" I shout. Is my mentor watching me, even now? Can he hear me? Is he really just going to stand aside and let all these people die while I fail?

"Please!" I beg, spitting water with each syllable, but no one answers. Tears stream down my face, mixing in with the raindrops.

Mom—the demon—presses her foot against Nolan's back, holding us both down. Blood from Nolan's wound mixes with the rainwater and drips onto my face. I gasp, struggling to fill my lungs with air as the water edges ever higher. I know that no matter how deep it gets, it can't really drown me—the demon can't kill me. But it can drown Nolan.

Writhing and twisting, I manage to wrap my fingers around the knife beneath me. It's cold as ice, so holding it hurts. Wriggling beneath all this weight, I finally pull the weapon out from beneath us.

It's still just a knife, but I hold it up anyway, slashing at Mom's leg. She just grins her horrible glowing grin. My arms aren't long enough; I can't reach her.

Thunder rumbles above us, followed immediately by a flash of lightning so bright that for a second it blinds me. The storm is right above us. The wind is howling, but in between gusts I can still hear sounds of celebration from the TV in the living room. "All right everyone," an announcer shouts, "ten seconds to the New Year!"

The roof must still be in place in the living room. Maybe it's still dry. Maybe I can drag Nolan and Victoria in there, get them out of harm's way.

A crowd begins chanting: *10, 9 . . .*

Who am I kidding? I can't even get out from under Nolan, let alone drag two bodies into the other room. Mom digs her heel into his back, pressing down on us both. I gasp for breath and my mouth fills with water. It's the most disgusting thing I've ever tasted, rotten and sour.

8, 7 . . .

This is how it's going to end. Everyone I care about is about to die. Victoria is helpless, unconscious across the kitchen. Nolan will drown just like Anna did. Will I feel his spirit when it leaves its body? My mother's spirit will be destroyed. And

Anna's along with it. Nolan's will be next, once the demon moves on to its next victim.

Victoria will forget that she was ever a mother—she'll forget every diaper change, every bottle feeding. Forget that she ever helped Anna with her homework, forget the first time her daughter read a book by herself, forget Anna's hands and her laugh and her smile.

6, 5 . . .

I close my eyes, trying to blink the icy-cold water away. I will forget my mother. Not right away, like Victoria said. It will happen slowly, inevitably, even if I plaster the house with photographs. Maybe in a few months I'll forget the sound of her voice, the way she laughed. Then I won't know how she smelled. It could be two years before I forget pizza dinners and arguing over the remote. After a decade I'll even forget why she named me Sunshine.

I've failed completely. We lost, and the demon won. What happens to luiseach who fail their tests? Will my mentor keep testing me over and over until I pass? Or will he disappear and leave me all alone, a luiseach without her powers, just like Victoria?

4, 3 . . .

"I love you, Mom!" I shout up at her face as thunder and lightning explode in unison above us. She's got to be in there somewhere, maybe she can still hear me. Maybe I'll remember that I loved someone this much, even if I can't remember who.

Suddenly someone is wrapping her hands around my wrists. I open my eyes and glance around frantically: Nolan is still unconscious, and Victoria is out of my sight somewhere on the other side of the counter. The grip tightens; I'm being pulled out from under Nolan's body, pulled up to stand by a phantom helpmate.

"Anna?" I sputter, water dripping down my face. I hear a small, distant voice answer, "*It's me.*" She squeezes my fingers into a fist around the knife.

The house starts to shake, a localized earthquake. In the morning geologists for miles around will check their Richter scales, wondering what on earth happened.

I squeeze the knife, feeling the cold steel prickle my skin.

Wait, it's not a knife, and it's not cold. Not anymore.

It's a *torch.*

An enormous wooden torch with a hot orange flame coming out of its tip. A flame that only gets stronger in the driving rain. I hold it out toward my mother but she jumps away, dancing out of my reach.

2, 1 . . .

The flames grow higher, warming me. Suddenly I am magically, magnificently dry. I hold the torch above me like an umbrella; it creates a bubble of warmth around me. A bubble whose edges are growing, inch by inch. Still, my mother dances away from it. The kitchen wall gone, she's able to back into the driveway, well out of my reach. She grins her wet grin from just outside the bubble.

"What good is a torch that can't reach her?" I yell. How do I get to her?

The sound of paper ripping makes me turn from my mother to the kitchen counter. Invisible hands are ripping open the bag that holds Nolan's fireworks.

I know exactly whose hands. "Anna, you're a genius!" I shout. I reach for the sparklers and pull them into my bubble, where they magically dry just like I did. I use the torch to light one; it brightens the room, looking festive even now. I throw it at my mother. It hisses when it touches her skin. The flame brightens, but when she looks at it, it extinguishes immediately.

I light a handful more and throw them all. Still, the sparklers extinguish when they hit her skin. Still, she is able to dance out of my reach.

Lightning flashes again, but this time the thunder is almost a minute behind it. The storm must be moving away.

It's working!

I light another sparkler. This one I throw into the driveway behind her. Despite the water all over the ground, it still burns—this rain cannot extinguish the fire from my torch. I light and throw another, then another, until there is a bright *U* of sparklers around my mother's body, blocking the demon so it can't back any farther away from me.

I take a step closer, out of the kitchen and onto the driveway. Then another step, closer still. The demon hisses at me, but I don't retreat. Instead, I get so close that my mother's body is enveloped in my bubble of heat and warmth. Her wet skin sizzles as it dries. She crouches on the ground, wailing in pain.

No, not she. *It.* This is the demon I'm facing, not my mother. I hold the torch over her body, and her skin is no longer sizzling. It's *boiling.* Steam rises off her skin like a thick blanket; it's so thick that I can barely see her.

She screams. Now her voice sounds like her own: "Please stop, Sunshine! You're hurting me!"

My heart races at the sound of my mother's voice. Can she feel what's happening, even with the demon possessing her? Oh gosh, should I stop—what if I'm hurting her every bit as much as I'm hurting the demon?

I hesitate, and as I do I feel Anna pressing one last firework into my left hand. I look down at it; in the light that the torch gives off I can see the scar where my mother cut me, already fading away.

This firework isn't another sparkler–it's a Roman candle.

Victoria said that dark spirits are often those whose lives were taken too soon. They might have been the kindest humans, but the urge to stay here on earth twisted them into something unrecognizable, something evil. I wonder who this demon used to be. I wonder whether exorcising it will allow it to finally move on to where it's supposed to be.

I feel Anna's fingers squeeze my shoulders, her way of telling me that I know exactly what I have to do. And now is the time to do it.

Mom screams again, calls my name again. "Sunshine, please!" she begs, but I shake my head, tears streaming down my face. She told me once that the body can't remember pain. I just hope it's true.

I light the firework and hurl it at my mother's crouching body. It explodes in a fire of colors at my feet, the most horrifying and beautiful thing I've ever seen.

CHAPTER THIRTY-TWO

Drenched

I lower the torch, but I remain dry. My hands are black with soot, my ears ringing from the sound of the explosion. I'm back in the kitchen with Mom's body at my feet; it looks like she's fainted. Above me the ceiling is back, and the second floor is above us, right where it's supposed to be. The wall between the kitchen and the driveway is back in place, not even a scratch around its edges to show that it was missing just seconds ago. Water still drenches the floor, but the tile around my mother and me is dry.

From the TV shouts of *Happy New Year!* echo through the house, which has stopped shaking. The mournful first lines of *Auld Lang Syne* drift into the room.

How is that possible? It feels like I heard the chanting of *3, 2, 1* hours ago. Okay, maybe not hours, but at least several minutes. I look at the torch in my hand; it's shrinking, turning back into a knife. I wonder what it might have manifested as if I'd been facing a different kind of demon.

Just how magical is this weapon? Did time stand still while I wielded it? Did the earth freeze while I was locked in that bubble, warm and dry?

I study the weapon in my hand– it's just a dull knife again, although now, when I look closely, I can see the shadow of the torch that it was just seconds ago. Maybe it will always look that way to me, the way it was a rope to Victoria.

"Sunshine?" My mother sounds groggy, like she's waking from a deep sleep. I look down at her, still crouched at my feet. "What happened?"

"You don't remember?"

Mom shakes her head. She looks around the kitchen like she's seeing it for the first time, reaches her arm out of the dry ring surrounding us, and touches the wet floor. "Why is the kitchen soaking wet?"

"What's the last thing you remember?"

"I was going to make you popcorn," she answers. Slowly she stands and begins to walk around the room, up to her ankles in water.

I'm not sure what to tell her. I don't want to lie anymore, but I'm really not sure that now is the time or place. "There was a flood," I answer finally. "The rain was crazy tonight. A pipe must have burst or something."

Before Mom can ask another question—and she must have plenty of them—she sees Victoria lying face down in the doorway between the kitchen and the living room, her long skirt tangled around her legs, her hair damp.

"She's unconscious!" Mom shouts, and runs across the floor, splashing up rust-colored water as she does. She turns Victoria over and begins giving her mouth to mouth. "Call 911, Sunshine," Mom says in between breaths. But before I can call anyone, Victoria is coughing up water. Mom pulls her to sit up and smacks her on the back.

"Anna!" Victoria cries hoarsely, reaching out a wet hand to point. I turn around. She's pointing almost exactly to the spot where I was standing just seconds ago.

"Anna," she repeats, her arm outstretched.

"There's no one there," Mom coos in her soothing nurse voice.

Victoria looks meaningfully at me. Maybe she sees something I can't see, maybe something I don't yet know how to see.

I kneel beside my art teacher and take her hands in mine. "I know, Victoria," I say softly. "She helped us." I could never have passed this test without her.

"Anna," Victoria says once more, whispering this time.

Then she passes out again.

"Call 911," Mom demands once more as she resumes CPR.

I crawl through the demon water back around the counter to where Nolan's body lies. He hasn't regained consciousness since the demon smacked his head against the counter, but he's still breathing. I lean over him and reach into his jeans' pocket, baggy around his skinny hips. Carefully I pull out his cell phone and dial.

"9-1-1. What's your emergency?"

I glance frantically around the kitchen. I have no idea how to answer that question.

I recite our address. "Our house flooded," I sputter. "My friend . . . fell into the water," I add, scrambling for a reasonable and nonparanormal explanation. "She lost consciousness. And my other friend . . ." I glance at Nolan, trying to come up with a second cover story. He slipped on the wet floor and smacked his head against the counter? But before I can tell another lie, Nolan moans from the floor beside me.

"Nolan!" I shout. "Are you okay?"

"Ow," he says in response, pressing the heel of his hand to his forehead. Blood from his wound has dried onto his face, chin, and neck, making him look like a vampire after a feeding frenzy.

"Nolan," I repeat, more softly now. He looks up at me and nods, silently telling me that he's okay.

"Ma'am?" the 911 operator prompts. "I've dispatched an ambulance to your address. I need you to tell me if you need more than one. I know this is difficult. But can you please tell me how many people need aid?"

"Ummm," I pause, looking at Nolan and then at my mother. They don't look *good,* exactly. Mom is covered in sweat from the effort of doing CPR for so long, but other than that, she looks fine—not a scratch on her. Slowly, carefully, Nolan pulls himself to sit up. Nolan's wound has already stopped bleeding, and other than the blood on his face and his soaked clothes, he looks practically normal, his blond hair falling into his eyes. He doesn't look perfect, but I'm not sure he needs an ambulance all to himself either.

Finally I answer, "I guess just one."

The doctors don't even examine Mom and me. They don't ask how the kitchen flooded. They just give us some dry scrubs to change into and cover us in blankets. I slip Nolan's damp jacket on over my scrubs.

Victoria is still unconscious when the EMTs wheel her into the hospital. Her pulse is weak and her breath shallow, but she's alive. They hook her up to about a million machines and tell us to go home—she won't wake until morning.

"But she will wake up?" I ask. The doctors don't answer my question but again gently urge us to go home.

"Get some rest," the on-call doctor instructs. "You've been through a lot."

I shake my head. He has no idea.

Nolan and I stay up all night. By the time we get home from the hospital it's already almost four in the morning. The doctor stitched up the gash on Nolan's forehead and said he shouldn't sleep for twenty-four hours, just in case of a concussion. I make us some coffee, and we start mopping up what's left of the water in the kitchen. Despite the fact that this place has never been wetter, the smell of mildew is fainter than it was before. By the time the kitchen is dry, the smell has vanished completely.

At eight in the morning Nolan says he better get home.

"It hasn't been twenty-four hours yet," I argue.

"I promise I'll come back this afternoon," he says, then gestures to the green scrubs the doctors gave him. "I just want to change out of these clothes. And maybe shower," he adds. His fine blond hair is matted with dried blood, falling over the bandage that covers his stitches.

"Good idea," I agree. I haven't looked in the mirror recently, but I'm pretty sure I don't look the least bit presentable. I can feel my curls sticking straight up from the top of my head, like a messy sort of crown.

I offer Nolan his jacket back. I tried to dry it in the hospital's bathroom, pressing paper towels against every drip and spatter.

But it's still pretty much soaked. "I hope I haven't ruined it," I say.

"Keep it," he insists. He holds his hands out in front of him; once more, the closer he gets to me, the warmer I feel. (And the more nauseated, but I'm concentrating on the good feelings for now.)

I shake my head. "I can't. I know how much it means to you—"

"It's just a jacket, Sunshine," Nolan says with a sad sort of smile. "I mean, I love it, but it's not my grandfather, however much it reminds me of him."

"I know, but—"

He cuts me off before I can argue anymore. "And I owe it to you—consider it a thank you present."

"There's no such thing as a thank you present. Besides, what do you have to thank me for? For putting your life at risk? If anyone should give anyone a thank you present, it's me."

"Because of you, I know that my grandfather . . ." Nolan pauses.

"That he wasn't just spouting crazy theories about ghosts and spirits?" We've known that for a while now.

"Not just that. I mean, yes, but now I know that wherever he is, he's not alone. When he died some luiseach, somehow, was there to help usher his spirit to the beyond." He smiles. "And it's nice knowing that. So . . . thank you."

I smile and hug the jacket to my chest like a Teddy bear.

"You know it still smells like him?" Nolan says.

I shake my head and lower my face to the jacket, inhaling. It should smell wet and mildewy, but it doesn't. "Not to me," I say. "To me it smells like you."

Nolan grins. "Looks better on you anyway."

"I can't keep it."

"Consider it a loan, then."

I nod. "Okay. Just for now. And hey," I add, before he closes the front door behind him.

"Yeah?"

"Thanks for the fireworks."

"I knew we'd have something to celebrate."

"That makes one of us. I really didn't think I'd pass this stupid test."

Nolan smiles wide. "I didn't doubt you for a second."

CHAPTER THIRTY-THREE

Flowers

After Nolan leaves I go into my bedroom. All my toys are put away—no checkerboard, no Monopoly money—and Dr. Hoo is right where I left him. I thought I would be relieved when the test was over—and believe me, I am—but my room feels so empty without Anna here. I kind of miss her.

"Where did you go, little girl?" I ask, but for once I'm talking to no one.

I get into the shower. I guess it's kind of strange that I'm using water to wash away water. But the water pouring down from the showerhead feels clean; the water that dried to my skin and hair last night was filthy. I close my eyes and imagine that whatever is left of the demon is disappearing down the drain.

"Sunshine!" Mom shouts almost as soon as I step out of the bathroom. "Get dressed."

I wrap my hair in a towel as she follows me into my room. "What's the rush, Mom? It's New Year's Day. Nothing is open anyway."

"We're going to the hospital to visit Victoria. It's the least we can do."

I raise my eyebrows. I mean, of course I want to visit Victoria, but what does Mom mean by *it's the least we can do?* She doesn't even remember what happened last night, doesn't know that she's the reason Victoria needs visiting at all. Unless . . . is she beginning to remember?

Before I can ask, Mom says solemnly, "She was a guest in our home when she was hurt. Anyway, I want to have one of my doctor friends check up on her."

"You have friends at the hospital?"

"I've been working there for months now. Of course I have friends—or did you think I'd become some kind of social pariah?" She folds her hands across her chest and smiles. Despite the fact that she was up most of the night, the dark circles beneath her eyes are lighter than they've been in months. There's some color on her cheeks, and even her hair looks shinier than it did a few days—a few hours—ago. She's dressed in jeans and a gray turtleneck sweater that brings out her eyes. She looks pretty. In fact, to me, she looks absolutely beautiful.

"Of course not," I say with a grin, not quite ready to explain that—since she was possessed by an evil water demon—I'd assumed she hadn't been particularly social at work recently. Right now, we're teasing each other the same way we used to. It feels familiar and wonderful.

Mom glances around the room. "I really have to call the landlord about this carpet. I don't know how you've lived with this pink for so long."

"I don't mind it so much." I shrug. "In fact, let's stop and get Victoria some flowers just as pink as the ones on this wallpaper."

"Sweetie, I don't think this particular shade of pink actually exists in nature."

"You might have a point there."

Mom smiles, then suddenly reaches out to hug me tightly. She might not truly understand that she's been gone all these months, but she holds me as though maybe she's been missing me as much as I missed her.

I'm clutching a bouquet of a dozen roses when we walk into the hospital. I settled on pale pink in the end, so light it's almost white. The color reminded me of Victoria's living room. I press my face to the cool petals and inhale.

The hospital feels like it's well below freezing. I know now that this chill is connected to my luiseach powers somehow. After all, I'm in a hospital, a place where people are born and die every day. Which means there are probably tons of spirits moving in and out, forcing my temperature to dip down while Mom doesn't feel the slightest bit cold.

Mom leads the way to the ICU.

"ICU?" I ask nervously. "That's where they put the really sick people, right?"

"Don't worry, sweetie. They'd have put her there because it's where they can keep the closest eye on her."

But Victoria isn't in any of the beds in the ICU.

"Excuse me?" Mom says, reaching out to grab a nurse's arm as she walks past us. "Can you tell us where we can find Victoria Wilde? Did they move her to recovery?"

The nurse looks at us blankly. Maybe she doesn't know who we're talking about. "Long dark hair," I offer. "Pale skin. Flowing witchy clothes."

The nurse furrows her brow like I'm a crazy person. I guess I can't really blame her. It's certainly not the first time someone's looked at me that way. I've been saying inappropriate things since long before I heard the word luiseach.

"Are you her family?" she asks. I look at the badge hanging around her neck and see that her name is Cecilia.

"Not exactly—" I begin, but Mom cuts me off.

"I'm Kat Griffith from neonatal." A shadow of recognition crosses Cecilia's face. "We met a few months back?"

"I didn't recognize you in street clothes," Cecilia says with a small smile. Her scrubs are blue, nothing like the pastel colors of the neonatal unit. Her light blond hair is pulled into a messy knot at the nape of her neck.

"Cecilia, we really need to know where Victoria is."

Cecilia nods; I guess there's a kind of understanding between nurses that's enough for her to give us information that would normally only be released to family members. "I'm so sorry," she says softly, her mouth resetting into a straight, sympathetic line, her pale blue eyes narrowing slightly. The look on her face frightens me, maybe as much as the demon did last night. Despite the chill in the air, the tiniest bead of sweat forms at the nape of my neck, just below my ponytail. I tighten my hold on the roses, hugging them to my chest.

Ow. One of the thorns stabs me in the thumb. I drop the bouquet abruptly. It hits the ground with a soft thud, the pretty pink petals scattering across the hospital's linoleum floor.

The scent of roses is heavy in the air when Cecilia finally confirms my fears: "Victoria passed away early this morning."

Mom holds my hand as we walk back through the hospital.

"I'm so sorry, sweetie," she says, but I don't say anything in return. I don't think I can. Not with this lump in my throat choking me. "I looked at her chart," Mom continues. "She was just without oxygen for too long."

I nod as though that explains things, but none of this makes the least bit of sense. I passed the test, didn't I? I got rid of the demon! How could Victoria still die?

I have to get out of this hospital. The creepy feeling is stronger than ever. It wasn't like this last night, in the emergency room, on the other side of the building–Victoria was one of the only patients, and the others were mostly New Year's Eve partiers who had partied a bit too hard, nothing life threatening. But right now, walking through the ICU, it's overwhelming. So many people hovering on the brink between life and death. I'm certain now that this feeling–the one I felt on my sixteenth birthday, the one I felt in our house with Anna there, in the professor's office–is my body's way of telling me that a spirit is near.

I walk faster, toward the exit, toward the car that Mom will drive away from here. But all at once I stop.

"Honey?" Mom asks, but I shake my head. The creepiness has shifted; instead of the weight of thousands of spirits that have come and gone from this building, I feel only one.

I close my eyes and concentrate, focusing on the sensation: the chill in the air, the hair prickling on my arms and at the nape of my neck. Then I gasp with understanding and open my eyes. Though Mom can't see her, there's an elderly woman with white hair and paper-thin freckled skin leaning against the wall across from where I stand. At once I know that she was sleeping two floors above us mere seconds ago, but then her heart simply gave out. Her spirit was drawn to me—like a moth to a flame, just like Victoria said.

A light spirit. One that's ready to move on.

I extend my arms in her direction, and as she begins shuffling toward me I can feel her spirit—all the memories, all that she did and saw and knew—rushing toward me.

Her fingertips brush against mine, and suddenly I know that she had a good life: two children, four grandchildren, a beloved husband who passed away just six months ago. She's ready to see him again. An amazing feeling washes over me. It's not the least bit creepy—it's the opposite of creepy.

It's peace.

I smile.

"Honey?" Mom says again. I turn to face her. "Are you okay?" She wrinkles her nose the way she has a thousand times before, every time she tried to figure out what her dopey daughter was up to.

The feeling of peace is dissipating, replaced by grief over the loss of Victoria. Still, somehow it feels more manageable now than it did before.

"Not really," I answer. "But I'm getting there."

Mom takes my hand in hers once more. Arm in arm, we leave the hospital behind.

She Has Succeeded

I watched her confront the demon. I stood in her yard, a device of my own keeping me hidden and dry, even when the water demon drenched her house with rain, flooded it with water that seemed to appear from out of nowhere, from beneath the tiles of her kitchen floor, from the very air that she breathed.

The creature had saturated the house for months, thriving in this damp climate. The demon that Victoria couldn't conquer, who murdered her human family. The creature she gave up her powers to help destroy. I sensed Victoria's need throughout the night: she wanted the girl to succeed as much as I did, her feelings every bit as intense. But unlike me, she was focused only on saving her daughter; I'm trying to determine the future of our entire race.

I watched Sunshine every step of the way. Even as she was begging her powers to manifest I could feel that she was hoping for some other luiseach to come and finish the job. I felt it when she gave up hope, then sensed the change in her when she found stores of strength she didn't know she'd had. Still—even now—she is trying to plot her way out of her destiny.

But destiny is inescapable. I will teach her that. Perhaps it will be our first lesson.

The weapon took longer to manifest than I would have liked. The girl simply couldn't concentrate. Easily distracted by her concern for Katherine, for the boy—even for Victoria and Anna, whom she barely knew and couldn't possibly have loved already. She needs a stronger will, a sharper focus. There will always be distractions; she has to resist such things. If she isn't careful, they will become her greatest weakness.

Perhaps that will be our second lesson.

Today she helped her first spirit move on. She trusted her intuition long enough to allow the spirit to flow through her. She granted the spirit peace and, in so doing, found an instant of peace herself. I sensed the moment the spirit was released into the ether. I felt the smile on Sunshine's face.

She is ready. It is time for me to make my presence known.

CHAPTER THIRTY-FOUR

The Mentor Arrives

The drive home from the hospital is (of course) foggy. Last night's rain has all but washed away the snow. Only tiny patches of white remain. I lean my head against the window and stare at the homes we drive past. A shrunken snowman melts in someone's front yard, looking pathetic and defeated.

What exactly did I do back there? Did I help that woman . . . move on? It just felt natural, like Victoria said it would.

Not just natural. It felt *good.* I *liked* helping her find peace. For an instant I was at peace too. For once, just like Victoria said, I didn't feel awkward and clumsy and out of place. I felt like I was doing exactly what I was supposed to be doing, like I was exactly where I was supposed to be. Maybe Victoria was right: I've never fit in because being a luiseach was what I was *supposed* to be doing instead. If I give up my powers, does that mean I'll never feel that kind of peace, that kind of *right*-ness, again?

I wish I'd been there when Victoria passed. I wish hers was the spirit I helped move on.

Maybe, finally freed from the confines of my house, Anna was with Victoria when she died. Maybe they'll never have to be apart again.

I really hope so.

Finally the tears make their slow, sad descent across my cheeks.

"Oh sweetie," Mom says. "The doctors did all they could."

I nod, but the truth is, I'm not sure the doctors had a chance. They had no idea what they were *really* dealing with. They thought it was a woman who'd been submerged in rain and flood water. Not that it would have made much difference if they *had* known. It's not like the hospital has a doctor who specializes in demonic injuries who could have saved the day if only we'd told them the truth about what happened last night.

Shouldn't my mentor be here by now? I hated this test, but I passed it. I got rid of the demon, saved my mother's life, and protected Anna's spirit. I'm ready to meet him, ready to make a deal, just like Victoria did. Ready to give up my powers, no matter how good it felt to use them this morning.

Mom turns into the driveway. Through the fog I see Nolan sitting on our front porch. He doesn't have his jacket–I'm wearing it, and I don't plan on taking it off anytime soon–so he's bundled up in a heather gray sweatshirt with a scarf, his breath coming out in puffs of steam. His blond hair peeks out from the corners of his gray hat, pulled down low over his amber eyes.

"What's he doing here?" I ask. His big Chrysler isn't in the driveway; he must have walked here from his house.

Trying to lighten the mood, Mom smiles. "Guess he just can't stay away."

"It's not like that," I insist, but I'm blushing. Because maybe it's not like that, but it's also not entirely *not* not like that, and I'm pretty sure Mom can tell.

I guess that's the one good thing about her absence the past few months. She would have been teasing me about Nolan the whole time.

Nolan stands up as I approach. He holds out a folded piece of paper.

"What's that?" I ask without taking it. From inside the house Oscar barks. Mom opens the front door, and he bounds out onto the porch, leaping for joy. I guess we're not the only ones who are happy the demon is gone. Mom crouches down to pet him, and he starts covering her face with doggy kisses, his way of saying, *I missed you I missed you I missed you.*

"Victoria asked me to give it to you."

"Victoria?" I echo. "When? Before last night?"

"No," Nolan shakes his head. "She stopped by my house this morning."

Mom turns from Oscar to us. "What?" she says, straightening up to stand.

"You mean, her spirit visited you?" I say carefully, and Nolan looks at me like I'm crazy. Butterflies flutter gently in my stomach as I wait for his answer.

"Of course not. Victoria dropped it off and told me to give it to you. Besides, if it were her spirit, I wouldn't have been able to take the letter. I'm not the luiseach here—you are."

"What's a luiseach?" Mom asks.

Nolan and I exchange a look with a capital L, and the butterflies in my belly flap their wings harder. I shake my head. I know I can't keep this a secret forever, but I'm just not ready to tell Mom yet. She's a scientist, and it's not going to be easy to convince her that her daughter is some kind of paranormal-guardian-angel thing. No way do I want to start arguing with her all over again. Not when I just got her back.

"I'll explain everything eventually," I promise.

"Does it have to do with all that creeptastic stuff you haven't been able to stop talking about since we moved here?" she asks.

"I never called it creeptastic, Mom. You did."

"What did you call it?"

"I preferred just plain old creepy."

"Well, I like creeptastic better." Mom grins and I groan. I lean forward and wrap my arms around her. I inhale deeply, smelling the familiar combination of her perfume and shampoo. She rocks me back and forth like I'm a baby. Which, I guess—to her at least—I still am.

"I'm sorry I haven't been myself lately," Mom whispers into my hair. I shake my head, because she has nothing to be sorry for. None of this is her fault. My mentor did this to her—did this to *us*. Put my mother at risk, Victoria at risk, Anna's spirit at risk—all just to test me.

If he ever shows up, I'm going to give him a piece of my mind, as Mom would say. For the first time the expression sounds horrifying to me, needlessly *graphic*, like I'm literally going to split open my skull and offer up a chunk of my brain. This guy has messed with my mind enough; I'm not about to give him any free access to it.

Mom lets me go. "I'll let you and Nolan talk," she says solemnly, stepping inside the house. Oscar trots along behind her.

As soon as the front door is closed Nolan asks, "How could Victoria's spirit have visited me anyway? She'd have had to be—"

"Gone," I finish for him, a lump rising in my throat once more. "We just came from the hospital. They told us she passed away early this morning."

I expect him to look devastated, but instead he calmly shakes his head. "Not possible. It was after ten when she rang my doorbell."

I feel shivers up and down my spine but not the same cold ones I felt in the hospital. These are shivers of something else. Understanding. I chew my bottom lip and pull the jacket's leather sleeves down over my wrists, trying to work out what all of this means.

"But . . . Victoria wasn't a luiseach anymore," I begin softly.

Nolan understands what I'm thinking immediately. After all, he's the one who told me: *A luiseach's spirit—unlike the spirits of mere mortals—cannot be taken, damaged, or destroyed by a ghost or a demon.*

"She gave up her powers," he says slowly. "But she was still *born* luiseach."

She must have retained some of the qualities of being a luiseach despite what she gave up. After all, she saw Anna last night somehow. And her house was so warm and cozy, as though she had the power to keep spirits—and the chill that comes with them—away.

"So the demon could hurt her," I say, thinking out loud, "but not *destroy* her."

"She must have flatlined at the hospital," Nolan surmises. "They declared her dead and sent her off to the morgue—"

"And then, when no one was looking, she simply stood up and walked away," I finish. The lump in my throat vanishes.

"To my house so she could give me this." He holds Victoria's letter out in front of him. Carefully I take it from his hands. Nolan and I lower ourselves onto the front porch steps as I unfold the pages.

Victoria's handwriting is old fashioned, something out of another century. It looks like she must have written with an antique quill pen, the kind I've always wanted to find for myself.

"Read it out loud," Nolan says.

"*Dearest Sunshine*," I begin. "*Congratulations. You've passed your test. I'm so glad I was able to play a small part in your success.*"

"A small part?" I interrupt myself. "I couldn't have done it without her."

"Keep going," Nolan urges.

"*Thank you for saving my daughter. Although memories of my husband continue to fade, the knowledge that my daughter will live in my heart forever will temper the pain of losing him. Finally, Anna has a chance to find peace.*

"Please thank Nolan for his aid. And help him understand his part in all of this."

"My part?" Nolan echoes. I keep reading.

"*I don't think either of you has realized yet that Nolan is your protector. The two of you are inextricably connected for the rest of your lives.*"

"That's ridiculous," Nolan protests immediately, jumping to his feet. He begins pacing back and forth on the porch behind me. "I was *useless* last night. You're the one who protected us, not the other way around." Hc takcs off his hat and runs his hands through his fine hair nervously; it sticks up almost straight with static electricity, making me smile. "I'm just a bookish teenager who likes doing research."

"And I'm just a dorky girl who likes shopping for vintage clothes," I counter. "If I can be a luiseach, then you can be my protector."

Maybe this explains everything—the way that I'm warm when he's near, the way the creepy feeling diminishes. It could be my body's way of telling me to keep Nolan close.

But then why does it feel so wrong when he gets too close? Why doesn't it feel right to hug him, to hold his hand?

I turn back to the letter, hoping that Victoria has explained, but there's no mention of the way Nolan makes me feel. Instead, I read, "*A protector doesn't just protect his luiseach. He protects knowledge. Nolan, you will be responsible for helping Sunshine learn.*" I look up at my friend again. "Sounds like you're *exactly* what a protector is."

The knowing smile Victoria flashed when I talked about Nolan—it wasn't because she was amused by our adorable puppy love; it was because she had just figured out he was my protector.

I keep reading. "*Please look after Anna while I'm gone*—gone?" I ask, interrupting myself again. "Where? Why?"

Nolan adds, "Why hasn't Anna moved on? Now that the demon is gone, what's stopping her?"

"I don't know," I answer anxiously. If Anna hasn't moved on, have I really passed the test? Wasn't that part of it? I go back to the letter. "*My daughter still has work to do in this world, but I hope all of us will be in each other's presence again someday. For now know that your mentor—who was also my former mentor—will be pleased and proud to work with you.*"

"You and Victoria have the same mentor?" Nolan asks.

"Apparently," I answer, trying to remember everything she told me about him. For the first few years they worked together she only helped light spirits move on. That doesn't sound so bad. I wouldn't mind that, I think, remembering the way it felt this morning. I might even like it.

But if that's the case, why did my test involve a dark spirit—not just a dark spirit, but a demon? I turn back to the letter.

"*Together you and he will resume the work that he and I had been doing.*"

I drop the note onto our damp front steps like it's hot. Now I'm the one pacing back and forth.

Resume the work they'd been doing? I press my fingers into my forehead. Victoria said that they weren't doing normal luiseach work. That he had a secret project to restore the balance. What balance? And why do I have to dive right into the secret work when Victoria had years of training first? What's the rush with me?

I purse my lips and concentrate. Victoria also said that I was descended from two of the most powerful luiseach in history, that Nolan was right—I was the last luiseach to be born. That my birth father abandoned me for my own protection . . .

All of this has to be connected somehow, right?

I look at Nolan, certain that he knows there are about a zillion questions dancing around my brain.

But I won't need any of the answers. Not if I strike a deal and give up my powers like I planned. But . . . what if my mentor says no? What if I'm somehow, I don't know, *necessary*? And if I am, how can I refuse when there is so much at stake?

"Sunshine?" Nolan asks. "Are you okay?" He smiles faintly, like he knows the question sounds ridiculous right now.

I open my mouth, positive that Nolan—my protector—can help me fit all these puzzle pieces together. But before I can say a word a fancy black car turns into our long driveway, shiny even in the fog. The chain-link fence around the yard shakes when the car rolls past it, years of rust falling onto the patchy grass.

The car moves at a snail's pace, like someone has magically set the world on slow motion. The car's windows are tinted dark, and I can't see who's inside. The car eases to a stop just behind our own—which is not nearly as clean or bright—and its engine fades into silence as the driver pulls the key from the ignition.

Without meaning to, I hold my breath, waiting to see who will emerge from the driver's side door. The world is still in slow-mo when a tall, slender man steps out of the car. He's dressed in a dark suit, a perfectly knotted gunmetal-gray tie tight around his neck. He doesn't smile as he walks up the driveway toward us.

As he gets closer I gasp. Nolan looks from the stranger to me, trying to figure out what's wrong, but I can only shake my head and point.

The stranger's eyes are a milky, light kind of green, the pupils small, despite the fact that it's a dim, cloudy day. No one has eyes like that. *Almost* no one. They look like cat's eyes.

They look exactly like mine.

Acknowledgments

From the very start *The Haunting of Sunshine Girl* has been an adventure. And as with most great adventures, it's not something I could have done all alone. So many wonderful people have been part of Sunshine's journey so far, and I am tremendously grateful to them all. Go Team Sunshine!

For starters, thanks to Nick Hagen—the idea man from the very beginning and the driving force behind making Sunshine's world bigger and better. And then even bigger and even better than that. (And Nick asked me to thank his wife, Nikki, on his behalf!)

Thanks to the rad Alyssa Sheinmel for bringing Sunshine's voice and world so vividly to the page. (Alyssa asked that I send her thanks to her friends and family, especially JP Gravitt.)

Thanks to the incomparable Mollie Glick for believing in Sunshine, in Nick, and in me. She saw the potential in this project from the start and knew how to take us exactly where we'd dreamed of going. (And Alyssa says to tell you thanks for inviting her to join the team!) Thanks to everyone at Foundry, especially Jessica Regel and Emily Brown.

Great, big, enormous gratitude to the folks at Weinstein: Amanda Murray, Georgina Levitt, Kathleen Schmidt, and, of course, Harvey and Bob Weinstein. Thank you all for your amazing and overwhelming faith in and support of this project.

Thanks to Cindy Eagan for her enthusiasm, kindness, and editorial savvy. Thank you to David Davoli, Christine Marra, and Levy Moroshan.

Thanks to my wonderful family: Papa and Gamma and Greta, for helping in so many ways. To my brother and sister—two of my favorite writers—for all the inspiration. To Daddy, 2½%. And a special shout-out to my mum for being with me every step of the way.

Most of all, thanks to all of the amazing Sunshiners out there. Without you, Sunshine's adventures—and mine right along with her—wouldn't be possible.

The Sacrifice of Sunshine Girl

COMING SOON

Sunshine may have passed her test . . . but her adventures are far from over.

Sunshine's luiseach powers are fully awakened and spirits follow her everywhere. Hoping to get her supernatural abilities under control, she agrees to begin work with her mentor in his eerie lab in the Texas desert. But his work is more terrifying—and, yes, even *creepier*—than she ever could have imagined. Thousands of miles from Kat and Nolan, Sunshine feels utterly alone—until she befriends another young luiseach, Lucio. But can she trust him? Can anything—her father's work, her friendship with Lucio, even Nolan's careful research—prepare Sunshine to face the sinister woman who haunts her dreams, to finally learn the truth about the rift that threatens the future of the luiseach and the human race . . . and the deadly part she may play in it?